FLAT-OUT SEXY

MY IMMORTAL

"The writing is seamless, the story a page-turner, and the romance is one to defy all odds."

—*Romance Reviews Today* (A Perfect Ten)

"Sultry, steamy New Orleans is the perfect setting for Erin McCarthy's story of shocking sin and stunning sensuality."

—*USA Today* bestselling author Rebecca York

HEIRESS FOR HIRE

"If you are looking to read a romance that will leave you all warm inside, then *Heiress for Hire* is a must read."

—*Romance Junkies*

"McCarthy transforms what could have been a run-of-the-mill romance with standout characterizations that turn an unlikable girl and a boring guy into two enjoyable, empathetic people who make this romance shine."   —*Booklist*

"Amusing paranormal contemporary romance . . . Fans will appreciate Erin McCarthy's delightful pennies-from-heaven tale of opposites in love pushed together by a needy child and an even needier ghost."   —*The Best Reviews*

"One of McCarthy's best books to date . . . *Heiress for Hire* offers characters you will care about, a story that will make you laugh and cry, and a book you won't soon forget. As Amanda would say: It's priceless."

—*The Romance Reader* (5-heart review)

"A keeper. I'm giving it four of Cupid's five arrows."

—*BellaOnline*

"An alluring tale."
                                        —*A Romance Review* (5 roses)

"An enjoyable story about finding love in unexpected places, don't miss *Heiress for Hire*."
                                        —*Romance Reviews Today*

A DATE WITH THE OTHER SIDE

"Do yourself a favor and make *A Date with the Other Side*."
                        —*New York Times* bestselling author Rachel Gibson

"One of the romance-writing industry's brightest stars . . . Ms. McCarthy spins a fascinating tale that deftly blends a paranormal story with a blistering romance . . . Funny, charming, and very entertaining, *A Date with the Other Side* is sure to leave you with a pleased smile on your face."
                                        —*Romance Reviews Today*

"If you're looking for a steamy read that will keep you laughing while you turn the pages as quickly as you can, *A Date with the Other Side* is for you. Very highly recommended!"
                                        —*Romance Junkies*

"Fans will appreciate this otherworldly romance and want a sequel."
                                        —*Midwest Book Review*

"Just the right amount of humor interspersed with romance."
                                        —*Love Romances*

"Ghostly matchmakers add a fun flair to this warmhearted and delightful tale . . . An amusing and sexy charmer sure to bring a smile to your face."
                                        —*Romantic Times*

"Offers readers quite a few chuckles, some face-fanning moments, and one heck of a love story. Surprises await those who expect a 'sophisticated city boy meets country girl' romance. Ms. McCarthy delivers much more."

—*A Romance Review*

"Fascinating."

—*Huntress Reviews*

PRAISE FOR THE OTHER NOVELS OF ERIN McCARTHY

"Will have your toes curling and your pulse racing."

—*Arabella Magazine*

"The sparks fly."

—*Publishers Weekly*

"Erin McCarthy writes this story with emotion and spirit, as well as humor."

—*Fallen Angel Reviews*

"Both naughty and nice . . . Sure to charm readers."

—*Booklist*

FLAT-OUT SEXY

erin mccarthy

BERKLEY SENSATION, NEW YORK

THE BERKLEY PUBLISHING GROUP
Published by the Penguin Group
Penguin Group (USA) Inc.
375 Hudson Street, New York, New York 10014, USA
Penguin Group (Canada), 90 Eglinton Avenue East, Suite 700, Toronto, Ontario M4P 2Y3, Canada
(a division of Pearson Penguin Canada Inc.)
Penguin Books Ltd., 80 Strand, London WC2R 0RL, England
Penguin Group Ireland, 25 St. Stephen's Green, Dublin 2, Ireland (a division of Penguin Books Ltd.)
Penguin Group (Australia), 250 Camberwell Road, Camberwell, Victoria 3124, Australia
(a division of Pearson Australia Group Pty. Ltd.)
Penguin Books India Pvt. Ltd., 11 Community Centre, Panchsheel Park, New Delhi—110 017, India
Penguin Group (NZ), 67 Apollo Drive, Rosedale, North Shore 0632, New Zealand
(a division of Pearson New Zealand Ltd.)
Penguin Books (South Africa) (Pty.) Ltd., 24 Sturdee Avenue, Rosebank, Johannesburg 2196,
South Africa

Penguin Books Ltd., Registered Offices: 80 Strand, London WC2R 0RL, England

This is a work of fiction. Names, characters, places, and incidents either are the product of the author's imagination or are used fictitiously, and any resemblance to actual persons, living or dead, business establishments, events, or locales is entirely coincidental. The publisher does not have any control over and does not assume any responsibility for author or third-party websites or their content.

FLAT-OUT SEXY

A Berkley Sensation Book / published by arrangement with the author

PRINTING HISTORY
Berkley Sensation trade paperback edition / November 2008
Berkley Sensation mass-market edition / June 2010

Copyright © 2008 by Erin McCarthy
Excerpt from *Hot Finish* copyright © 2010 by Erin McCarthy
Cover design by Rita Frangie
Cover art by Craig White
Interior text design by Kristin del Rosario

ISBN: 978-0-425-23517-1

BERKLEY® SENSATION
Berkley Sensation Books are published by The Berkley Publishing Group,
a division of Penguin Group (USA) Inc.,
375 Hudson Street, New York, New York 10014.
BERKLEY® SENSATION is a registered trademark of Penguin Group (USA) Inc.
The "B" design is a trademark of Penguin Group (USA) Inc.

PRINTED IN THE UNITED STATES OF AMERICA

10 9 8 7 6 5 4 3 2 1

For Meaghan and Connor,
who let me live in my cave
to write this book

ACKNOWLEDGMENTS

I had a lot of help from my friends on the story line for *Flat-Out Sexy*, and I want to give a shout-out and a huge thank-you to them.

Special thanks to Barbara Satow for conceiving the original story idea with me way back when on one of our conference car trips. What started out as "Could we write a race car book?" became the beginnings of *Flat-Out Sexy*. Barbara, extra thanks for giving Elec his name.

Many thanks to Kathy Love, Jamie Denton, Rhonda Stapleton, Mary Ann Chulick, Christy Carlson, and Chris Nolfi for listening to me whine and for helping me take a premise and make it a book. I couldn't have done it without all of you!

CHAPTER
ONE

I'VE met teenage girls with more testosterone than that man has."

Tamara Briggs didn't even have to look to know that Suzanne was talking about Geoffrey Ayers, because in a roomful of race car drivers, the anthropology professor would be the only one her friend would find lacking in male machismo.

But she pleaded ignorance because she didn't want to acknowledge that Suz might have a point about the man she was trying to convince herself she could actually have sex with on a regular basis. "Who are you talking about?"

"You know I'm talking about Geoffrey. And I'm sorry, I know he's your new boyfriend and all, but honestly, Tammy, the man couldn't grow a chest hair if his life depended on it. *Look* at him."

Did she have to? Tamara was feeling like if she did, all her delusions might shatter. She was working really hard to convince herself that she could be in love with Geoffrey, but if she had to look too closely, she suspected she would have to admit that wasn't going to happen. Ever. Gathering all her willpower, she forced herself to eyeball Geoff, and it wasn't pretty. They were at a cocktail party to raise money for a charity that funded research for children's cancer, and he was right smack in the middle of a group of well-dressed drivers, pit crew chiefs, and car owners. Geoffrey was the only one wearing a sweater. A brown sweater at that. It couldn't even aspire to the heights of mocha, espresso, or mahogany. It was just plain old brown.

All the other guys had left their jumpsuits at the track and had polished up in snappy suits, or at least black pants with a classy shirt and tie. Tamara wanted Geoff's boring sweater not to matter, but somehow it did. He had no discernible hairstyle, graying eyebrows that begged for tweezers, and yellow teeth, but Tamara had been telling herself for the month she'd been seeing him not to be shallow. She was no beauty queen herself and Geoffrey was above all things a nice man. Yet all those nitpicky things like his need for a comb and a thorough dental cleaning jumped out at her every time she looked at him, and tonight it was even more obvious that she was not in the slightest bit attracted to the man. He looked dumpy and careless and thin and . . . lacking in testosterone. Suz was right, dang it.

"He just made a bad outfit choice for the night. I should have given him better instructions." Like not to wear those god-awful scuffed brown shoes with the ancient unraveling tassels. Tamara sipped her wine, annoyed that she was being so petty. "Clothes don't make a man."

"That's true. It's what's under the clothes that does." Suz fiddled with her diamond earring, one of a whopper pair that had been given to her by her ex-husband Ryder in better times. "I mean, I could handle a metrosexual man, I suppose. That's all about good grooming and nice clothes, and there's nothing wrong with that. Hell, waxed balls make my life easier. Smoother, anyway."

Staring idly at Geoffrey, wondering about the mystery of chemical attraction, or lack thereof, between men and women, it took Tamara a second to process what Suzanne had just said. "Waxed . . ." She spun around to face her friend so quickly, she almost splashed her Merlot out of the glass and onto the carpet. "Suz!" Was she really talking about testicles at this charity fund-raiser?

Suz was. And she continued, "Taking it all off and out of my way is a good thing, but a girl should know that her man can at least *grow* hair on his balls. That's all I'm saying, Tammy. Geoffrey isn't metrosexual at all given those saggy clothes, he's more like completely asexual. He just looks like a dud. So you end up with hairy balls *and* no big bang. What's the point?"

Indeed. Tamara had no legitimate response to that.

Suz didn't need one. She was on a roll. "For me personally, I want to know that if I bend over in front of him, my man is going to pitch his tent. I don't see that happening with old Geoff there."

No, Tamara didn't see that happening either. There was no spontaneous tent pitching from Geoffrey.

"But I'm not the one who has to have sex with him. So if it works for you, if he gets your engine firing, then it's all good."

Right. It would be all good. If he got her engine firing. Which he didn't. He couldn't even get the key in the ignition. They'd only attempted sex once and it had been just shy of appalling. Not that Geoffrey knew that. It had seemed to work for him, because he was the one who'd had an orgasm. Tamara took another sip of wine because she suddenly needed it. God, what was she doing? Was she really this lonely that she was willing to try to force herself to like a man she found dull as dirt?

Apparently she was. It had been two years since her husband Pete had been killed in a wreck at Talladega and yes, damn it, she was lonely. "I just want some company, Suz. Someone to go to dinner and the movies with. He's good for that."

"So he's your manpanion. A male companion."

Accurate, Tamara supposed, yet that sounded so totally unappealing, she had to wonder if she really had any clue what she actually wanted.

She shifted so that a member of the catering staff could clear the table behind them. They really should be mingling, not standing in the corner talking about her sex life—or lack thereof. But Tamara was feeling downright cranky and fussy as she started to realize that this weekend—which was supposed to be a test-drive of her relationship with Geoffrey and if they could take it to the next level—had her sucking down wine for fortification. And she was stuck with him for another twenty-four more hours. At least the next day Pete's parents were dropping her kids at the track to watch the race, and they would serve as a welcome distraction from Geoffrey's lectures on the negative effect of corporate sponsorship on professional sports. However, that was tomorrow, and tonight there was no denying she was dreading going back to the hotel room with him.

Time to throw the caution flag if anticipating a night in a hotel with a man and no kids to interrupt just made her want to turn tail and run.

She was also thinking that if she needed her kids as a shield between her and her boyfriend just to sit through a four-hour race, there was a big old problem. It really didn't make any sense. Geoff was a nice guy and she liked him. Truly and genuinely liked him as a human being. He was solid and caring and safe. Exactly what she wanted this time around the relationship track. He had been nothing but kind and tender to her, and this was how she reacted? By wincing at the thought of sliding into bed naked with him?

She needed to be kicked in the head.

Or maybe she just needed more wine.

But the truth was, you couldn't force chemistry between two people, and she had been pretending that she could. Since she wrestled everything else in her life into submission, she had figured this would work the same way. Unfortunately, her libido wasn't listening and refused to ignite.

"*Manpanion* in the goofiest word I've ever heard," Tamara said, turning and exchanging her empty glass for a full one, not even able to bring herself to feel guilty about it. She was starting to feel a little desperate.

"It fits him. Goofy."

"Don't hold back. Tell me how you really feel about him." Bad enough that she knew he was basically a nerd, did Suzanne have to point it out, too?

That brought a contrite expression to Suzanne's face. Her friend, the one who had stood there in the hospital with her and held her hand when the doctors told her that Pete was dead, squeezed her hand now. "I'm sorry, sweetie, I'm being rude, aren't I? I just want you to be happy, and you really don't look happy. He's not your type at all. You're a driver's wife, Tammy."

Tamara felt her chest tighten. "Was. I was a driver's wife. I said I wouldn't go there again, Suz, you know that. I'd rather have boring than live with that fear again. I don't want a life where racing consumes every minute of every day anymore." She had loved the sport, still did, but this time around she needed a man with a regular nine-to-five job, who came home for dinner, and who cut the grass on the weekend. A man who didn't drive around the track at one hundred and eighty-five miles an hour every weekend, tempting fate. She meant that.

Suzanne squeezed her hand again, then dropped it. "I understand. But there has to be a happy medium, sugar. Because unless that man over there is hiding a penis the size of an anaconda in his shit brown pants, you are too young, too pretty, too successful, and too much fun to settle for that."

That made Tamara laugh, though she wasn't sure she deserved the label *fun* anymore. Truth be told, she was as unadventurous as Geoffrey these days, and that had come about partly as a result of the demands of single parenthood and partly from conscious choice. She had aspired to a predictable lifestyle, and Geoffrey would fit perfectly into that equation.

So why couldn't she bring herself to like him?

Because maybe somewhere deep inside her she still felt the need for speed. For excitement. For the thrill of the race. Which was ridiculous given that she was a thirty-two-year-old widow with two kids and a career. There was no place for wild, not when she was her kids' whole world, their only parent, their security. But maybe there was room for a little plain old fun. Maybe she had swung too far the other way and did need to loosen up. "Thanks, Suz. You know I love you."

"I love you, too." Suzanne glanced over at her, eyebrow raised. "*Is* there an anaconda?" she asked, like it had suddenly occurred to her she could be totally wrong.

Tamara should only be so lucky. "No, there's no anaconda, I can promise you that." Not even a garden snake.

"Damn, I'm sorry."

"Me, too."

There was a pause when Tamara imagined they were both trying not to picture Geoffrey naked, then Suzanne smoothed her hands down the front of her red dress and tucked her hair back.

"Just do me a favor and think about what you really want. Don't settle, sweetie, okay?"

Tamara wanted to fluff Suzanne's words off, but she knew her friend was worried about her, and frankly, she was worried about herself. Forcing herself to date a man she felt no attraction to, and as a result finding herself slinging back wine to fight off a panic attack, wasn't exactly taking a positive turn.

Suz was right—there had to be something in between

deadly dull and wild girl. "Thanks, hon, I do have some thinking to do." Like how to break things off with Geoffrey before he whipped it out for the night.

"Good girl. Now I have to go network and earn my keep as a board member. You okay by yourself?"

"Yeah. You go ahead. I know half the people here." It was time to mingle. To move on.

Suzanne had managed to voice all of Tamara's niggling concerns out loud, and she knew what she needed to do. She needed to quit standing in the corner feeling sorry for herself and acknowledge that the weekend was her doing, and now she needed to undo it. She was the one who had invited Geoffrey. If she truly didn't like him as anything more than a friend and coworker, she needed to cut bait when they got home. She'd rather be alone than miserable, and he deserved someone who fully appreciated him. There was also no way she could have sex with him that night, not given that just entertaining the idea had her body feeling like she'd jumped into the Arctic for an extended swim.

It wasn't fair to Geoffrey to lead him on, and it wasn't fair to her to have to fake an orgasm. Again.

Maybe she could say she had a headache or claim the shrimp hadn't agreed with her to avoid the whole sex thing altogether. Of course, she could just break up with him, but it seemed downright awful to dump the man in the middle of the weekend. The nicer thing to do would be to wait until they were home, but then she was stuck wiggling out of whatever amorous plans he had for the evening. She'd put herself into a hell of a pickle.

Tamara glanced around the room, resolutely looking away from where Geoffrey was standing. It was a well-planned party, with lovely hors d'oeuvres and a quality quartet playing softly at the opposite end of the room. She would probably be enjoying herself if she weren't hiding from her date. Determined to stop being a stick and make the most of the disastrous weekend she had created, Tamara turned resolutely to follow Suzanne out into the crowd.

And walked straight into someone. Tamara jumped back, but it was too late. Her wine had splashed all down the front of the guy she'd slammed into.

"Oh my God, I'm so sorry!" Tamara winced as she accessed the damage. The red wine had turned his pale gray shirt rust from collar to waistband. It wasn't just a few droplets, it was the whole glass, and it was everywhere.

She looked up and immediately felt her cheeks start to burn. One, because she had never seen this man in her life, and therefore couldn't joke it off with a long-standing acquaintance. And two, because he was damn cute, with caramel-colored hair that was getting a little long on his forehead, shoulders that were broad and begging to be tested for firmness with a squeeze, and compelling, deep, brown eyes that had widened in shock from the impact.

"It's not a problem," he said, a Southern drawl to his voice.

Well, that was obviously a total lie, given that he looked like he'd taken a bullet to the chest and bled out, but she appreciated the effort to make her feel better. "I am really sorry. I've totally ruined your shirt. Let me replace it, pay for dry cleaning, do something," she babbled, reaching out with the napkin in her hand and brushing at the stain. Which was a complete and total mistake since he had a rock-solid chest under that wine-splattered shirt and she was suddenly very aware of the fact. She paused with her hand on him and felt her blush deepen.

Great, now she was groping the poor man. Tamara dropped her hand and winced.

"That's really not necessary," he said. "And honestly, you did me a favor." He nodded toward the room at large. "Perfect excuse to ditch this thing early, since I only know about four people and they're sick of me dogging their footsteps." His mouth turned up in a small smile. "If I'd been thinking,

I would've spilled wine on myself an hour ago. Course, I would have had to be drinking wine." He lifted his Bud bottle and shrugged. "I'm no more a wine guy than a tie guy."

Tamara relaxed a little. He was already tugging at his neck to loosen the tie, and he did look like he'd be more comfortable in the garage than at a corporate party. Maybe she hadn't exactly ruined the man's night, given that he kept glancing back at the room at large like it was going to pursue him, and he'd clearly been inching his way toward the door. She smiled back, and surprised herself by flicking her hair off her shoulder in a coy gesture she couldn't remember the last time she had used. "Are you telling me that you're not enjoying standing around making small talk with strangers and eating appetizers the size of your fingernail, when even after swallowing three of them, you still can't figure out what they are?" She could certainly sympathize with that. It had been a few years since she'd attended this kind of event, and she didn't miss it one bit.

He whipped his tie completely off his neck with a brutal tug and stuffed it into his pocket, looking relieved to be free of it. "That's exactly what I'm telling you. So I owe you a big thank-you . . . what's your name?"

"Tamara," she said, surprised to hear that her voice sounded a little breathy. God, she was flirting, wasn't she? He was too young for her. He was probably a pit crew member. And she was technically still with Geoffrey, yet she was flirting with this man, because he flipped her switch. Plain and simple. That chemistry that had been so elusive with Geoffrey had been there with this guy from the very second she had turned and laid eyes on him, and there was nothing wrong with a little flirtation, was there?

"Tamara . . . that's a beautiful name." He leaned a little closer to her and those deep, brown eyes swept over her. "Perfect for a beautiful woman."

Uh-oh. He felt it, too. Tamara swallowed. "Thank you. And you are . . . ?"

"Elec."

Damn it, even his name was sexy. She struggled against the urge to run her hand down his chest again. "Well, it's nice to meet you, Elec, despite the circumstances. And I really am sorry. I should have been paying closer attention."

"No harm done. And a wet shirt was worth the opportunity to meet you. It's been a pleasure."

It was just good Southern manners. That's all. He was trying to put her at ease, but Tamara felt warm in previously dormant places, and she was fairly certain it had nothing to do with the slightly excessive amounts of wine she'd tossed back. She wasn't drunk and she wasn't imagining the look he was giving her. Good manners didn't dictate he stare at her like he was picturing her naked, and she was not imagining the way his eyes kept darting down to her mouth then back up again. Elec was as attracted to her as she was attracted to him, and it felt . . . bewildering. She had no clue how to deal with it, given that she'd married Pete at twenty-one after a two-year courtship and had only recently ventured back into dating, with the dubious choice of Geoffrey.

This intrigue, this interest on both their parts, this sort of anticipation hanging in the air between them, was something she had zero experience with. So she stared at him, totally flustered, for a long, drawn-out second, then said, "Yeah. You, too." Which made no sense at all, which embarrassed her and confused her even more. Feeling like she'd suddenly regressed to the shy sixteen-year-old she'd been, she gave him a quick smile, turned, and tried to walk, not run, away from him, with her heart pounding and her palms sweating.

"What the hell was that?" she muttered to herself in complete disgust.

That was her libido leaping back to life without warning for the first cute guy who looked her way.

She suddenly knew that there was no putting off dealing with Geoffrey. Given that in two minutes standing next to Elec, a man she didn't know from Adam, she'd had more sexual stirrings than she had in a solid month with Geoffrey, including the times he'd been pulling out all the stops à la oral sex, she couldn't even wait until tomorrow to break up with him.

Geoffrey had been a colossal mistake and she needed to rectify it, immediately. Then get her own hotel room so that she could stare at the ceiling and picture what it would be like to have Elec over her, naked, his dark eyes flickering over her body, his fingers trailing across her . . .

Lord. Tamara fanned herself. What the hell had she been doing?

Right. Finding Geoffrey.

TAMARA waited for Geoffrey to say something to the careful words she'd just delivered to him, explaining how she wasn't ready to date after all, that she respected him as a friend, and felt she'd made a mistake in rushing their relationship. It had sounded good to her. Believable. It was the truth, if not the whole truth.

But Geoffrey was staring at her like she'd just said something in pig Latin, and she stared back, itching to take tweezers to those gray eyebrow hairs that poked out at random intervals from the rest of his brown brow. One, two, three, four . . . Tamara lost her place and started counting again. Dang, that was a lot of hairs that needed yanking.

"It's the money, isn't it?" he asked. "I should have expected that, but I confess, I'm still disappointed."

"What?" She dragged her eyes from his runaway eyebrow hairs and met his disappointed gaze, wondering what he was talking about.

"I know I can't keep you in the lifestyle you're accustomed to."

Was he joking? She could give a rat's ass about his money. She had her own income, had Pete's estate, and yet she still lived modestly, because labels and a fancy lifestyle weren't important to her. Never had been. Her handbag cost fifteen bucks at Target. When had she ever given off a vibe that she was high maintenance?

"It's not about money, Geoffrey. I just don't think we're well suited to each other as more than friends. I like you as a person, but I just don't think we're more than that."

"You came here tonight, didn't you, and it reminded you of how you miss all of this—the champagne, the parties, the track, the money."

Um . . . no. What she had realized during the course of the night was that Geoffrey wasn't a man she felt one ounce of sexual attraction to. And now she was doubting that she even liked him at all, period, given he seemed to think she was a gold-digging high roller.

"No. I realized that our relationship isn't going to work," she said firmly, no longer feeling an ounce of guilt that she was having this conversation with him by the empty coat check at the cocktail party. He was deliberately being obtuse.

"I don't think it is either," he said with disdain. "You're not the person I thought you were. I think it would be better if you stayed somewhere else tonight."

You bet she was staying in a different hotel room than him, the pompous ass. "If that's what you prefer."

"Unless you want one last night together," he said, looking suddenly hopeful.

Tamara felt her mouth drop open. He had to be joking. He thought she was a greedy name-dropper, yet he was willing to overlook that for a little nookie?

Like there was anything even *remotely* tempting about that for her, even if she ignored the fact that it was totally insulting.

Calculating that she'd left nothing in his hotel room except for an overnight bag with toiletries and a pair of jeans and a cotton shirt to wear to the race, she threw her shoulders back and glared at him. She could sacrifice her facial cleanser and a T-shirt to be done with him even sooner.

"I'd rather get my own room and spend the night alone," she said. "At least that way I might have a crack at having an orgasm. See you at the next department meeting, Geoffrey." She turned and stomped off, ignoring his spluttering protest.

She'd find Suzanne and beg her for a ride home, since Geoffrey had driven Tamara the forty-five minutes from her house to Charlotte. Or maybe she'd just get a room in the hotel the cocktail party was in and deal with a ride to the track in the morning, which sounded easier than going home. And she was definitely in no shape to drive as a result of the wine, though she supposed she could grab a cab to take her all the way home even if it would be pricey.

Tamara stopped midstride. Where the hell was her purse? She could have sworn she'd been carrying it all night, but now she had no idea what she'd done with it, and she was starting to think she should have eased up on the wine. Not having any cash or credit cards might be a serious problem.

"You alright, Tammy?"

She turned and saw Ryder Jefferson, Suzanne's ex-husband and one of Pete's best friends, standing next to her, looking handsome and full of testosterone. Tamara could see Suzanne's issues after spending nearly a decade with manly-man Ryder. "Hey, Ryder. I just broke up with that idiot I brought here and now I don't have a hotel room to stay in and I can't find my purse."

Still too annoyed to be concerned yet, she glanced around for her purse. It was hot pink, to offset her black dress and give her outfit a more summery look since it was May. How hard could it be to find a pink purse?

"I'm sorry," he said. Then Ryder gave her a grin. "Okay, not that you ditched the professor. He's dead boring, Tammy, and he doesn't know a damn thing about racing, or any sports for that matter. When he brought up his collection of antique thimbles, I thought about asking him to turn in his man card, but didn't out of respect for you."

A pang of embarrassment further flushed her cheeks. She probably looked downright feverish at this point, and she just wanted to get the hell out of there. Her day was officially and monumentally in the toilet. "Thanks, but you're free to say whatever you want from here on out since he just called me a gold digger."

Ryder raised an eyebrow. "What? You? That's ridiculous. You can squeeze a dime like nobody's business."

That was probably meant to be a compliment so she would just take it as such. "Anyway, I need to find my purse so I can get a hotel room."

"No need for you to get a room. Stay in my coach at the track." He winked. "I won't be needing it tonight. I have plans at my condo."

"With who?" Even as the words left her mouth, Tamara threw her hand up, realizing she really didn't want to hear his answer. "No, never mind. I don't want to know because if I know, then I have to tell Suzanne, and I don't want to go there."

He frowned. "Why would Suzanne care? She divorced me, remember? I doubt she's sleeping alone tonight either."

Tamara wasn't touching that one, since she knew Suzanne was in fact not sleeping with anyone, but who knew? Maybe Suz wanted her ex to think she had a string of able-bodied men in her bed. Better to keep her lips zipped and stay out of it. "You sure you don't care if I crash at your place? I don't want to start rumors."

"If I'm not there, how can there possibly be rumors? Come on, let's look for your purse, then we'll grab you a cab."

Biting her lip, she followed Ryder around the room. There was no sign of her purse, and she started to wonder if she'd even brought it in with her. She'd been so stressed out all night, she was no longer clear on if she'd even had it when she'd arrived. After ten minutes of searching, she was panicking, but Ryder took her by the arm and led her out of the room.

"Tammy, relax. It's no big deal. I'll let the hotel know it's missing, and tomorrow if we still can't find it, you can cancel all your cards." He was talking and walking, leading her straight to the front door. "Now I think you need to just go back to my place and crash out. You've had a long night and breaking things off with someone is never easy."

Feeling sympathy for toddlers who were dragged through the mall by their mothers, Tamara started to wonder if she was keeping Ryder from his overnight date since he seemed so determined to get rid of her. As he hustled her out the front door, she said, "I can't pay for the cab without my purse."

He pulled out three twenties and handed them to her before stepping out into the circular drive in front of the hotel. She didn't even have time to protest that was more money than she needed when he pointed. "Oh, hey, look, there's a buddy of mine. Bet he's going back to the compound. You can rideshare with him and then I'll know for sure you're safe."

Tamara only saw legs getting into the cab to the right of them and she hesitated. Great. Nothing like getting fobbed off on some poor unsuspecting guy who was probably done up and looking to just go home. "I don't want to impose on anyone."

"Nah, it's cool. We go way back and he joined my team this season." Ryder took her hand and pulled her over to the cab. He stuck his head inside and chatted for a minute, then turned back to her and smiled. "You're all set. Elec will get you to my coach."

Oh, no. He did not just say . . .

"Elec?" Tamara blurted as she took a step back and almost fell over the curb. There couldn't possibly be two Elecs at the party, which meant that . . .

Elec, just as gorgeous as she remembered, leaned out of the cab. "Hop on in, Tamara. I'll make sure you get home safely."

Said the spider to the fly.

But she climbed in beside him anyways, watching him watching her, because she had no other choice, and because if she were totally honest, she wanted to. Not Tamara, the sociology professor, or Tamara, the mother. But Tamara, the woman, felt a little hitch of excitement at the thought of sitting in the backseat with Elec, her leg brushing against his, those dark brown eyes focused on her.

There was nothing wrong with a little flirting, after all, and she could sorely use some.

"Thanks," she told Elec a little breathlessly as she settled in next to him on the vinyl seat and adjusted her dress so it wasn't riding up her thighs. "I appreciate it."

He smiled at her, not a grin, not a smirk, but a serious, he meant business kind of smile, and said in a low, sexy drawl, "Best thing to happen to me all day."

Tamara suddenly knew there was nothing harmless about this flirtation at all.

She was in all kinds of trouble, and she seriously liked it.

TWO

ELEC Monroe watched Tamara's eyes widen as she looked at him from under those luscious eyelashes. She was a drop-dead-gorgeous woman, with pin-straight rich brown hair, long bangs that she swept to the side, and full, pouty lips. Elec hadn't recognized her as the late Pete Briggs's wife until Ryder had mentioned it when he'd quickly explained her predicament and asked Elec to see her back to the compound. Elec hadn't yet been driving in the cup series when Pete had, and so his path hadn't crossed Tamara's much. But what he remembered from seeing her in Victory Lane with Pete on TV, and from early days hanging out by the haulers when Elec had been a teenager and she'd been a young bride, was that she had been a shy, fresh-faced little thing, her hair always scraped back in a ponytail, her favorite outfit jeans and a polo shirt.

There were shades of that young girl in the Tamara Briggs sitting next to him, but she had obviously grown into a sophisticated, confident woman. One that made him hard as concrete and wonder if he had any chance of getting anywhere with her. He doubted it, and that was probably for the best. She was not the type he usually dated, because a woman like Tamara wanted commitment and he couldn't offer much in that way, but there was nothing wrong with a little flirting. Nothing wrong with seeing how far it could go, because he was seriously attracted to her, the edgy desire he felt when looking at her surprising him. He wasn't usually one to tumble for a woman, but there was something about her that had him leaning closer and hoping it was his lucky night.

"You're just trying to make me feel better," she said, tucking her hair behind her ear in a gesture Elec found sexy as hell.

It wasn't meant to be—he didn't think anyway—but it was. She wasn't an obvious or aggressive flirt. She was just looking at him sideways, moist lips slightly open, her long legs crossed in that elegant little black dress, yet it was doing a serious number on him. There was something so intelligent and classy, yet open and vulnerable, about her, and he found that incredibly appealing.

"I'm not just saying that," he told her. "Like I said, I hate those parties. I'm not much for small talk with strangers, and I'm lousy at it, frankly. I'm much better one-on-one." He hoped she'd pick up on the innuendo. Not subtle, and edging into corny territory, but the cab ride wasn't that long. Elec needed to get his intentions across loud and clear so that when he asked her out, she wasn't caught off guard.

He shouldn't go out with her, but damn, did he want to go out with her. He just wanted her, flat out. Since the second she had turned and collided with him, he had been intrigued and had spent the last half hour watching her wandering around the party, talking to some guy in a sweater and then to Ryder. Seeing Ryder with his hand on the small of her back was what had sent Elec out the door. He knew Ryder was a ladies' man, and it had looked like

Tamara was with him, Ryder's latest conquest. Elec had felt a burst of annoyance that had surprised him so he'd decided it was time to pack up and go home.

Which had somehow landed him with Tamara figuratively in his lap.

Couldn't get much better than that.

"Me, too," she said. "You'd think since I'm a teacher that I would be used to hordes of people, but mingling is different. It's hard work trying to remember names and who is married to who, and I'm always a little bit terrified I'll totally screw up and offend someone."

"I feel the same way," he said. Exactly the same way. He was no schmoozer, and he dreaded media interviews like some folks did the dentist. Put him behind the wheel, and he was aggressive and confident. Stick a mic in his face, and his tongue mysteriously stuck to the roof of his mouth and his brain moved like molasses uphill in winter. "I can't ever remember anyone's name." He smiled at her so she'd know he was joking as he said, "I've probably already forgotten yours."

She laughed. "Really? That's okay, I answer to just about anything, even 'hey, you.'"

"A woman with a classy name like Tamara shouldn't answer to 'hey, you.' You should hold out, in my opinion."

"So you do remember my name."

Her tongue slid across her plump bottom lip in a way that had Elec mentally groaning and questioning how he could be so damn turned on. His body was acting like he hadn't had sex in a good five years, yet he didn't even think it had been a month since he'd last done a little sheet diving with a willing woman.

Getting women was never a problem when you were a driver, and he'd done his fair share of sucking up the attention. But Elec had never been one for a string of meaningless hookups with women he had nothing in common with, even when he'd tried to convince himself he was.

It had occurred to Elec not too far into his career that he was plain old over busty bleach blondes with half a brain throwing themselves at him on a regular basis. They made him uncomfortable, feeling like a notch in their proverbial bedpost. Item ten on their life list: Nail a race car driver.

That wasn't what he wanted. He wanted a woman he could talk to.

A woman like Tamara Briggs.

Yet he had spent years actually avoiding dating anyone like her because the bottom line was that women like Tamara wanted children, and he couldn't have any. He was shooting blanks, and nothing short of a miracle was going to change that. Aside from his own personal disappointment that he'd never be a daddy, he had steered clear of maternal types. Why fall in love with someone only to tell her the truth and have her dump his ass in pursuit of a man who could give her babies? It didn't sound like a good time to Elec. So he'd dated women like Crystal, his latest failed attempt at companionship, who was more interested in the limelight than him, and he'd been left feeling like there wasn't ever going to be the right relationship for him.

But Tamara Briggs was very, very tempting. And she had children already, he was fairly certain. That had to count for something.

"You caught me. I do remember your name. And just so you know, I'll answer to anything but Junior."

"Why? Because it makes you feel like you're in your father's shadow?"

"No. It's because I'm not a Junior."

Tamara laughed, a soft, throaty laugh that spiked his desire up yet another notch. He wouldn't have thought it was even possible to be so turned on just sitting fully dressed in the back of a cab, but life took unexpected turns, and this was new knowledge he was happy to have.

"Oh. Well, alright then." She gave him another side smile. "That makes total sense."

"I'm sorry you lost your purse," Elec added. "I hope it turns up."

"Me, too. I don't even know what I did with it, and that's driving me crazy. I never lose things. Never." She waved her hand in the air. "God, this weekend has been a total disaster. Maybe I should have just stayed home."

That would have been seriously unfortunate because then Elec wouldn't have been treated to the view of her long legs or her luscious lips, and that would have truly been a damn shame. "Why? What else has gone wrong?"

She shot him a sheepish look. "I brought a man I've been seeing with me."

Elec felt a serious kick of disappointment. She was dating someone? That was just all sorts of wrong. "So where is he tonight? Why isn't he taking you home?" And could Elec pay him off to get rid of him?

"I broke up with him."

Thank the Lord. Now he didn't have to worry about stealing the poor sap's woman, because he was fairly certain he was going to take a crack at it, morally wrong or not.

"There just wasn't any . . ." She cleared her throat. "He's very nice, but there was no . . . between us, you know. Do you know what I'm saying?"

"You mean no sexual attraction?" he asked, not sure why she wasn't just saying that outright. It happened all the time. That's what friendship was for. Sometimes you just didn't feel any sort of physical connection with someone of the opposite sex.

She nodded rapidly. "Exactly. Only, I feel like I led him on by inviting him for this weekend." She turned more fully to him, uncrossing her legs and drawing them up onto the seat in a way that created a tunnel between her dress and her inner thighs. "The thing is, I haven't dated at all since my husband was killed."

Distracted by the fact that he could almost see up her skirt—almost, but not quite—which was teasing him something terrible, Elec was having a little trouble concentrating on her words. He forced himself to drag his gaze away from those legs and look up at her face. Focus. Form words. He could do that. "Well, that's understandable. It hasn't been all that long, has it? Two seasons ago, right? You don't get over something like that in the blink of an eye."

Hell, how did a wife ever get over losing her husband in a wreck? He wasn't sure.

"Thanks for saying that." Her hand came out and softly touched his knee before pulling back. "And I've been busy raising my kids, juggling my career. This was the first guy I've gone out with and I thought I could make myself like him since he's nice and safe and stable. Tonight I figured out I can't do that."

Elec wanted to touch Tamara back, to stroke his own hand over her bare knee, or slide his fingers into her thick hair, but he restrained himself. "No. You can't force yourself to feel attracted to someone." He'd learned that with the bimbo brigade. Just because a woman looked good on his arm before a big race didn't make up for the awkward silences, or worse, the mindless chatter she threw at him until all he wanted was a remote control to turn her volume down.

"No. You can't." She gave a soft laugh and pressed fingers to her temples. "God, I have no idea why I'm telling you all this. You're probably regretting getting saddled with me. I'm babbling."

"Obviously you needed someone to talk to, and sometimes a person you don't know is the best bet. You feel like they have no bias on whatever you're saying." He gave her a smile. "And I've been told I have one of those faces. People like to tell me things." Sometimes things he could do without, frankly, like the bank teller's description of her hysterectomy.

"You do have one of those faces," she said softly. "Like

you're actually listening, not just looking for an opening to turn the subject back to you."

The look on her face led him to believe she'd known a lot of men like that. He shrugged. "I like listening to people talk. Most people are fascinating. And I'm not all that comfortable in the limelight, anyway." Which had been a major setback in his career, something he fought against every day. "My mother used to call me Elec the Eyeball, because I was always sitting and watching. Staring, I guess." He grinned. "Not really a flattering nickname, but I actually think she appreciated me being a quiet kid, and meant it in an affectionate way. My brother and sister were kind of loud." In the way that the roar of forty-three cars circling the short track at Bristol was kind of loud.

She laughed. "Elec the Eyeball? Mothers give their kids the most appalling nicknames. I call my son Peter-Pants and I really need to stop. He's nine years old and it's not so cute anymore."

Ouch. Poor kid. He'd take Eyeball any day of the week over being referenced as a fairy boy in tights. Elec grinned. "Just don't call him that in public. That's a fistfight with the other boys waiting to happen."

"Ugh. I can't stomach the thought of my baby getting into a fistfight. I'm not ready for any of that. Ryder is Petey's godfather and I'm going to be calling on him for help the first time a punch is thrown." She laughed. "I try not to be overprotective, but there are some things I just don't want to think about or deal with. And don't even get me started on how I handle the day my son discovers girls don't have cooties . . . I won't be turning to Ryder for advice there, trust me, since he's got a new woman every week. I think I'll just lock my son up until he's thirty instead."

"I don't think that will go over well."

"I'm hoping that since Petey's main interest in life is bugs and nature, he won't discover girls until he's eighteen."

"Just because he likes a good cockroach doesn't mean he won't be fantasizing about girls between tromps in the woods."

"That's true, I guess." She sighed. "Lord, I don't even want to think about it."

"I bet you're an amazing mother," Elec murmured, wondering if she had any idea at all how damn hot she was. He was such a skunk. For all he claimed to be a good listener, and for all that he really was interested in getting to know her, he was seriously distracted by how close she was to him in the cab. Her perfume drifted over to him every time she shifted on the seat and her legs came dangerously close to bumping his over and over, tormenting him. He wanted to just reach out and taste those plump, juicy lips and see if they were as delicious as they looked. He wanted to slide his hand up her leg, under that dress, and discover if she wore practical panties, a sexy thong, or nothing at all. If he were a betting man, he'd put his money on black lace covering her soft, feminine sex, cupping her firm ass delicately.

And while he was thinking all of that, she was talking about her child, which meant he really should be heartily ashamed of himself.

He wasn't feeling it.

"Thanks," she said in a soft voice, her eyes widening, like she realized which way the wind was blowing.

Like she knew he was two seconds away from kissing her.

Elec leaned forward.

Tamara sucked in a breath.

The cabdriver announced, "We're here."

She jumped back and said, "Oh! That was fast."

Damn it. Elec gritted his teeth in frustration and sank back against the seat. Tamara was already jumping out of the cab, though, so he didn't have any time to waste lamenting the lost chance. He threw double the fare at the driver and climbed out before she could completely escape on him.

Fortunately, she was standing there looking around in bewilderment. "I don't even know which coach is Ryder's. I don't remember what it looks like, or if he even has the same one."

"I'll show you." It was the gentlemanly thing to do. Walk her to Ryder's place, ask her out on a date. That was the plan. That was the right thing to do. Not to kiss her in the cab, or invite her back to his own coach, which was parked three over from Ryder's. Not to mash his mouth against hers and dip his tongue inside to see if she tasted as delicious as she looked. She would think he was on the make, which he was, but there was a difference. Elec was on the make with every intention of calling her, so while it might seem a little lecherous, it was lecherous with a follow-through. She'd never believe that, though, so he had to be patient, play it cool.

They went through the gate and entered the restricted area where all the drivers kept their motor coaches. Elec's portion of the coach, which he shared with his older brother Evan, wasn't as rigged out as some of the other guys', since he did tend to go home to his condo in Charlotte Monday through Wednesday during the race season, and because he was still just a rookie—as the other drivers all liked to point out—but he did have a flat-screen TV and his Xbox. Both kept him company now that he'd ditched the last of the simpering, camera-hungry females who had been dangling after him, though Crystal still insisted on sending him a boatload of text messages. He hadn't figured out how to make that stop without getting rude on her and he didn't like to be rude, so for the moment, he'd just been ignoring her.

Elec knew from barbeques Ryder had thrown that his coach was fully loaded, looking straight out of a decorating magazine with plush furniture in earth tones, and containing every gadget known to man. Ryder's driver, a man who was probably pushing sixty, but was sporting killer biceps, gave Tamara a wide smile in recognition when he opened the door to them.

"Well, hello, Mrs. Briggs, how are you? Ryder called me and gave me a heads-up. I'm sorry you lost your purse but it's good to see you again." He shot a curious look over her head at Elec. "Elec," he said as a greeting.

Elec nodded in return, getting the message loud and clear that the driver was wondering what the hell he was doing with Tamara. "Jeff."

"Thanks," Tamara said with an answering smile. "It's good to see you, too, Jeff. How have you been?"

"Can't complain, can't complain." Jeff stepped down out of the coach. "I'm heading over to my girlfriend's for the night, so if you could lock up in the morning, I'd appreciate it."

"I hope I'm not running you out," she said in alarm. "Don't leave on my account if you usually stay here when Ryder isn't."

"Oh, no, no. Ruth and I have a standing Saturday night date. But I left my cell phone number on the table so call me if you need anything, Mrs. Briggs."

Then the older man left, with a stern glare and a nod in Elec's direction. He hardly even noticed, reflecting on what Jeff had been calling Tamara.

Mrs. Briggs. Damn, what the hell did Elec think he was doing? The title bothered Elec, gave him serious pause. Who did he think he was, competing with the late, great Pete Briggs? Tamara had loved him, probably still missed him. That was a lot to live up to, and Pete had been a social guy, the life of the party. He had been the first one to smile for the cameras, to climb up on a table and give a speech, and to do a burnout for the fans when he won a race. Elec winced when the cameras turned on him. He was a racer, never happier than when he was building an engine or sitting behind the wheel, and he wasn't good at public speaking.

Elec was nothing like Pete Briggs. So no doubt he was not Mrs. Tamara Briggs's type at all.

Pete had given Tamara marriage, children, fame in racing, money.

Elec had none of that to give.

Yet he was more attracted to her than any woman in a good long while. Maybe ever.

Which was why he couldn't stop himself from saying, "Tamara."

She turned around, standing in the doorway of the coach, her head tilted, chin tucked toward her chest, her restless hand playing with the ends of her hair. "Thanks for seeing me back, Elec. I know Ryder foisted me off on you and you've been very patient."

Patience had nothing to do with anything. What he was, was damn frustrated, and wishing he'd been gifted with a silver tongue instead of one that tripped over words, and a brain that had no clue how to articulate to her what he was thinking. Which was that he wanted to get to know her better. Much better. So he just stuck his hands in his front pockets and hoped for the best, knowing he wasn't going to be able to dredge up any pretty or slick words. "I told you it's the best thing to happen to me all day."

He was standing only a foot or two in front of her and he wished he wasn't wearing a stained dress shirt and shoes that pinched the hell out of his feet. He'd kill to be in jeans, a T-shirt, and a ball cap. Maybe then he'd feel like less of a jackass. "I'd like to go to dinner with you next week," he said before he turned into a total chickenshit and hauled ass out of there without asking her out. "Are you free?"

Her eyes widened, like she'd honestly had no idea he was going to say that.

"Oh," she said and blinked.

Well, that was quite the ego stroke. Not. Elec figured he

could say something smooth and flirtatious and coaxing, or he could just wait and see if she expanded on her nothing of a response. He knew anything he tried to say would sound desperate so he just shut his mouth, watched, and waited.

"I . . ." Her hand fluttered up to her chest. "I don't know what to say."

Hell, she was going to turn him down. Elec really didn't want to hear that, so he stepped closer to her, stared into her blue eyes, and said, "Say yes."

Then he raised his hand and cupped her cheek. He leaned toward her, still watching her, gauging her reaction, giving her time to pull back. She didn't. Her eyes went even wider, but she didn't stop him. So he kissed her.

Oh, man, he was dead. The minute his mouth connected with hers in a smooth, soft, full-contact kiss that started a burn low in his gut, Elec knew he was in for some serious trouble, and it was going to take all of his willpower to step away. Which he had to do. Yet his mouth still hovered over hers, his body tense, fists clenched, eyes closed as he inhaled her scent, listened to the rush of her breathing, felt the brush of her thighs against his arm. In a second he would move away. After another kiss. Just one more, then he'd back up and go home. For real.

But he had to have another one—bigger, fuller, deeper—to take away with him.

Elec eliminated all the space between them and gripped her cheek, sliding his hand all up into her thick, silky hair. Then he took her mouth, harder this time, enjoying the feel of her body close to his, the sweet taste of her soft, moist lips. For a good long while, they both just explored the feel of each other, the hot press of his mouth to hers, until he couldn't resist. He slipped his tongue into her, and Tamara's hands snaked around his neck and met his tongue with her own in a seductive little thrust. Just like that, heat exploded between them. He heard her breath suck in as they broke contact, felt her breasts press against his chest, was aware of her fingers digging into the back of his hair. They paused, staring at each other, poised between stopping and starting what he knew they couldn't stop.

Their heavy breathing filled the warm night air and he stared into her soft, blue eyes, then down at her plump, kiss-swollen lips. Her cheeks were flushed from arousal, her hair mussed and hanging in her eyes, and Elec wanted her in a way that made all logic disappear, and his body tense in places he hadn't even known existed.

Elec went with it, because, well, he couldn't stop himself. She tasted like wine and woman, and she had opened her mouth for him eagerly. She had willingly wedged her leg inside his, pressed her breasts against his chest. She wanted him, too, and when he reached for her, arms, hands, and lips, she met him halfway with enough force that their teeth knocked together. He wasn't even sure who was kissing who anymore, they were just colliding into each other, taking and tasting, nipping and gripping each other, his common sense gone, his erection bumping right into her inner thighs. She was a step up from him in the doorway of the coach and it made for damn good positioning, which he took advantage of by grinding himself against her.

When they broke apart to pull in air before they both suffocated, Elec tried to think of what to say, not an apology, but some kind of reassurance, a promise that he'd knock it off and get control of himself, no matter how hard that might be. He was pushing it, he was losing it, he was being downright offensive and aggressive and he would really, really try to cool it and be a gentleman. But before he could form any words, Tamara glanced left and right.

"Oh, Lord, get inside before someone sees us."

Green flag. Elec had one foot on the step when his conscience got the best of him. "Are you sure? I can leave if you want."

"Do you want to leave?" she asked him, wiping her damp bottom lip.

He couldn't help it. He stared at that lip, thinking just how badly he wanted to suck that plumpness into his mouth, while his erection throbbed painfully in his stupid dress pants. "*Hell*, no, I don't want to leave."

MOMMA had always warned her to watch out for the quiet ones, and have mercy, had she been right. Tamara stared at Elec staring at her, and she forgot how to think. Did he have any idea what he did to her when he looked at her like that? The way his deep, sensual eyes just bore into her, making her feel like he could strip away all her reservations right along with her clothes and take whatever he wanted from her.

Pete had been a lot of fun, and an enthusiastic lover, but ultimately at the end of the day, she'd often felt like the moon sucked into his gravitational pull. It was always a good time, but it was always about him.

When this man in front of her looked at her, she felt like she had his full and total attention, that right at this very moment, his focus was one hundred percent on her. And that was the hottest thing she'd ever experienced in her life.

Which was why she heard herself saying, "So don't leave."

Her heart was pounding, but it was from excitement, not nerves, as he stepped up into the coach and shut the door behind him. Tamara had moved back only far enough to let him in, and he erased that space in half a step. There was a lot of man in front of her, and she was aware of just how long it had been since she'd touched one.

A real man, that is. Geoffrey pretty much didn't count, and frankly, she hadn't done that much touching. Not that she wanted to think about Geoffrey. Because she really, really didn't. She just wanted to think about, to appreciate, that it was Elec standing in front of her and what a truly lovely twist of fate spilling her wine on him had been.

She had expected that he would start kissing her again, but he surprised her by gliding his thumb down her cheek, across her lips, over her neck. "You are very beautiful," he said in a husky whisper.

It had been such a very long time since she'd heard anything like that. She sighed out loud in pleasure, and she thought she could almost be satisfied with just that. Almost.

Her cheeks started to burn under his scrutiny and from embarrassment that she needed to hear that kind of compliment, but she managed to murmur, "Thank you." She'd had no idea until that very moment how much she had missed being just a woman. More than a mother. More than a sociology professor. Being a woman, who could make a man look at her like he wanted to eat her all up with a spoon.

But she had that standing in front of her now, and she wanted Elec, wanted those words, his touch, and he gave it to her.

Elec bent his head to kiss her and she met him halfway, hungry for more, desperate to run her hands across his chest, to feel his body hard against hers. His tongue plunged inside her mouth and she closed her eyes as desire tugged at her inner thighs, leaving her hot and wet and ready faster than she could have ever imagined possible. There wasn't a single rational thought left in her head as she dug her hands into his hair and kissed him for all she was worth. He felt hot and hard and good, his hands in her hair, on her back, squeezing her backside.

She hadn't realized how long two years could be until she was tasting what she'd been missing, and now she knew it was damn near an eternity. Way too long to go without feeling this freedom, this intensity, this giving in to what her body ached for.

It wasn't pretty and it wasn't smooth and she didn't care. It was frantic and fumbling as they both tried to touch everything they could all at once.

They were grinding their hips together, stumbling around a few feet as they tried to get closer still, Elec's tongue doing crazy sexy things to her mouth, her jaw, her ear, her neck, trailing down to her breasts and back up again when he found her nipples were inaccessible through her dress. Tamara moaned, both in delight from all the fizzy feelings stirring in her, and from the need for more. Now that she was getting it, she wondered how she could have ever lived without it, and she needed him to take her all the way to the finish line before she literally lay down on the coach floor and died from want.

"Thank you for spilling wine on my shirt," Elec said, stepping back and unbuttoning his shirt. He yanked it off with little care or concern for the fabric and tossed it on the floor with hard movements. His T-shirt, which also sported a smaller wine stain, was peeled off and sent after the dress shirt.

Tamara almost choked on her drool. Oh. My. God. "My pleasure," she said and gawked mercilessly at his ripped chest and abs. He clearly wasn't scarfing potato chips and playing video games on his days off because that was one fine-looking male form, and she reached out and did what she'd been dying to do since she'd first set eyes on him. She squeezed a bicep, just to feel how firm it was. It was as hard as rock. Hard as steel. She glanced down at his pants. Hard as his erection.

"Impressive," she said, not sure if she was really talking about his arm muscles or another equally promising muscle. Not that it mattered. It was all impressive, and it was all hers for the taking.

He pulled her into his arms and Tamara ran her hands all over his chest and back, surprised at how bold and greedy she was being, but unable to work up any shame or regret.

He was just altogether too much temptation, and after the disaster with Geoffrey, she was in need of some serious comfort. She needed to know she could have good sex again at some point in her life. Starting now. Elec had her more aroused than she could have ever actually thought possible, and while part of her brain was hinting that just maybe she should think about slowing down, most of her brain and all of her body were screaming for her to take it. To enjoy it.

His hand snaked around her back as he kissed her, and he found her dress zipper. Elec paused. "Is this okay?"

For a woman who had never had a one-night stand in her life, she was amazed at how easily she announced, with zero hesitation, "Yes."

She should probably think about the fact that she didn't know squat about Elec, including his last name, but Ryder knew Elec and so did Jeff, the coach driver. Ryder had vouched for him, and had mentioned that Elec worked on his pit crew, and under the circumstances that was good enough for her. Drivers didn't let just anyone onto their crew. They had to trust them implicitly because they could make or break a race for a car. So while Elec was a new acquaintance, he wasn't a complete stranger, and given the heady combination of wine and rampant sexual longing, she was inclined to talk herself into believing just about anything.

He wasn't leaving the damn coach without giving her an orgasm. Plain and simple.

Fortunately, he seemed to have the same goal in mind. Elec undid her dress slowly, teasing her, his fingers tickling down her spine, his tongue sliding across her bottom lip.

"Let me know if I'm going too fast," he murmured into her ear, before his tongue dipped inside.

Tamara almost jumped out of her dress, which probably would have been a good thing since then they could get straight to the good stuff. She was dying from want, and she couldn't prevent a moan from leaving her mouth as she gripped his arms for support. "You're not going too fast . . . you're going too slow. I haven't had sex in two years, three months, and three weeks." Not that she'd been keeping track or anything.

Geoffrey didn't count. It had been two years, three months, and three weeks since she'd had satisfying sex. With a man.

Though maybe that was a mood kill to tell a guy something like that. She stiffened a little in his arms. Maybe she'd just put pressure on him, and had created performance anxiety. Men could be so arrogant and yet so insecure and what the hell did she really know about seduction? Diddly. A glance up at Elec to gauge his reaction showed that his eyes had gotten even darker and he was breathing hard, his chest rising and falling rapidly.

He didn't say a word. He just ripped the front of her dress off her shoulders and down past her breasts. It caught for a second on her hips, but he was having none of it. One more tug and it was at her ankles and she was standing in her bra and panties and high heels. Thank God she'd worn a black lace bra. A quick glance down reassured her she also had on the flattering boy shorts that covered some of those unfortunate stretch marks above the pelvis that her first pregnancy had left her as a souvenir.

Elec popped her bra open before she could blink.

Okay, so maybe she hadn't given him performance anxiety. That was encouraging.

"Well, let's make it worth your wait," he said.

Oooh, she liked the sound of that, especially since his words were followed up by his mouth moving down over her nipple and sucking it. Yeah, no vibrator on the planet could do *that*, and she let out a low moan, gripping his arms to keep herself standing. She had missed that feeling, that hard tingling pull on her breasts that echoed low in her belly and made her drop her head back automatically. That sensation of a man over her, surrounding her, his grip tight on her arms, his breath tickling her flesh, making her appreciate it all the more for having gone without.

Her bra had slipped down her arms and Elec managed to divest her of it altogether while still licking and sucking, moving from one breast to the other, his free hand cupping the weight of the breast he was working on. Tamara fought for air as he moved faster, tugged harder, nipping at her, then startling her by sliding his fingers down into her panties from behind, clear down into the divot of her bottom. She wasn't expecting that, or that she wouldn't be freaked out by it, but she welcomed it, enjoyed the boldness of it, the intimacy, the sensuality of him confidently exploring her body.

She jerked involuntarily at the jolt of pleasure she felt from that simple touch as he traced all the way down and around to her wet core, and she wondered how she was going to see this through to the end without shattering like glass. If he so much as brushed against the front of her, she wasn't sure she would be able to stay standing. More likely, she'd just puddle on the floor in boneless, gooey ecstasy while he stared down at her in total confusion.

Figuring if he had the right to touch her butt, she could certainly check his out, Tamara snuck around the side of his pants and lightly rested her hands there, a little unsure. She couldn't say that anytime recently she'd just blithely groped an unknown ass and she wasn't sure how to proceed.

Then he bit her nipple, not hard, but with enough force to send a sharp throb rushing through her body, and she instinctively grabbed on to his butt and shoved herself against him. Whoa and whoa. He had some nice muscle definition on his back porch, and an even nicer muscle on his front, and she greedily ran her hands all over him, squeezing and exploring, enjoying the hitch to his breath. Forget hesitation or modesty when he was sporting a body like that, and she was all too aware it could be her one and only chance at it, so she might as well touch it all and then some. When she bumped against him a second time, he actually moaned out loud, and Tamara joined him. Damn, despite being so out of practice, she'd managed to hit her clit dead-on, and even with his jeans and her panties in the way, she felt the force of that collision all the way to her toes.

"Tamara," he said in a low voice, undoing his belt with quick, urgent movements. "Do you have a condom?"

She froze. Oh, damn it all to hell and back. "No," she said, stepping back so she wouldn't be tempted to touch him again. She was as fertile as the freaking Nile and she might be taking a walk on the wild side, but she wasn't insane enough to risk getting knocked up with a younger pit crew member's illegitimate child. The very thought of the scandal, of having to explain that to her seven- and nine-year-olds, and to her own mother—good God, her mother—was almost enough to douse the fire of her desire. Almost.

"Isn't there a drugstore up the road?" she asked. He had to have a car, right? Maybe. Hopefully.

"Yeah." Elec ran his hand through his hair, making the long front ends stand up at a funny angle. He looked a little crazed and she almost laughed. "But this is Ryder's coach. He's got to have condoms around here somewhere, don't ya think?"

Good point. Suzanne's ex-husband was never lacking for female companionship. "You check the bathroom. I'll look in the nightstand."

"Okay." He turned and headed to the bathroom, his unzipped pants riding low on his hips.

Oh, my. That was one fine-looking butt she'd been feeling up. Tamara just stood still, struck dumb at her good fortune, and glanced down at her tummy pooch. She should have been going to the gym. Eating better. She was past thirty now after all.

"Are you even looking?" Elec called from the bathroom, the obvious sound of drawers opening and closing accompanying his voice. "Cuz I'm not finding anything in here and I don't have my car at the compound, and I'm about to crawl to the damn store if I have to."

Her tummy pooch, poor diet, and advanced age clearly didn't seem to be bothering Elec, so she kicked off her heels and hightailed it into the bedroom in nothing but her panties. But she still dashed past the bathroom at high speed so he wouldn't have time to see her almost-naked self. It was one thing for him to see her bare breasts when he was licking them, it was another altogether to just be strolling around demonstrating the effect gravity and breast-feeding had had on them. "I'm looking."

Ryder was one messy boy. Glancing around the room, Tamara saw his bed wasn't made, his clothes were scattered all over the floor and on an easy chair, and he had nothing short of three thousand ball caps crowding his dresser in stacks at least ten high. It took her a minute to wade through the flotsam to the nightstand, but the second she yanked the drawer open, she knew she'd hit pay dirt. There was not one, but three boxes of condoms. With spermicide, ribbed for her pleasure, and extrasensitive. Options. How considerate of Ryder.

Lying next to the condoms was a pair of fur-lined handcuffs, lubricant, and a rubber whip. She'd just leave those right there for Ryder. She didn't think she and Elec were to the bondage stage yet, and she had absolutely no need for the lubricant given how damp her panties were.

"Found them!" she called, debating which kind to choose. She grabbed the spermicide box. Elec was young and looked awfully healthy, so she might as well have the extra insurance.

He must have run, given the speed with which he appeared next to her.

"Oh!" she said when she turned and bumped right into him.

Elec smiled. "We have to stop running into each other like this."

"I don't know," she said. "I kind of like it."

"That's funny," he said. "Cuz I like it, too."

Oh, my. His bare chest was touching hers and his hands had found her butt and were squeezing. She should explain that she hadn't been able to work out because of her schedule. She should warn him about the stretch marks. Apologize for the damage breast-feeding had wreaked on her once perky, now not so perky, breasts.

The only man ever to see her fully naked had been Pete, and he had been there with her through the changes to her body. She felt a moment's hesitation, a rising panic that she couldn't be attractive enough or sexy enough for a man like Elec.

But then he kissed her mouth, slowly, sensually, kissed her jaw, her neck, each breast, just on the tip of the nipple. Then he bent down and slid his tongue along her navel, down into her belly button, and farther on, licking a trail right and left along the waistband of her panties. He knelt on the floor and kissed her on the front of the lace panties, on each inner thigh, his fingers tickling across the backs of her legs, and she forgot to worry, forgot everything but the desire he ignited in her, the ache that demanded she have more, the need to feel him fully inside her.

She forgot to feel anything but sexy when he so clearly desired her, wanted to explore her, and she stood straight, shoulders back, hair tumbling forward, teeth sinking into her bottom lip. It was good, all so good, and she was going to have sex with this man.

When he stood back up and nudged her backward, she

went down on the bed willingly. When he touched her panties, the last scrap of clothing covering her, and pulled them down, she ignored the momentary pang of modesty and swallowed hard, staring up at the ceiling to get control. She wanted to do this, wanted to know that she was still a woman, and when he kissed her right between the thighs, she knew she was still a woman capable of giving and receiving passion and pleasure and that this was her time to take back her identity, her turn to be selfish and sexual and empowered.

Elec moved his tongue slowly over her, top to bottom, like he was savoring the taste of her. He pulled back, making her moan at the loss, then he returned with just the tip of his tongue, teasing her with light, quick movements, circling around her clit, but never touching it.

Tamara moved her hips, wanting more, tight with pleasure, feeling the ache build deep inside her.

"Do you want more?" he asked, casually stroking across her, his hands lightly resting on her thighs.

Um, yeah. Obviously he was a mind reader. "Yes," she said, wondering if it would be rude to grab his hair for leverage. She gripped the sheets instead and tried to remember to breathe, tried not to squirm and flop around in an ecstasy that came dangerously close to agony. She didn't want to look desperate and unattractive, she wanted to be sexy and artful and elegant.

"Okay."

Then Elec plunged his tongue inside her and Tamara decided to screw elegant. When had she ever been that anyway? And what was the point in holding back, denying herself any piece of this experience? She was this far in, might as well toss out the last of the old inhibitions and just say what she felt. So she arched her back, grabbed his hair with both hands, and let go of the most outrageous moan she had ever emitted in her entire sexual existence.

That felt so good. Beyond good. Better than great. More than amazing.

It was two years of celibacy, of clamping down on her desire, erupting all at once, and when he flicked his warm tongue over her tight clitoris, she broke, and let the orgasm rush over her.

CHAPTER
THREE

ELEC held on to Tamara's thighs for leverage and kept tasting her, his body hard and aching and totally over-whelmed at how freaking sexy she was. When she came for him, her hands yanking on his hair, her back up, her thighs wrapping around him, the rich scent of her arousal filling his nostrils, he almost lost it himself. He could feel her muscles contracting, feel the tremors that raced through her legs, and the spasms of her fingers jerking on the roots of his hair. It was a big one, and he felt both pride and want so intense he closed his eyes and swallowed hard, his cock throbbing on her leg.

Get control, that's what he needed to do. He didn't want it to be over before he started, and that was a very real pos-sibility given that he was dangling on the edge already just from giving her oral sex. Once he went in, it was going to take everything in him not to just explode in thirty seconds or less. Tamara was wiggling beneath him, her breathing ragged.

"Where are you going?" he asked, prying his eyes open

and giving her a searching look. He hoped she wasn't having regrets already.

"I'm just shifting," she said, her eyes glassy, her hair falling forward on the left side and sticking to her lip. "Sit up."

"What? Why?" If she made him leave now, he was fairly
certain he would weep.

But Tamara was sitting up and getting on her knees and
tugging him up and . . .

Holy shit.

It finally clicked what she was doing.

She was offering to give him head.

Elec should tell her that wasn't necessary. That he didn't
expect reciprocation. That he was too close, anyway, and
maybe they should just proceed to the main event.

But then he was on his knees, and she was on all fours
in front of him, and her hair was falling forward in a sensual
cascade, and he could see the bumps of her spine down her
delicate back to the peek of her very cute ass, and his protest died on his lips. Then her mouth was on him and he
about died along with his protest. Apparently oral sex was
like riding a bike—once you knew how, you never forgot.
There was no evidence that it had been two years since
Tamara had been with a man. She was working him over
from tip to shaft, sucking with skill and enthusiasm, forcing
him to grit his teeth and grip her shoulders.

"That feels so goddamn good," he said as her warmth
surrounded him, pulling and sliding along his erection.

She made little sounds, like she was pleasing herself
pleasing him, and Elec closed his eyes again. He couldn't
see her *and* feel her, it was too much, he was too close. He
kept his eyes screwed shut, mind empty, feeling the suck
and pull of her hot mouth on his throbbing cock, the slick
slide of her saliva over his flesh, and wanting it to never end
at the same time he knew he only had about thirty seconds
of control left in him. When she went deep, taking all of
him, he groaned and jerked back on the bed, panting.

"That's enough. Lie back down." He sounded urgent, he knew it, his hands reaching for her shoulders, gently trying to urge her back, and he should apologize for being demanding, but damn it, he was desperate.

She handed him a condom before going onto her back again and he slapped the thing on so fast it was a miracle he didn't just burst right on out the other end. Job done, he looked up, and found her spread out in front of him, her hair spilling across the pillow, her arms above her head, her breasts and nipples arching up at him, her legs delightfully spread out for him to move in between. Elec paused, just to savor his good luck, to appreciate the classy, mature woman who was willing to take off her clothes for him.

It was humbling to know that she hadn't been with anyone since her husband, and he reached out, slipped two fingers inside her, and stroked. She rewarded him with a soft moan and eyes that fluttered shut. He brushed the pad of his thumb over her swollen clit and she squirmed in a very satisfying way.

"Elec," she whispered, eyes still closed.

"Yes?" He plunged his fingers deeper, then pulled them back out, pleased at the way she tried to follow him with her hips and prevent him from leaving.

"Give it to me. Please."

He could make her spell out exactly what it was she wanted, but Elec knew when to push and when to let it go. The fact that she was asking at all was a total turn-on, and he knew probably a big thing for her. And truth be told, he didn't want to wait one more lousy second to be inside her.

So he said, "You got it, sugar," and he replaced his teasing fingers with his cock at her warm, wet opening.

Her legs slipped around behind his knees, almost drawing him into her, but he resisted, just bumping lightly against her, torturing himself at the same time he was enjoying the way she gripped the pillow on either side of her head. He stayed there, drawing out the anticipation, getting himself under control so it lasted more than four seconds, while she moved restlessly beneath him, spreading her wet desire all over the tip of his erection and driving him crazy.

When she said, "Elec, please . . ." he gave up trying to own the situation and just pushed inside her with abandon.

Then he just about stopped breathing. Dammit, she was tight and felt so *good*. Her eyes had rolled back into her head, and he knew the feeling. Unable to stop himself, he forget about slow, about finesse, about coaxing her to another orgasm. He just pounded, taking her hard, desperately, in and out with hard, urgent thrusts, her body wrapping around his. To his amazement, and gratitude, she came again, her mouth opening on a silent cry.

She was barely easing back down when he followed her, exploding in an orgasm that had him forgetting his own name. He could honestly say that nothing—no woman, no win on the track— had ever been as good as that moment when he pulsed inside her, his whole body tense, his brain empty of anything but the way it felt to be buried deep inside Tamara, her swollen lips parted on a sigh, her eyes filled with sensual triumph and satisfaction.

When he pulled out of her, sweat rolling down his back, his muscles replete, whole body damn happy, he rolled onto his side and took Tamara with him. She reached down and dragged the sheet up and over them, then gave him a small smile.

"Definitely worth the wait," she said.

Oh, yeah. Elec felt a ridiculous level of pride, vowing to make the next time even better. After he caught a quick little nap. He brushed her lovely hair off her face and ran a finger down her smooth cheek. "Glad to hear it, sugar."

Then he promptly fell asleep like the guy that he was.

* * *

TAMARA woke up with a start, a knock on the door jerking her out of deep sleep. She had a hazy half second of trying to figure out why her door would be closed at all, when she realized she wasn't at home. She was in Ryder's coach. She glanced to her left.

And Elec was in bed with her.

Oh, Lord. She'd had sex with him, a total stranger that she'd convinced herself didn't qualify as a stranger since Ryder knew him. And she'd loved every dang second of it. But now it was the morning after and she had zero experience with that concept, and there was clearly someone standing on the other side of the door.

Mere feet away from where she knew she was still naked lying in bed with most likely an equally naked Elec. She didn't remember falling asleep, but she did recall him pulling her against his body, still naked as a jaybird. She eyeballed him now as he slept. He definitely looked naked, even though the sheet was covering him from the waist down. His chest was bare and he looked big and strong and satisfied. Naked. All sorts of naked.

Tamara swallowed hard, her mouth dry as she gripped the sheet tighter over her, wondering exactly how she should handle getting her clothes back on and getting both her and Elec the hell out of Ryder's coach before the person knocking or anyone else caught them. The pounding came again, louder and persistent. Shoot. She really did not want to get caught in bed, rumpled and bare-butt naked. Maybe if she kept very, very quiet, they would go away and let her get dressed and sneak out before any other human being had to be a party to the fact that she'd had a one-night stand with a pit crew member in her best friend's ex-husband's coach.

"Tammy?"

Shit. It was Ryder. Her best friend's ex-husband and owner of the coach she had been so tacky as to have sex in. In Ryder's very own bed. Lord. Her cheeks burned. She didn't answer, heart pounding, the sheet clenched tightly up to her neck. She was all kinds of mortified.

"Tammy, I hate to bother you, but it's late, sweetie, and I need to come into my room and get my bag."

Elec's eyes had opened and he rolled over toward her groggily, his big hand landing on her stomach. "Morning."

He kissed her shoulder, in a gesture she would have appreciated if she hadn't been on the verge of hysterical. And did he have to touch her stomach, of all things? It was the bane of her existence between the stretch marks and the unexplainable fact that it stored all her fat deposits in it, and she really didn't want him hanging around there exploring it. Tamara shifted so his hand would be on her hip instead. Much better, now she only needed to panic about Ryder on the other side of the door.

"Is that Ryder? Aren't you going to answer him?" Elec asked.

"No." If she just ignored Ryder, maybe he, it, and everything would all just go away.

"Did you say something?" Ryder called through the door. "Tammy, I'm serious, I have to get my uniform. Are you okay? Pull the sheet up, I'm coming in."

Ohmigod. "No, Ryder, *don't*!" Tamara half sat up and held out her hand, which was stupid, since he couldn't see her, but she needed to stop him before . . .

Too late. Ryder had the door open and was strolling in. Tamara dove back down, like that was going to hide anything, clutching the sheet with an iron grip as she waited for the fallout.

"It's not like you to sleep so late—"

Ryder glanced up, and immediately stopped talking, his mouth falling open in a nearly comical expression of surprise. His lips moved, but nothing came out, and for the first time in the decade she had known him, Ryder Jefferson was well and truly speechless. It might have been funny, and under different circumstances, she would have ribbed him for it, but the truth was she was absolutely and utterly without words herself. She was frozen in mortification.

"Morning, Ryder," Elec said, breaking the awkward silence in the bedroom. "How are you doing today?"

Tamara realized that Elec was snuggled up against her, his arm over her hip, his face still right next to her shoulder, his leg nestled with hers.

She flushed, feeling the heat rise up her neck and into her cheeks. "It's not what it looks like," she said to Ryder, which was perhaps the stupidest thing she had ever said in her entire life.

That ridiculous lie in the face of the obvious seemed to break through Ryder's shock. He burst out with a laugh. "Oh, I think it's exactly what it looks like." He grinned. "Guess Elec saw you home safely. Knew I could count on him."

Ryder moved through the room to his closet, still grinning. "I hate to be the voice of reason—I mean, when does that ever happen? But it's damn near noon. I have to grab my uniform and head to the pre-race meetings with my team. I would imagine you have to do the same, rookie."

Elec sat up next to her. "Jesus, it's almost noon? I had no idea it was that late."

Tamara looked from Ryder to Elec. Between the wine and the lack of sleep, her brain was fuzzy. She also desperately needed a drink of water to get rid of a major case of cotton mouth and she was painfully aware that she was both naked and that her body was aching in places she hadn't even been aware she had muscles. Which reminded her of why she was sore and the different ways she had been touched and licked and entered and she was really, really not at the top of her game.

But she could have sworn Ryder had just called Elec a rookie.

"Rookie?" she said. "What kind of rookie?"

Ryder had pulled his bag out of the closet and was

moving back toward the door. "Tammy, geez, girl, get some sleep. If Elec keeps driving the way he has been, he's well on his way to being rookie of the year."

Then Ryder was gone with a wave and another big old grin. "See you all at the track."

And Tamara was left staring at Elec as he turned to her. "You're a driver?" she asked stupidly.

Now it was his turn to look confused. "Of course. You didn't know that?"

She shook her head and swallowed, wondering why it felt like she'd stuffed marshmallows into her mouth. It was hot and sticky and she was having trouble getting her spit down her throat. "I thought you were on Ryder's pit crew."

Those soulful brown eyes—the ones that were completely responsible for her current state of nakedness—penetrated her.

Then his mouth turned up in a smile. "No kidding? Well, hell, at least I know you wanted me for me, not because I was a driver."

Hah. If she had known he was a driver, she would have run.

Then she remembered the way his tongue had felt on her, and she knew she was lying. She totally would have stayed anyway; she just would have felt more guilt in doing it.

"What's your last name?" she asked, thinking maybe she should have asked that a tiny bit sooner. Though she hadn't followed racing all that closely in the last two years, so even if he had told her his name, it was possible she wouldn't have recognized it as belonging to a rookie driver.

"Monroe."

Oh, no. "Monroe . . ." That was a name she knew. Tamara sincerely hoped that he wasn't . . .

"Elliot Monroe's son."

Yep. That's exactly who she was hoping he wasn't. He was just the son of one of racing's legend drivers. His entire

family was involved in the sport and the older brother Evan
had been driving in the cup series when Pete had. The Monroes and the Briggses had socialized together for years before a legendary fallout the year Pete had died. Tamara
remembered a particular barbeque at her in-laws' house
probably a decade ago where all the Monroes had attended,
including Evan, who was her age, and their younger son,
who had been a quiet, dark-eyed teenager named . . .

Oh my God.

It was Elec. "I know you," she said, struck dumb. "You
were at a barbeque at the Briggses a long time ago. You got
drunk on pilfered beer and took your daddy's car and did
doughnuts on the front lawn."

Elec rubbed his chin and gave a sheepish smile. "Guilty
as charged. But they shouldn't have left the beer keg unat-
tended. It was too much of a temptation for a teenage boy."

Tamara started to think she just might faint. Dear God
in heaven, she had slept with a teenager. She was a mo-
lester. She scooted back on the mattress, trying to get off
the same pillow as him, put some space, any space, between
them. "You were like twelve then! How old are you now?
My Lord, Elec, I'm old enough to be your mother!"

"Don't be ridiculous," he said, not looking at all concerned that she had just done a Mrs. Robinson on him. He
reached for her, touching her hip, hauling her back a little toward him. "That was more than ten years ago, I imagine. And if you're old enough to have a twenty-six-year-old
child, I'll eat my car, part by part."

"You're twenty-six?" Tamara's heart rate slowed a little.
That didn't sound quite as bad. She'd been thinking early
twenties, but at least he was heading toward thirty.

"Well, almost. In a couple of months."

"Oh my God!" She panicked and ducked under the
sheet. She could not even look at him in all his sexy cute-
ness. It was too tempting and just so *wrong*. Unfortunately,
diving under the sheet only forced her to confront her own

nakedness as well as his. And his nakedness was a beautiful thing, all muscular and hard and hairy in the right places, with a big old morning erection. Nope, going under hadn't been one of her better ideas.

Nor did he leave her alone under there. He actually came under, too, tenting the sheet with his left hand and turning to her. "Tamara, calm down. It's not a big deal."

"It is a big deal. I'm the mother of small children! Yet I slept with a man half my age without even knowing his last name. God, I'm a . . . I'm a . . . a *cougar*."

Elec burst out laughing. "You are not a cougar. That's ridiculous."

"It's not!" Didn't he get it? She had lost her mind. Give her three lousy glasses of wine and she was knocking boots with a baby driver, who she had let do all kinds of . . . *things* to her and who even at that very moment was seeing her naked.

Ack. Tamara covered her breasts with her arm and clamped the sheet between her legs. That brought the sheet straight down over his face, which was fine by her.

He punched it back up with his fist. "What exactly is the problem here? Are you regretting that we made love last night? Are you telling me I was a drunken accident?"

Tamara bit her lip. That wasn't what she meant. Just thinking about how it had felt to have Elec filling her up, moving over her, kissing her so eagerly, had her pausing. She didn't regret a damn thing. Not really. But she felt guilty. Embarrassed. Like she should regret it. Like she had betrayed her husband, her children, her image, all of her responsibilities by having sex with Elec. Young, buff, rookie driver Elec.

"No, it wasn't a drunk accident. I knew what I was doing." She would be a total bitch if she let him think otherwise, and she had to own up to her actions. The wine had just made her bolder in taking what she had wanted to. She'd have done it with or without the liquid courage.

"Same holds true for me."

He was looking at her that way again. All intense and serious and sexy. It was warm under the sheet, and she was very aware of his nakedness. The scent of their bodies, warm, and still tinged with the sweet aftermath of sex, filled the small space. Tamara wanted to touch his chest again at the very same time she wanted to bolt and get the hell out of there. Neither seemed like a great idea so she just lay there waiting for guidance from a higher power. Which could take a while. If she were lucky, Elec would get bored and leave in the meantime.

He had a race to run, after all.

A driver. She had slept with a driver. Whose life revolved around sponsors and crazy hours and poles and winning purses. After swearing she would never get involved with anyone in racing ever again, she had nailed—literally and figuratively—the granddaddy of all in the sport. The man who climbed behind the wheel. Yikes.

"What night do you want to go to dinner?" he asked. "Tomorrow works really well for me. What's your schedule like?"

What the hell was he talking about? She blinked at him, still clutching the sheet, vowing that she would not, would not, would not—maybe if she chanted it enough she'd actually believe it—touch any part of him with any part of her. "Dinner?"

"You said you'd go to dinner with me. I want to make plans before I head out."

She could honestly say she had no memory of agreeing to that. If she had, it had been before she'd known he was a rookie driver a minute out of high school. "Oh, I don't know . . . maybe that's not such a great idea."

Elec frowned. "Are you giving me the morning-after brush-off?"

Did he have to phrase it like that? It was only marginally true. She wasn't brushing him off so much as coming to her senses and realizing that she could not date Elec. Even if she'd had amazing, hot, lovely sex with him. Tamara blew her hair out of her eyes. This dating thing was hard and she was seriously not up for the challenge.

"Of course not," she said because he looked hurt and she didn't want that. Didn't mean that. She owed him a great deal for giving her such a fabulous reentry into post-marriage sex. He had made her feel sexy and uninhibited and that was no small thing.

"Okay, so how about tomorrow night then?"

She had a built-in excuse, thank goodness. "I have my kids tomorrow night." Her children. Those small human beings who had no idea their mother had lost her everlovin' mind.

Elec proved himself to be stubborn, imagine that in a driver. "Tuesday then," he insisted. "Or Wednesday. I don't fly to Dover until Thursday."

"I can't get a sitter on such short notice." Tamara was starting to panic all over again. He was going to pursue this dinner date and she didn't think she should go at the same time she kept thinking she actually did want to go. It seemed like a bad idea, but her girl side, the one who had hopped into bed with Elec, seemed to feel it was a rockin' good idea to see him again. And how she could feel both counter-emotions at the same time was mind-boggling.

"Okay," he said. "So we'll plan on next Monday then. I'll get your number in a minute when I stand up and get my pants. I think my phone is in the pocket."

So they were going out the following Monday. Just like that. Well. Tamara tried to figure out how she felt about that, but suddenly Elec moved in beside her, letting go of the sheet so it fell over both of their heads and they were ensconced in cotton, his body all up alongside hers, his face so close she could see the fawn-colored stubble on his chin.

"What are you doing?" she asked nervously. His third leg was pushing against her thigh with enough force to indicate it was fully hard, and she was alarmed at the proximity of all that hardness to the part of her that was suddenly alert and ready to roll out the welcome mat. Again. Her lonely body was betraying her, that was for certain.

"Getting my good luck kiss. Every driver needs one before a race." He gave her a devilish smile.

Tamara melted a little. Hell, a lot. Still, she managed to voice an unconvincing protest. "I don't think they're usually naked when they get them. That would look kind of funny in the pits."

"Guess they'll be jealous then, because my kiss is going to be extra lucky."

They were both lying on their sides and Elec's hand stroked across her waist and hip as he leaned forward and claimed her mouth. Mercy, the man could kiss. He used his tongue to absolute perfection, with just enough pressure and depth to make her crazy with desire, but not so much that he was drilling for oil, nor so little that a girl had to wonder why he was even bothering. It was just right, commanding but not forceful, slick and smooth and delicious.

She had really missed kissing, and feeling a man's chest against hers, she had missed the way it felt to have arms wrapped around her, hard to her soft, big to her small. Orgasms could be achieved on her own, but nothing replaced the press of a man's mouth over hers, the flick of his tongue across hers, and the grip of his hand in the back of her hair.

Even as Elec's fingers started to wander to cup her breasts, Tamara knew she was lost again. It had just been too long, and Elec knew all the right places to touch, and while she knew she should stop him, the words never seemed to leave her mouth. It was too busy opening for his assault, too busy kissing back, licking and nipping at his bottom lip. God, she was aroused over nothing, and she squeezed his biceps just for the thrill of it, ran her hands over his firm back, down to his tight behind.

Cupping that firm, bare flesh, she might have actually pulled him forward hard, forcing his hips and erection to collide with her again, but if anyone ever asked her about it, she was going to deny it.

"I'm feeling luckier already," Elec said, breaking off the kiss and staring at her, his breathing ragged.

That was it? He was going to take the kiss and leave? Tamara felt profoundly disappointed. "Have a good race," she said for lack of anything better to say.

"Oh, I'm not ready to leave just yet. I want another kiss."

She didn't know him well enough to read the expression in his dark eyes but it was obvious he was telling the truth. He was making no move to leave the bed and somehow she doubted another kiss was all he was asking for. Common sense and years of being around the track compelled her to remind him, "You'll be late. If you miss the drivers' meeting, they'll send you to the back of the qualifying pack."

"I won't be late. If we stop talking and start kissing."

So now he was all logic. Tamara couldn't help but smile. She flicked her finger against his chest, loving how muscular it was. "You're the one who started this conversation."

"Good point. Okay, I'm shutting up now. After I ask you to kiss it."

It? "Kiss you, you mean?" she asked, feeling her cheeks heat up. She knew beyond a shadow of a doubt that she had given him oral sex the night before, but that had been spontaneous. Hearing him ask for it, well, it was a touch embarrassing. Unless that wasn't what he had meant. It probably wasn't what he meant at all. *It* must mean his mouth and she was a total hooch for thinking otherwise.

"No, not just me. *It*. My penis. Hard-on. Erection. Dick. Whatever you want to call it. Kiss it. Please."

Well, okay, clearly he wasn't talking about his mouth.

He gave her a charming smile. "That's the good luck kiss I want."

"You are really pushing it," she told him, shocked to her curled-in-arousal toes.

"Probably. But if I'm going to be late, I'd like to remember your sexy little mouth wrapped around me while I drive my way out of last place."

Oh, my. Heat flooded her inner thighs. "Oh. Okay." She didn't know what else to say because she was way too turned on to say no, or to let him get away from her. It suddenly felt like they'd just gotten started the night before and she needed to do a little more, really quick-like exploring. She didn't want him to be late, but if she was quick . . .

It was warm under the sheet and all she could hear was their breathing, the rustling of the cotton, and the tick of a clock somewhere in Ryder's bedroom, as she turned and moved her way down to Elec's impressive erection. She had a moment of fear that the position put her butt dangerously close to Elec's face and who knew what kind of cellulite was hanging around back there, but suddenly his hand was gripping her backside.

"I just love your ass," he said in a husky voice. "So tight, so cute."

Elec had a way of making her worries disappear as soon as they popped up, without her ever even voicing them, and that was definitely appealing. He made her feel incredibly sexy and sure of herself.

"Thank you," she murmured before taking the length of his erection into her mouth. She enjoyed the gasp he gave, and fully appreciated the power a woman could wield when she had a man literally by the balls. She wasn't sure she'd ever really understood how sensual and arousing it could be to know that every flick of her tongue, every slide of her mouth, could affect a man's pleasure, but under the sheet with Elec, their breathing hot and heavy, nothing but cotton and his bare flesh beneath her, she understood how exciting it was.

The hard smoothness of him pleased her, the desperate

moan he gave when she took him deep thrilled her, and the swearing that flew out of his mouth when she raked her fingernails across his testicles made her smile. There was no wine to blame her actions on, and she was actually pleased to know that she still enjoyed sex, still was a whole woman who could go down on a man with no apologies, simply because they both enjoyed it. After the sexual debacle with Geoffrey, she had felt *bad*, and it was a total relief to know it had just been her lack of chemistry with him.

The night before hadn't been a onetime fluke either. She was really, truly attracted to Elec, and it felt as good, if not better, to be with him than it had the first time. When he shifted her legs so that her thighs spread on either side of his head, she paused for a second in surprise, but forgot to be embarrassed when his tongue flicked across her.

"Ohhh," she said when any other words failed her.

It felt so good, so hot and intimate, his mouth pressed so deep into her, she just lay there stunned, her body tight and tense with pleasure.

Elec stopped and she said, "Why did you stop?"

"Why did *you* stop?" he asked, his words muffled since he was beneath her thighs.

Oh, right. The nature of the position was that neither of them was supposed to stop. "Sorry," she whispered, swallowing hard. The second her tongue touched the tip of his shaft, his tongue lapped across her clit, and she sucked in a hard breath.

She should really reflect on why it was so damn easy to be doing something so personal with Elec, but she could do that later. After she came, which, if he kept on the way he was, was going to be any second now.

Her weight rested on him, and she could feel all his hard muscles beneath her, and the press of his fingers into her thighs as he gripped her flesh and held her legs apart. The sheet had fallen down onto her back and head and in the warm cocoon, with his mouth doing such delicious things to her, she was pretty sure she would agree to do anything he asked of her. Everything felt good and wonderful and sensual and she sucked him harder and harder, slicking his thick penis up with her saliva. Tamara added her hand, wrapping it around him, and followed her mouth with it, so that every inch of his flesh was always feeling a hot, warm squeeze. Elec groaned briefly, and she knew he liked it, before he returned to her, his mouth enclosing her clit as he sucked.

It was a fight to not pull back and moan at that, but she stayed on him, excited by the challenge of keeping her rhythm when she really wanted to just collapse in agonized ecstasy. She moved her hips while she sucked and he sucked, so that they were both colliding with each other, and she lost all rational thought, all sense of where they were, time, space, and what her first name was. There was only that moment, the two of them locked in mutual pleasure, and when Elec plunged his tongue inside her, she came hard. When she would have jerked off him, he held her tightly so she didn't move, and while she paused with him in her mouth, she didn't let go, so that her orgasm swept over her with him fully embedded in her, and she closed her eyes to ride out the intense waves of pleasure.

Oh my. The man was just full of good ideas.

The second her orgasm eased up, she refocused on him, taking it slow and steady, then speeding up when his breathing grew erratic and his fingers dug into her thighs. She felt the throb of him inside her mouth, knew when he was going to come, and knew he was trying to pull away. She wanted to take him into her mouth, wanted to feel that final pulse, wanted to know she had done that to him, so she held on until he groaned, then he filled her mouth with his hot, salty come.

Having made an art form out of avoiding her husband doing just that in her mouth, Tamara was shocked at how much she had wanted Elec to, and how good it felt. It was raw, and messy, but it was damn satisfying.

She collapsed on his legs, every muscle in her body quivering from overstimulation, and Elec lightly smacked her backside.

"Holy shit," was his thought on the matter.

She had to agree.

"I have about three minutes to get my ass out of here and I can't move a single muscle," he said.

Tamara shifted a little and stroked his penis. It jumped. "One muscle's still moving."

"Leave it alone, darlin', or we're going to have a situation on our hands."

She laughed. "I don't want you to be late. That's bad form for a rookie. But I'm having a hard time peeling myself off of you."

In fact, she couldn't believe she was still lying with her ass inches from his eyes, but her body felt too damn satisfied to care. About anything. Ever again.

But he had to go. She knew that well enough. So she forced herself to roll off him. "How was that for a good luck kiss?"

Elec grinned as he tore the sheet off them and sat up. "Couldn't ask for more than that. That ought to see me straight through to the finish line. How was it for you?"

It ought to see her through the next ten years, that's how it was.

CHAPTER
FOUR

ELEC dragged his dress pants on, watching Tamara bustle around Ryder's bedroom. She had pulled on her panties and her dress in two seconds and was now stripping the bed.

"What are you doing?" he asked, feeling lazy and content and in no way inclined to hurry, which was what he really needed to do.

"Changing the sheets. Ryder knows what happened on them since he saw us in bed. It's tacky to just leave them." She dug through drawers until she found fresh sheets, and before Elec even had his T-shirt on, she had snapped open the fitted sheet and efficiently tucked it all around the bed.

Damn, she was sexy. Her hair was tousled, her cheeks pink, her dress all rumpled, and she smoothed the sheet out with her hand, doing what needed to be done. While he just stood and stared at her. Elec got his head out of his ass and stepped forward to catch the bottom of the top sheet as she spread it out, and he tucked the bottom while she tucked the top. Together they threw the comforter and pillows back on, and Elec found himself grinning like a fool for no apparent reason.

There was just something about Tamara that he really liked. She was the absolute opposite of the women he'd been dating, and he really appreciated her compassion, her sense of responsibility, hell, even the way she worried. She worried because she cared, and that was damn sexy to him.

"So what are your plans for the day?" he asked, fishing his shirt off the floor and putting it on without buttoning it back up. It was safe to say that particular shirt was going into the trash when he got home.

"I have to meet my in-laws at the race. They're bringing my kids."

Elec eyed her outfit. "You're going to the track in a cocktail dress?"

"I don't have a choice. I left my bag at Geoffrey's and I lost my purse, remember?"

There was no way she could show up at a race wearing a black dress and heels. Somehow he knew Tamara didn't covet the spotlight any more than he did, and wearing that sort of getup was bound to get her all sorts of unwanted attention. "You don't want to do that. Just come back to my coach and we'll find you something else to wear. I have to go get my bag anyway."

She was biting her fingernail. "Nothing you wear is going to fit me."

"Probably not, but a baggy T-shirt is better than a wrinkled cocktail dress. Think of all the media scrutiny you'll get strolling around in last night's clothes."

Tamara blanched. "You're right. Okay, thanks."

"We'd better get a move on." Elec scooped up his shoes in his hand. He was not stuffing his feet back into those things. He'd rather walk across glass.

Tamara actually put her heels back on and headed for the front door. Elec put his hand on the small of her back. "Third coach to the left."

She glanced back at him. "You're that close? Yet we stayed here?"

He grinned. "Well, I do share it with my brother, though he wasn't planning to stay here last night. Mostly I figured no sense in ruining the moment. Besides, if we had taken the time to walk to my place, you might have changed your mind. I couldn't risk that."

That was spoken to tease her. The true story was that once she'd told him to get inside Ryder's coach, it had never even occurred to him that his own place was spitting distance away.

Tamara glanced back at him, but she didn't say anything. She looked worried, her gaze darting left and right. Elec dropped his hand from her back to alleviate her feeling even more self-conscious than she already did. The compound was quiet, and they didn't pass anyone in their quick dart to his coach. Elec had the door unlocked and they were inside, Tamara's hand over her heart.

"I'm not cut out for sneaking around," she said.

"Then maybe we shouldn't sneak around. Who cares if people know we're dating?" He certainly didn't. But even as he said it, he knew the situation was different for her. She had kids, in-laws, a spotless reputation. "But I understand. I do. No one saw us, I'm sure of it."

"I hope not." She bit her lip. "I mean, no offense or anything, it's just that . . ."

"I know. It's okay, I do get it." He did know, and he didn't really want to hear her spell it out. Reality sort of sucked all the fun out of their spontaneous night of sex, and he didn't want to let go of that satisfaction and pleasure just yet. "Let me find you some clothes to wear. Have a seat, make yourself comfortable. If you're thirsty or anything, feel free to dig through the fridge."

Elec glanced around his living room. There was a half-eaten bag of chips on the coffee table, some beer cans, and a multitude of video games splayed across the couch. His furniture didn't really match, since he'd just gathered it here and there over the years and there were no pictures or anything hanging on the walls. It looked like he was a college kid, and he was suddenly embarrassed. His condo looked way better, like he was actually an adult, and he really wanted her to lose the focus she had on their age difference. The coach wasn't helping the matter. Not to mention he was starving and he really wanted to toss a handful of those chips into his mouth, but didn't dare.

He went into his bedroom and saw similar turmoil . . . lots of dirty clothes, a bed minus a headboard, and his remote control car. Best to get her out of the place before she thought too long and hard about his housekeeping. Elec ripped open a drawer and dug through it until he found the smallest shirt he owned. He did the same thing with his jeans, and even dragged out a pair of gym shoes, then tossed them back when he realized her tiny feet would swim in them.

Elec was mortified when he came back into the living room and found that Tamara had tossed out his empty beer cans and was rolling the bag of chips closed. "You don't have to do that," he said.

"The chips will get stale," she said, setting them back on the coffee table, her hands going to her hips, then falling away. "And I'm nervous and needed something to do with my hands."

His embarrassment disappeared. "I wish we had more time. I can think of a thing or two you can do with your hands."

Her cheeks turned pink. "We don't have any time. We have no time whatsoever and I'll feel really terrible if you're late and get reprimanded. So are those clothes for me?"

Elec handed them to her, knowing a lazy smile was spreading across his face. "Why don't you change in the bathroom so I can get my stuff together in the bedroom. Bathroom is the first door on the right. And I suggest you get a babysitter for a good long while next Monday night. I think we're going to want a lot of time for . . . dinner."

Tamara's eyes went wide. "You're a very naughty boy, Elec."

It didn't sound like it bothered her in the least. She pulled the clothes out of his hands and he made sure their skin brushed against each other. "So punish me."

She arched her eyebrow. "You'll like it too much."

Elec laughed. "You're right."

Then she surprised him by leaning over and giving him a sexy, lingering kiss. She stared at him for a second, then turned on her high heel and walked down the hall, pausing to gaze in like she was making sure it was the right room, before she went inside the bathroom.

Elec found himself just standing there feeling like he'd been hit with a stupid stick. He was grinning in an empty room over being with a woman who didn't want anyone to know they were getting it on, because he was falling for her already—hook, line, and goddamn sinker.

TAMARA came out of Elec's bathroom feeling less than prepared to face him or a crowd at the track. His jeans were resting on her hips and sagging in the butt and his golf shirt was gaping in the armpits and just about everywhere else. The grin he gave her when he saw her didn't help.

"Do I look that bad?" she asked, self-consciously. She had patted her hair down and washed her face, but it wasn't the same as having a shower, your blow-dryer, and a hairbrush. Not to mention she probably had foul breath from not having a toothbrush.

"You look adorable," he said, and he sounded and looked like he meant it.

Had the man been drinking? "I look ridiculous, is what I look like."

"I don't agree. And before you run off on me, give me your number." Elec was dressed in jeans and a T-shirt, his sponsor's ball cap on his head, his gym bag at his feet.

It was a look Tamara was very familiar with, and she suddenly had a lump in her throat, unsure how she felt about all of this. But Elec was flipping open his cell phone and typing her name in, so she recited her number for him. She wanted to go out with him, she did, she wanted to have good sex again, at the same time she was damn well terrified of what might happen if she did. Elec was too young for her. Pete's family hated Elec's family. Tamara had children who would resent their mother dating another driver. It was just all sorts of complicated and she didn't want any of that.

But Lord, she did want to have some fun with him.

"Got it, thanks. Tamara Briggs, Hot Mama," he said as he punched buttons on his cell phone.

"Very funny."

"It's the truth." Elec grinned at her, then went back to his phone. He pushed a button, then frowned.

"What?"

"Oh, it's nothing. There's just this woman, a fan, who keeps sending me text messages. I'm almost afraid to read it. She's been a little aggressive."

He was holding the phone away from his body like he expected it to bite him. Curiosity got the best of her. "What did she say?"

Elec pushed a button, then his eyes went wide. "Wow, okay, didn't expect that."

"What?" Tamara moved a little closer to Elec, feeling something she was refusing to label as jealousy.

"It's a picture text," he said, one eye squinting a little as he stared at it. "One I could have done without, frankly."

"She sent you a picture of herself?" Tamara started to get suspicious. "What, is she naked or something?" she asked, half joking, half convinced that's what it was.

"Unfortunately, yes."

Unfortunately was good. Unfortunately probably meant that Elec was in no way attracted to the woman and that she was not a pretty sight naked. Tamara should just leave it at that. But she found herself asking, "Can I see?" Which was rude and tacky, but she couldn't stop herself. She tried to cover her over-the-top interest. "I just can't believe someone would send a picture of themselves like that to a total stranger. How did she get your number, by the way?"

"Are you sure you want to look? It's crude." When she nodded, in spite of herself, Elec turned the phone toward her.

Tamara saw an amazingly perfect nude body with perky breasts and a waxed bikini area at the same time Elec said, "Well, she's not a total stranger. We went out a couple of times. I'm just not interested in her and she's not getting the hint."

Feeling like all the air had been crushed out of her lungs, Tamara gaped at the text picture. Not interested? He hadn't been interested? On top of the long legs and the firm abs and the toned arms was a beautiful face surrounded by the quintessential halo of blond hair. Pouty lips smiled out at them. She could have been a model. A Playboy bunny.

And Elec had gone out with this woman. Dated her.

Tamara felt like a big old schlumpy soccer mom. *Old* and *schlumpy* being the operative words.

"She's very attractive," Tamara managed to force out.

Elec just shrugged. "She's alright, physically. But I can't think much of a woman who would do this . . . I mean, if we're dating and we're a couple, sending naked pictures of yourself is sexy as hell. But when you're not dating, doing what Crystal is doing is just sort of like trying to sell yourself. I don't know. I just don't like it."

While she could appreciate that, and the fact that it said wonderful things about Elec's character, all she could think about was that smoking hot body and how it compared to her ten-years-older cottage cheese ass. And the naked beauty's name was Crystal. Of course.

"Erasing this," Elec said, pushing the button to get rid of

the pic on his phone. "Good thing I have free texts. I'd hate to think I'd paid to get that." He shoved his phone in his pocket. "Guess we should go."

"Definitely." Tamara shook her head when he tried to hang back and let her go first, like a gentleman would. Screw manners, she needed to be covert. "No, you go first," she insisted, shoving Elec toward the door. "I'll follow you."

He turned and shot her a look of amusement over his shoulder. "No one is going to care if we walk out of this coach together. For all they know, we're just friends. It's almost one in the afternoon."

What was he not understanding about this? "I am meeting my children and Pete's parents in thirty minutes. I came down here yesterday with a different man. I don't think they're going to be thrilled to see me tumbling out of your bed."

"Technically, it was Ryder's bed. And only Ryder saw you in it."

Tamara smacked him on the arm, feeling like she just might have an anxiety attack if anyone saw her with Elec. She just wasn't mentally prepared to deal with the questions and curiosity, especially now that she had naked Crystal to fret about as well. "Whatever. Just go. I'll wait a few minutes, then I'll leave. I'll lock the door, I swear."

Elec looked like he was going to make some kind of smart-ass remark, but he just grinned and leaned forward and gave her a quick kiss. "Make sure you cheer on number fifty-six. I'll call you later, gorgeous."

Then he was gone with a wave and Tamara was left standing there in jeans that didn't fit, a golf shirt that swallowed her whole, and her black heels. She was going to sacrifice the cocktail dress and just leave it at Elec's because she couldn't imagine strolling up to her in-laws with it tucked under her arm. If he was as determined to see her again as he said, he'd get it back to her next week.

With no cell phone, she figured her only recourse was to head to the track and find Pete's parents. They always sat in the pit boxes or hung out in one of the suites, so she would just go and look for them. If worse came to worse, she could borrow someone's cell and give her mother-in-law a quick call to locate her, except without her own phone, she suspected she'd never remember Beth's number. Though it wouldn't be a bad thing if she spent hours wandering around and didn't spot them. She was sure she had "Guilty Slut" stamped across her forehead.

Unfortunately, she found them right away. The minute she walked into the media suite, Pete's mother was waving to her.

"Tammy, sweetie, over here."

The endearment made her wince. Her in-laws were good people and Beth would curl up in a botoxed, bleached ball and die if she knew how Tamara had spent the preceding night.

"Hi," Tamara said, giving Beth a cheek kiss and praying to the Lord her own cheeks weren't flaming red.

"I tried to call your cell phone and you didn't pick up."

"I lost my purse last night," Tamara said, glancing around the room. "It was awful." Well, not all of it. Definitely not the naked with Elec part. She felt a telltale jump of desire that mortified her. Floundering for a life raft, she asked, "Where are the kids?"

"Johnny took them for a hot dog. All this catered food in here and they won't touch it. Just like Pete was. Grease over greens. And Petey's turning into a bottomless pit. We feed that boy morning to night. When was the last time you measured him? I bet he's grown an inch since Christmas."

Tamara pressed her fingers to her temples. She was having a hard time following Beth's chatter. All she could think was that she still had the scent of another man on her. She had stubble burn on her breasts, sore arm muscles, which she couldn't even quite explain, a lingering dampness between her thighs, and kiss-swollen lips. She felt like she was standing there screaming, "I had sex!" and yet Beth was just smiling at her like absolutely nothing had changed when it absolutely freakin' had.

"Right. Great. I actually think I'm going to grab something off the table myself. I didn't get any breakfast."

"Oh, go right ahead. There's a huge spread. And there's coffee, too. You look like you could use it. Did you call about canceling your credit cards?"

"No, not yet." Tamara headed toward the table of bagels and Danishes furnished by corporate sponsors and winced as her high heels pinched her feet. "I was hoping someone would turn my purse in."

"Shoot, I doubt it. They probably stole all your cash and cards and pitched the rest in the trash."

Beth was probably right, but somehow it didn't make her feel any better to hear it out loud.

"I can't call until I go home and find all the right numbers. What a mess. I never should have set it down at the cocktail party." Beth had followed her to the buffet, and looking over the food, Tamara suddenly realized how hungry she was. She piled two pastries and a bagel on her plate, along with a healthy helping of fruit.

"You lost it at the party? Well, I bet the staff stole it then. You'll never see it again."

At the moment she could truly care less. "I only had about forty dollars in it, and it was just an evening clutch, so I didn't even have my wallet in it, just my license and one credit card, so it's not that big of a deal. I'll just have to be more careful from now on." She stabbed a piece of melon and ate it to occupy her mouth, figuring the less she said about the night before, the better off she was.

"Are you losing weight, Tammy?" Beth was looking at her curiously.

"No, why?"

"Your clothes don't fit right. They're really loose."

Oh, Lord. How did she wiggle out of this one?

"And where's your friend, Geoffrey?"

Hopefully somewhere far away from the track, washing his ugly sweater.

"Things didn't work out and Geoffrey went home." Tamara rammed a strawberry into her mouth.

Beth's eyebrow rose. "Oh, that's a shame. Are you okay?"

"Oh, I'm absolutely fine." About Geoffrey, anyway. She wasn't sure how she felt about Elec. "I'm the one who called things off. We only had a few dates, and I just realized that I'm really not attracted to him."

"He did sound kind of boring," Beth confessed. "But I know it hasn't been easy for you being all on your own. You know Johnny and I want you to be happy . . . We'd like to see you find a nice guy at some point."

Chalk it up to lack of sleep, but Tamara suddenly felt tears in her eyes. Her in-laws were good people. "Thanks, Beth. I appreciate that, and everything you both have done to help me with the kids. With my parents being in Seattle, I don't know how I would have managed without you." Her voice trembled.

Beth, who was a notorious crier, only needed that much encouragement from Tamara to choke up herself. "Well, shoot, you know we'd do anything for you."

They were hugging over the plate of melon and both swiping at their eyes when Tamara heard her father-in-law's voice next to her.

"What are you two getting all worked up for? We brought enough hot dogs for everyone."

Tamara turned and saw Johnny standing there with her kids. Petey was halfway through his hot dog, his mouth stuffed to capacity, and her daughter Hunter was clutching a hubcap in front of her Ryder Jefferson T-shirt.

"Hey, guys!" Tamara tried to hug her kids, which was

only mildly tolerated by both of them, and turned to Johnny. "We were just having a girl moment."

"Glad I missed it." Johnny was what Tamara had always assumed her husband would grow into—an attractive older man with salt-and-pepper hair and a wicked smile. "But I did pick this up for you. They were calling your name over the speaker to come to the lost and found." He held up her overnight bag. "Can't imagine where you left this but someone was nice enough to turn it in."

That someone had to be Geoffrey, and Tamara wasn't sure how nice it was to dump her bag at the racetrack lost and found, but she wasn't going to question it. At least she had her bag back with her clothes and a good moisturizer. "Oh, thanks!" She set her plate down on the table and unzipped the bag. It was too much to hope for but maybe her purse was in it.

It was. She yanked out the hot pink clutch and gave a sigh of relief. Cell phone, credit card, driver's license, all intact.

"Is that the purse you lost?" Beth asked.

"Yes, thank goodness."

"I wonder who turned it in?"

"I guess Geoffrey did."

"Why wouldn't he just bring it to you?" Beth asked. "What a wimp."

Exactly.

"Hey, Mom, did you see what I got?" Hunter asked, pushing in front of her grandfather for center stage.

"It looks like a hubcap. Very cool! Where did you get that?" Tamara tried to inject the proper enthusiasm into her voice, knowing Hunter was excited with her souvenir. Her daughter, an undeniable tomboy, was rolling her Heelie sneakers back and forth and grinning for all she was worth, her ponytail bouncing under her Ty McCordle ball cap. Hunter was devoted to both her favorite drivers, Pete's best friends.

"Uncle Ty gave it to me. He said it's nice and dirty because it came off his car yesterday."

"Wonderful." A closer glance showed it was filthy, and the grime had transferred to Hunter's fingers and her T-shirt. "You can put it in a place of honor with your tire collection." Hunter's room looked like a track garage, with worn-out tires, engine parts, and peeled-off plastic windshields, track dirt and bugs still intact. There wasn't a doll in sight in the girl's bedroom, except for the Barbie that Tamara had found wearing a racing jacket, and Hunter's bedding was a black checkered flag.

Saying her daughter was a racing enthusiast was an understatement, and while Tamara wanted to encourage her interest, and appreciated that Hunter's godfather Ty was involved in her life, she wished their relationship involved less race refuse. Her seven-year-old daughter's room smelled like rubber.

"Can we sit in the grandstands?" Hunter asked. "Do we have tickets?"

"I'm not sure where we're sitting, baby." Pete's parents had made the arrangements, and all Tamara wanted to do frankly was to just sit down and stare into space and reflect on the fact that she had engaged in enthusiastic sex with a driver. Eek. She was still having a little trouble processing that fact, even if she was barely an hour out from having his tongue in a certain place on her body that very few man had been allowed access to.

"We're in the suite this time, baby girl, but we can walk around a bit if you want," Johnny said. "We'll go after we watch the race, alright? You going to join us, Petey?"

Her son shook his head, licking ketchup off his finger. "No, I'll stay here."

Petey didn't have quite the affinity for racing that his sister did. Tamara never got the impression that he didn't like it, but he wasn't a die-hard fan. Most of the time he was happier poking around in the dirt or the woods than he was at the track. She often wondered how her husband would have felt about that, but usually reminded herself it was irrelevant.

"Alright, driver's intro is about to start. Let's watch the TVs, then we'll head to the suite for the white flag." Johnny pointed to the TVs mounted all around the room. "Slowest qualifier going across the stage now."

Tamara would never admit it out loud, but she always found the introductions boring to watch and horrible to participate in. The drivers came out, smiled, waved, sometimes with their wives or girlfriends, other times solo. When Pete had wanted her to walk with him, all those cameras had made her uncomfortable and self-conscious about her crooked smile, not to mention how wide her hips might look. The whole process just didn't interest her as much as the pastry she'd abandoned on her plate. Tamara reached for it.

"There's Elliot Monroe's youngest boy," Johnny said.

Pastry forgotten. Tamara whipped her head around and craned to see the TV. It was a giant flat-screen but clearly not good enough. Elec was the size of a Twinkie from where she was standing and she wanted a much better view than that. Without being obvious, that is.

"Oh, really?" she said, oh-so-casually. "I didn't know he drove."

"Yep. His first season in the cup series. Doing alright for a rookie, and for a Monroe."

Since Johnny was staring at the screen, Tamara figured it gave her permission to do the same. She couldn't really see Elec's face all that clearly, but he was definitely smiling. Grinning, actually. The commentators were even remarking on it.

"Look at that smile on rookie Elec Monroe's face. We don't usually see him looking so happy pre-race. Wonder what has him so up this afternoon?"

Tamara felt her cheeks burn.

"Must be confidence in his car, Rick."

Exactly. Tell him, Rick. It had nothing to do with a pre-race blow job. Tamara tried to breathe normally and not think about Elec naked, which should be easy given he was covered from neck to toe, but somehow all she could think about was peeling off that uniform piece by piece.

"He's ready to show folks what he can do."

"More like show off," Johnny muttered.

Elec was clearly in a good mood. He was talking to the driver next to him, and bouncing on the balls of his feet, like he was ready to climb into his car and go. Then he turned to Ryder, on the other side of him, and they exchanged words that didn't look quite as friendly.

What were *they* talking about? Hopefully wind conditions, not Ryder's midmorning surprise of finding Elec in his bed with Tamara.

"He's a show-off?" Tamara asked Johnny, having a hard time picturing that, but curious to hear anything she could about Elec.

Her father-in-law made a noncommittal sound. "He's a quiet one, actually. But he thinks he knows what he's doing."

Didn't they all? And didn't the fact that they were driving at that level prove they did?

"He acts entitled. Just like a Monroe."

So Johnny's attitude was more about his father than Elec himself. "What happened between you and Elliot, by the way?"

But her father-in-law wasn't going there. He just shook his head. "Nothing you need to concern yourself with."

Well, that was a maddeningly vague answer.

He turned to her kids and smiled. "Come on, short stuff. Let's go to the suite."

"Who's short stuff?" Hunter demanded.

"You," he told her. He pointed to Petey, then her. "Short stuff one and two."

"No, I'm one," Hunter said.

Petey didn't look like he cared one way or the other. Her son didn't have that same competitive drive that Pete and Johnny had, and which clearly Hunter had inherited.

Tamara laughed and told them, "You're both number one. Now be good for Grammy and Papa, I'll be there in a few minutes."

"Where are you going?" Hunter asked.

"To brush my teeth. I have something stuck in my tooth." Actually, she just needed to brush them because she hadn't been able to that morning, but she wasn't about to share with her child the logistics of her night of debauchery.

Her daughter made a face like she considered that seriously disgusting. "Yuck. Okay, see you later, Mom."

The minute they left the room, Tamara dug through her purse and found her cell phone. She had six text messages from Suzanne, each growing in worry and desperation when Tamara didn't respond. They were all variations of "Where the hell are you??"

Ducking into the hallway and glancing left and right to make sure her family was gone, she dialed Suzanne.

"Where the hell are you?" Suzanne asked by way of greeting.

"I'm at the track."

"Why didn't you tell me you were leaving? What happened with Geoffrey? Why didn't you answer your cell phone? I've been worried sick about you!"

"I lost my purse. It turns out it was in Geoffrey's room, which I never went back to last night because he proved to be a total jerk when I tried to break up with him gently. He called me a gold digger."

"No! What a loser."

"Exactly."

"So where did you go then? Home?"

"No, without my purse or a hotel room, I was wandering around getting frantic until Ryder found me and took pity on me. He sent me back to the compound." Tamara lowered her voice. "With Elec Monroe."

There was a gigantic pause. "What does that mean?" Suzanne asked carefully. "Like . . . Elec saw you to Ryder's where you crashed, or Elec took you back to his place . . . I can't quite picture what happened, Tammy. Help me out here."

"Well." She bit her fingernail. "He was supposed to just take me back to Ryder's, who was staying, um, somewhere else. But Elec sort of never made it back to his own coach."

Again, there was dead air on her cell phone. Then Suzanne said cautiously, "Are you telling me that you spent the night with Elec Monroe? Which would mean . . . you had sex with him? In Ryder's coach? That's what it sounds like, but I'm just having a hard time processing it."

So was she. "That's exactly what I'm telling you."

"You're shitting me." Skepticism dripped from her best friend's voice.

"No! Is it that hard to believe that he would be interested in me?" Geez. She had a hard time believing it, but it would be nice if at least her friend thought it could be *possible*.

"That's not what I meant! I absolutely believe he could be interested in you. You're gorgeous, you're single, you're intelligent . . . it's just that you are not exactly Miss One-Night Stand. Were you loaded?"

"No, I was only a little tipsy. And I have no idea what came over me, but the way he was looking at me, Suz. Oh, my God, it was so hot. And then he kissed me and the next thing I know, I'm naked," she whispered, glancing around again for anyone in earshot.

Suzanne's voice was full of awe. "Well, butter my butt and call me a biscuit . . . you had hot sex with Elec Monroe?"

She had.

And she was already wondering when she could do it again.

CHAPTER
FIVE

SUZANNE continued talking before Tamara could even respond. Her friend sounded downright gleeful. "Wow. Wow. I am so happy for you. He's so cute and buff . . . damn, I bet it was good. It was good, wasn't it?"

"Oh, yeah." No hesitation on that one.

Suzanne laughed. "That's a big old fat yes. Though I'm not surprised, he does seem to get around a bit."

Tamara stiffened. "What does that mean?"

"Just that he doesn't really lack for company. Those are the best kind to have a one-night stand with, because they know exactly what they're doing, and they understand you both plan to walk away whistling, no strings attached. Good choice, Tam."

There were about a thousand things about what Suzanne said that stopped Tamara cold. Elec had a string of women he was always with? He was a player? That just seemed so out of character for him that she was disappointed. And she was annoyed with herself for assuming she knew anything about him when she didn't, and for assuming that she could read him after just a few hours. She was irritated with herself that she had believed him when he said he wanted to see her again. Not to mention ticked off for wanting to see him again, even when she had known all along it was impractical.

Ugh. She wasn't sure what she had wanted from him, exactly, other than what she had gotten, but she didn't think she'd been quite ready to give up the possibility that she might get to do *that* all over again. Nor did she like thinking she was anything more than a handy opportunity for a piece of booty dropped into his lap. Which was ridiculous. Why should she think anything else, and where did she get off being offended when she had essentially taken advantage of that very same thing herself? When he had kissed her between the thighs, she hadn't been thinking, "Gee, let's see where this relationship can go emotionally." She had been thinking, "Bring it on, baby." There had been no thought of the future or even the next morning, and she had just been really, really happy to discover that she could actually still have rocking good sex.

So why was she standing in the hallway in Elec's golf shirt and jeans with grimy teeth, feeling deflated and disappointed?

Dang, she was such a girl.

"Tammy? Why aren't you saying anything?"

She forced herself to focus on the conversation at hand. "Sorry, someone walked past and I was trying to be discreet." Yeah, like that had really been her priority in the last twenty-four hours.

But Suzanne knew her too well. "Shit, I hurt your feelings, didn't I? I didn't mean that to sound insulting . . . I meant it as a positive thing, that Elec is experienced. You don't want your first post-marriage sexual encounter to be with some dud."

"It already was," she said, suddenly feeling all sorts of miserable. "It was Geoffrey."

"Oh, Lord," was Suzanne's opinion on that. "Honey, then you deserved a man who knows his way around a clitoris."

Were truer words ever spoken?

Suzanne went on. "And you should be feeling pretty satisfied with him and yourself this morning. Think of this as your reentry into the real world of adult sex."

Why did Suzanne make it sound like a porno? "It's fine. It's all good." Maybe. And maybe that sick feeling in her gut was the result of the acidic fruit she'd eaten on a thoroughly empty stomach. But she suddenly had the image of Crystal, the naked wonder from Elec's text messages, pop into her head.

"Uh-oh. You don't sound good. How did he leave things between you?"

"He asked me to dinner for tomorrow night. I said no. Then he asked me for Tuesday and I said no. Then he informed me we're going out next Monday." She hadn't dreamt his tenacity. He had been determined to see her again.

"Really?"

Suzanne's shock was not helping her ego. "Yes. Do you think he was lying?"

"Why would he lie?"

The total lack of conviction in her friend's voice had her stomach churning again. "I don't know. It seems stupid to lie about wanting to see me when we already had sex. It's not like he had anything to gain by it."

"True."

Tamara rolled her eyes. "Alright, I need to go. I need to spend some time with my children and try not to let everyone in the room know I'm a poster child for the morning after."

"Don't regret this, Tammy, you needed to do this. Think of it as fun, and enjoy the memory."

"But don't get attached to him because he can't truly be interested in dating me."

"That's not what I said."

"It's what you mean."

"I mean that you're looking to have fun, not a serious relationship. Don't confuse the two."

"I won't." Tamara gritted her teeth. "I'm not sixteen. I didn't sleep with him to win his heart."

"Oh, shit, you're pissed at me. I'm sorry, I'm screwing this conversation up. I'm really, really glad you had fun. I just don't want you getting hurt. You're much nicer than I am, and that makes you more susceptible to hurt feelings."

"Okay. I appreciate that you worry because you care. I do. But I really am going to go before Beth sends Johnny to look for me."

"Alright, but call me later! I want details. Love you."

"Love you, too, Suz." Tamara hung up the phone and sighed. Somehow that hadn't gone quite the way she'd expected. She'd thought Suzanne would press her for juicy details, not lecture her to guard her heart.

She was going back in the suite for that pastry. She needed it.

ELEC knew he was grinning like a fool, but he couldn't stop himself. He was feeling good. Better than good. Damn satisfied. He had met a woman he was seriously attracted to, had spent the night and morning doing all manner of delicious things with her, and now he was about to do his second-favorite thing in the whole world—drive his race car.

When he wound up standing next to Ryder Jefferson in driver's introductions, which surprised him since Ryder was usually way ahead of him in the lineup, he felt his smirk slip a little. He owed the man an apology for taking such liberties with his coach and his condoms.

"Hey, Ryder, uh, about this morning."

For a normally jovial guy, Ryder just glanced at him,

his expression serious. "Later. When there are no cameras on us."

"Alright, man, sure. But I just wanted to apologize." Elec was talking out of the corner of his mouth so no one in front of them could read his lips. He respected and admired Ryder and the guy had been good to him, introducing him to key players in their organization and making it clear he supported Elec. He didn't want to screw that up, nor did he want Ryder thinking he was taking advantage of Tamara.

"It's cool. No worries. Now shut up and smile. Camera to the left is zooming in on us."

Elec turned. Damn if Ryder wasn't right. An aggressive photographer was focused right in on them. He smiled and waved to the camera, wondering if he would ever get comfortable or be savvy with this aspect of his career. Especially when he went to leave the stage with the other drivers and saw his PR rep waiting for him, her foot tapping anxiously, arms across her chest.

"You were supposed to be here early," Eve said, her fists curled like she was fighting the urge to smack him. "You said you would autograph that merchandise I have to donate to the children's hospital."

"Oh, crap, I'm sorry. I totally forgot." No lie there. His mind had been seriously elsewhere. Like on the feel of Tamara Briggs's mouth on his . . . Elec cleared his throat. "I'll do it tonight. I swear."

"You better. Or I'll track you down and beat the ever-lovin' tar out of you." Tossing her caramel-colored hair over her shoulders, Eve gave him a stern and hateful look.

Elec fought the urge to roll his eyes at his sister and full-time PR rep. But he did say, "Is that any way to speak to your employer? I should fire you."

"Dad would never let you fire me." Eve's point made, she had eased up on the frown and the crossed arms, and fell into step beside him. "And I'm the only thing keeping you afloat on the business side of driving, admit it."

"That was never in question, darlin'. I wouldn't last a day without you, but you could be a little less hostile, you know. It was an accident, one that's easily fixed after the race." Elec knew his refusal to engage in a confrontation infuriated both his sister Eve and his brother Evan. But he had never seen any point in yelling about something that could just as easily be fixed by talking about it.

Eve sighed. "Damn it, you make it hard to be ticked off at you. Just be warned now—I don't care how tired you are after the race, you're signing these T-shirts tonight. They're for sick kids and you need to—"

"I'll be there," he told her easily.

"Argh," she said. "It is so not fun to boss you around because you just go with it. Where's Evan when I need him? He'll fight back with me."

"Why do you want to fight?" It was a question Elec had been asking for twenty-some years. He'd never understood the pleasure Eve and Evan took from sparing.

"Because it's fun," she told him with a grin. "Now get in your car, moron."

"Just let that love for me flow, Eve." But Elec wasn't actually the least bit offended. That was just Eve, and this was their relationship. Always had been, always would be, but at the same time he knew she'd throw herself in front of a bus to save him. And navigate his sorry carcass through the media frenzy of race car driving.

"And what happened to your hair this morning? It looks like you took a bushwhack to it."

Elec automatically put his hand on his head to smooth his hair down. It was sticking up. He couldn't help but grin thinking that it was Tamara's fingers gripping his hair like her life depended on it that had him looking a little rough around the edges. "Had a late start this morning."

Eve glanced over at him sharply. "Why do I think that means your morning involved a blonde?"

"Nope. Not a blonde." Tamara's hair was a soft, rich

brown, like the color of syrup with the sun shining through
the bottle, and he was clearly way far gone if he was giving
it that much thought.

"A brunette then?"

They had arrived at Elec's spot in pit row and his crew
was waiting for him, busy making last-minute checks. "Got
to go, big sister. See you at the finish line."

"Drive safely," Eve said, squeezing his arm.

"Duh," he told her with another grin. Then Elec went to
talk to his crew chief.

He was feeling fine, and he was ready to win himself a
race.

TAMARA didn't think she was going to have any fingernails left by the end of the race. She had bitten the entire right hand down to the quick, ruining a costly French
manicure.

Beth glanced at her curiously from her seat next to Tamara and said, "You have nail polish flakes on your lip,
Tammy. Are you alright? I've never seen you bite your
nails."

Swiping at her lip, Tamara tried to remember what it
felt like to behave normally so she could emulate it. Her
kids were sitting on the other side of Johnny, and Hunter
was glued to the edge of her seat watching the race. Petey
was working his way through a bag of cotton candy. "I
didn't sleep much last night. Dating is really difficult and I
felt guilty about bringing Geoffrey down here only to break
up with him."

Beth glanced out at the track, then over at her again.
"But you said he was unpleasant about the whole thing,
which shows his true colors. You should feel good that you
didn't invest any more time into someone who clearly isn't
worth it."

"I know. But you know how we are as women. We want

to fix everything." She did feel bad about Geoffrey, though she wasn't really sure why. Maybe it was just guilt that she had dumped him, then jumped into bed with another man about a minute later.

"Lord, that's the truth."

But the true reason for her stress was the number 56 car out on the track, and the man who was driving it. Elec was having an amazing race, sitting in eighth place out of forty-three cars at three hundred and fifty-three laps, which had him on the radar of the announcers, who kept referring to him over and over as the up-and-coming rookie. It was unnerving to be sitting there, watching, worrying, wanting him to do well, wanting him to be safe, yet feeling an undeniable anxiety that she was just another notch on the bedpost of Elec Monroe. Which shouldn't matter. The whole thing was ludicrous and she didn't like any of the feelings swirling around inside of her.

What the hell was the matter with her?

The announcer's voice came from the TV in the suite behind them. "What a great race so far for Hinder Motors. In the top ten, they have four cars right now. Ryder Jefferson in the lead, Ty McCordle right on his tail in second, Foster Davis in seventh, and the rookie Elec Monroe running in a very respectable eighth right now."

Both announcers were retired drivers and the second one said, "Very impressive. Hinder Motors must be very pleased with these performances, and I'm telling you, while Elec Monroe in the fifty-six car has shown a lot of promise and was always assumed to be a real contender in the near future, this kid is on fire today."

Kid. Tamara winced.

Beth turned to her. "Do you remember Elec Monroe? I think you met him a few times."

As if she could feel *any* more uncomfortable. "I met him a few times when Pete and I were first married. Then I actually met him again last night at the fund-raiser." Tamara took a sip of her diet soda. She seemed to have lost all the spit in her mouth.

"What did you think of him?"

Tamara swallowed hard and almost choked. Eyes watering, she gave a little cough. "He seems nice enough. Quiet. Not comfortable mingling." But very, very comfortable one-on-one. The mere thought made her want to crawl under the seat and die. After she had an orgasm.

She just wasn't cut out for this.

"Well, you know his father stabbed Johnny in the back."

"I knew there was some animosity, but I don't really know what happened."

Beth lowered her voice. "I can't tell you right now because it sends Johnny's blood pressure through the roof, but let's just say it wasn't pretty and it's not the kind of thing that these men will ever let go."

Great. "I'm sorry to hear that. I thought they were pretty good friends at one time."

"They were, which makes it all the worse," Beth said.

Tamara caught herself tearing off her pinky nail with her teeth and stopped. She picked at her—Elec's—golf shirt in the warm sun and tried to ignore her aching feet in her stupid heels. Fortunately, Elec's jeans were too long and they covered the bulk of her shoes so no one had noticed and commented on her strange choice in footwear. She was tempted to dig through her overnight bag and pull out her gym shoes, but that would just draw attention to her.

Sitting in the hard seat watching the cars loop around lap after lap for two more hours, Tamara ran through three diet sodas and the rest of her fingernails. By the time they were entering the final three laps under the lights after one of the longest days of her life, she knew this wasn't going to work.

She knew it. Hated it. But knew it.

She was kidding herself that she could go out with Elec.

Her in-laws would be hurt and angry, Suzanne thought he was playing her, she was worried sick about their age difference and about protecting her kids. It was too much to tackle when she had a whole handful of responsibilities and stress factors in her life.

It was impractical to get swept away in something that could only end badly.

She needed to tell Elec she couldn't go to dinner with him.

But first, all be damned if he wasn't taking advantage of a backdraft and going for a pass on the two cars in front of him. Tamara sat forward, alternating between watching the track and the TV screen.

"That was a good move," Johnny conceded to her right. "Look at the rookie go."

She was looking.

And he was going. Right on past the five and four cars.

Nails digging into her jeans—his jeans—Tamara finally remembered to breathe when Ryder and Ty crossed the finish line one and two, and amazingly enough, Elec came in third place.

Hunter was jumping up and down and whooping, showing an amazing amount of energy for a kid up way past her bedtime.

Beth said, "Oh, my. That'll get some talk going."

Johnny said, "Holy sh— shooters. The kid can drive."

Petey stuffed a handful of popcorn in his mouth.

And Tamara wanted to fight the urge to do as her daughter and leap up off her seat and cheer for Elec.

She couldn't stop herself from blushing though when the sportscasters interviewed a grinning Elec climbing out of his car as to what made the difference in the race.

After thanking his sponsors, his team, and Hinder Motors, Elec looked straight at the camera and said, "Not to mention the good luck kiss I got from an amazing woman before the race."

"Oh, really?" The female sportscaster smiled at him in amusement and stuck the mic back in front of him. "Care to tell us who she is?"

Tamara wondered how her brain could still function when she was absolutely certain her heart had just stopped. If he said her name, she was going to beat herself to death with her soda can.

But Elec just grinned and said, "Nope. I'm not the kind of man to kiss and tell. But it was definitely inspiring."

And for that, she could kiss him all over again.

But first, she had to cancel their dinner plans.

ELEC had never had so many mics stuck in his face or so many sponsor ball caps slapped on his head for photo ops. He couldn't stop grinning, despite the endless questions and his personal discomfort with publicity. It wasn't a win, but it was damn respectable and gave him confidence that he could come out strong the next week. Not even his sister running around looking equal parts frazzled and pleased as punch, like she'd won the race herself, could put a damper on his mood. It had been a good run for him, and he was feeling satisfied.

Starting the day off naked in bed with Tamara had set a positive tone and he was pretty much feeling it was one of the finer days of his life.

Then he read the text message from Tamara waiting for him on his cell phone.

It started out well enough, but headed south almost immediately.

Congrats on your finish! You drove a great race. ☺ Enjoy the moment. I know this is bad timing, but I wanted to give you plenty of notice . . . I can't make next Mon. It's just too complicated with my kids and work, etc. Maybe at some point in the future, but for now, I just don't see

it working out. I had a great time last nite, thx for
everything.

Elec read it three times. It sounded crappier each time
he read it. She was not only canceling their date, she was
effectively saying she wasn't going out with him. Ever.
Well, that sucked six ways to Sunday.

CHAPTER
SIX

RYDER had just finished his victory interviews and was feeling downright good as he headed back to his coach. He had four wins under his belt and the season wasn't even halfway gone.

It didn't surprise him to see Elec Monroe standing in front of his coach, obviously waiting for him, bouncing on the balls of his feet.

"Hey, Elec, congrats again." The rookie had driven a great race and Ryder was impressed with his aggressiveness.

"Thanks, Ryder. You, too. You're having a great season."

"Trying." He stopped in front of Elec and waited for the real reason the guy was standing there looking like he'd finished last instead of third.

"So, uh, about Tamara . . ." Elec managed.

"Yeah?"

"I'm sorry we were, uh, in your coach. That's not cool and I apologize."

"No big deal. Sex happens." Ryder almost laughed when Elec winced. "You want to come in for a beer?"

"Thanks, but I'd better get home and shower. Maybe another time."

"Sounds good." Then his curiosity got the best of him. He was damn fond of Tammy and thought it was great that she was finally enjoying herself again after Pete. "So, you like Tammy?"

There was no hesitation. "Yeah, I do. But I asked her out and she said no. Then she said yes, then she just canceled on me in a text message. I don't know what the hell any of that means."

The poor guy did look confused.

"I mean, I thought we had fun and all, so why the brush-off?"

Ryder eyeballed the rookie. He did look miserable. It was amazing what chicks could do to a guy. Here Elec had just had the best finish of his cup career and he looked like he was going to toss his lunch. "I'm guessing that Tammy is feeling a bit embarrassed. She isn't exactly a one-night-stand kind of girl."

"Well, I made it clear that's not what I wanted it to be."

"She's probably just worried about what people are going to think of the two of you hooking up. Tammy is a worrier, you know. Always has been."

"She's got nothing to worry about from me. I really just want to see her again, get to know her better. I'm really digging her, Ryder."

Oh, dude. Ryder recognized that look and knew what it meant. Elec was whipped already. It happened to the best of men, and Elec had his utmost sympathy. "So don't let her say no. Go after her."

"I don't want to come across as a stalker."

"It's not stalking if you happen to be at the same places she is."

"True. But where does she go?"

Hell if Ryder knew. He thought that Tammy pretty much went to work and raised her kids. He hadn't seen her out and about in years, which struck him as unfortunate. He was starting to really think Tammy could use someone like Elec in her life. "How about I throw a party and invite her?"

"That might work. You don't mind doing that?"

"Hell, no. I throw barbeques all the time. Nobody will think anything of it. I'll make some plans and I'll give you a call."

"Thanks, Ryder, I appreciate it."

Ryder clapped Elec on the shoulder. "My pleasure, buddy. See you later."

Whistling, Ryder stepped into his coach. It was a good day. He had won the race, and he was helping others. All in all, time well spent. His jubilant mood was snuffed out when his cell phone rang and he saw his ex-wife's name on caller ID. Suzanne rarely called him anymore, and while he always felt a jump of anticipation at hearing her voice, he was also wary of what exactly she could want. Their divorce was somewhat of a mystery to him, and he didn't understand her post-marriage any more than he had when they'd been wearing their rings.

"Hey, babe, what's up?" he said as a greeting, heading to his kitchen. He was really interested in an ice-cold beer.

"Congratulations, Ryder. That was an awesome race."

Touched for some stupid reason that she would take the time to call him, Ryder paused in front of his refrigerator. "Thanks, Suz. A little skill, a little luck, and it worked out for me."

"Well, I'm happy for you. You're having a great season."

Her voice was warm and honest, and Ryder was unable to resist poking a little. He missed Suzanne more than he generally cared to admit to himself, and he was thinking fondly of all the times he had won a race during their marriage and exactly how Suzanne had helped him celebrate. "Thanks. Though a victory just isn't the same without your pie as my reward."

She sucked in her breath. "Don't go there, Ryder."

"Why not?" Ryder dragged out a bottle of beer and popped the cap with the edge of his countertop. Suzanne had always feared for the safety of their granite counters when he'd done that, but he had always figured the whole reason they had spent an arm and a leg on the granite was because it was supposed to be indestructible. "You know the best part of winning was looking forward to your pie afterward."

"I'm not that good of a cook."

"But you make a mean apple pie. And you know that it was never just that flaky crust you were offering up."

"I appreciated the double entendre when we were married, but it's not really appropriate now."

Ryder made a face and took a sip of his beer. He had wanted her to flirt back a little. Why, he wasn't really sure, but it was damn disappointing that she didn't. "When have I ever been appropriate?"

"Good point. Which leads me to another reason I'm calling. What the hell happened between Tammy and Elec Monroe?"

That made Ryder grin. "If you don't remember what happens between a man and a woman at midnight in the bedroom, maybe you need to get out more, sugar."

"You know what I meant, smart-ass."

"Actually, I don't. They spent the night together. What do you think happened?" Ryder rolled his eyes for the benefit of his beer bottle.

"Why would they do that?" Suzanne demanded.

See, this was where he didn't understand his ex-wife. Or any woman for that matter. "Uh . . . because they wanted to?"

"Don't be obtuse."

He didn't even know what that was, so he didn't see how he could stop being it.

Suzanne didn't wait for his answer. She continued, "If

Elec had a thing for Tammy, why didn't he just ask her out? She's not a one-night-stand kind of girl."

"They just met last night, Suz. There was no *thing*, it was more like lust at first sight. And she clearly is a one-night-stand kind of girl because she did just that. It's no big deal. It's good for Tammy."

"Except that now she's upset and feeling bad about it. She thinks he's a player."

"Why would she think that?"

"Because I accidentally might have told her that. I always see Elec with some dumb blonde . . . I was trying to protect her and make sure she knew that she should take it for exactly what it was—a night of fun."

Ryder sighed. Suzanne meant well, but sometimes she needed to mind her own damn business. "Except that Elec is moping around crushed because he asked her out, she said yes, then she just texted him and canceled. Probably because you freaked her out."

"He really did ask her out? How do you know?"

"Because he told me. He was here not five minutes ago apologizing for making free with my coach and looking for some advice. He wants to go out with her, there's no question about it."

"Oh. Shit."

"Shit is right, sugar. Do you think Tammy likes him?"

"I actually think she does, because she's not the kind to sleep with a guy unless she does like him, you know what I mean? So I guess we need to fix it since we messed it up."

Ryder plopped down on his couch. "I didn't mess anything up. *You* did. But I told Elec I'd throw a barbeque and invite Tammy. Getting 'em in the same room is a start, don't you think?" Beyond that, Ryder figured it was up to Elec and Tammy to sort things out. They were big kids, and if they wanted to be together, they'd find their way there eventually.

"That's true, but maybe not a barbeque. Then she'll bring her kids and she'll use them as a shield. No, we have to have something more intimate or they'll both just avoid each other."

Clearly, Suzanne didn't share his philosophy of standing back. He also knew her well enough that she wasn't going to take no for an answer. "What do you want me to do? Just tell me so I can go to bed. I'm tired."

She gave a huff of impatience. "Sorry. Didn't realize I was keeping you from your bed."

"Care to join me in my bed?" He knew she would say no, but just the thought that there was any possibility that she might say yes had his worn-out body stirring to life.

"No, thanks. I prefer my own bed, where you're not stealing my covers all night."

"Sounds lonely."

"Everything's a trade-off. My vibrator has never once pissed me off, whereas you . . ."

He didn't want a list of all his flaws and infractions, so Ryder just said, "Point taken. But if your batteries ever die, you know where to find me."

"And you probably won't be alone."

Ouch. Okay, this conversation was going all sorts of wrong. Ryder could hear the bristling from Suzanne clear through the phone lines. He kicked off his shoes and tried to deflect the tension. "So you want me to throw a party or what?"

"Yes, a dinner party. A victory party for today's race. We'll have it tomorrow night at your condo. And we'll invite Ty and Elec as the top three. We'll let Ty bring a date, and you tell Elec that Tammy will be there. I'll drag Tammy over, telling her it's just Ty and you, then we'll feed her wine all night. This will be perfect, don't you think?"

He thought Suzanne was cracked if she believed that Tammy was going to be happy about being set up on a date with Elec after she had just canceled her own plans with the man. But there was no arguing with Suzanne when she was playing matchmaker. Hell, there was no arguing with Suzanne most of the time. That had been their problem—he had argued.

Old habits died hard, because he couldn't completely bite his tongue. "Tammy is going to be hopping mad at you, Suz. She's not going to like being set up like this."

"I'll tell her you ran into Elec last minute and invited him since he finished third."

"Okay, whatever you say. You handling food or am I? And what time?"

"Seven. I'll take care of food. You invite Elec and Ty."

"Alright, now let me grab some sleep since I'm suddenly entertaining tomorrow."

"Fine. Good night, Ryder."

"Bring your pie," he demanded before she hung up. If he was going to get stuck jumping through hoops, he wanted some apple pie, damn it.

There was a pause and he waited for a snarky remark and a refusal. But Suzanne said, "You'll get your pie."

Holy shit. That almost sounded like she was saying . . . Ryder opened his voice to ask for clarification, but Suzanne had hung up.

He sat in stunned silence for a second, then went for his shower. A cold one.

TAMARA stared across the table at Suzanne and set her iced tea back down. "Why are you throwing a victory party for Ryder?"

She had agreed to this spontaneous lunch with Suz between her morning and afternoon classes because she needed her friend's opinion on Elec. He hadn't responded to her text message and she found that odd, to say the least.

She thought that he would have either argued or else sent an "Okay, thanks" kind of text. But he had been totally silent and she didn't know how to read that.

Then Suzanne had blindsided her with an invitation to a dinner party she was hosting for Ryder. Which, frankly, just didn't sound like a good idea for a whole lot of reasons.

"Because I called to congratulate him and he was very forlorn," Suzanne said, dumping three packs of sugar in her coffee and stirring it vigorously.

"Forlorn? Ryder?"

"Yes. He went on and on about the parties I used to give him and how I always made him a pie, and I just felt bad. I opened my big mouth and said I'd have a party for him, now I absolutely have to have you there to help me get through this without murdering him."

That did seem likely, and a sour ending to a victory party. "I guess I can ask Beth to watch the kids, but I can't stay out late. My kids went to bed really late last night after the race and they're going to need to be in bed by eight. Beth can put them to bed at my house, but I can't ask her to sit around for hours. How many people are going to be there?"

"Not many. Like ten, tops. That's why I need you there. It's going to be awkward."

"Wow. I can't wait then." Just how Tamara wanted to spend her Monday night after one of the strangest weekends of her entire life. She had managed to avoid Geoffrey around campus that morning, and was hoping to do the same in the afternoon, but what she really needed was a good night's sleep after watching a chick flick in her pajamas, not a night making small talk.

"Thanks, babe. You don't know how much this means to me." Suzanne took a deep breath and glanced around the sleek deli. "Where is the waitress? I'm starving."

"I don't know. But I wanted to tell you I canceled my date with Elec."

Suzanne didn't exactly look surprised at that news. "Why?"

"Because I got to thinking about my in-laws and my kids and what you said about him being a player . . . and I thought about the text message he got when we were together and I just decided it's a bad idea." And she was sticking by her decision. Even though she felt mildly nauseous and discontent, and had developed a nervous tapping of the foot.

"What text message did he get?"

"Some woman sent him a picture of herself naked." She would be lying if she said that hadn't been bothering her for the last twenty-four hours. That woman had looked amazing. Tamara hadn't looked that good ten years ago, pre-babies and gravity. It was scary to compare herself naked to that waxed and perky body.

"Are you serious? How do you know?"

"He showed it to me."

"Why? To get you excited or something?"

Yuck. "Why would seeing some hot chick naked get me excited?" Nothing like comparing yourself and coming up short to really get the juices flowing. Please.

"Well, I don't know! Maybe it was some kind of ménage fantasy or something. So who the hell was she and why was he showing it to you?" Suzanne dumped yet another sugar packet in her coffee after tasting it and making a face.

"He was annoyed by it. He said he went out with her a few times and now she won't stop texting him. He didn't seem overly impressed with her method of pursuit. I'd almost say he was disgusted with her."

"That says good things about him. But he should know that's the kind of women he's been dating and that he can't expect much better than that. Did he say what her name was?"

"Crystal." Tamara made a face. "Blond. Built."

Suzanne grimaced. "Oh, I know who that is. A total pit

lizard. She's always tramping around the garage looking to hit on drivers. I swear, if that girl had as many sticking out of her as she has sticking in her, she'd be a porcupine."

Tamara grinned at the metaphor. "That's a beautiful way to put it."

"Why, thank you." Suzanne flagged the waitress, who indicated she'd be there in a minute. "God, I could eat my arm. What is taking so long? We haven't even ordered yet." She refocused on Tamara. "So what did Elec say when you canceled your date?"

"He didn't answer. At all. What do you think that means?" Feet still sore when wearing heels for an entire day at the track, Tamara halfway kicked off her sandals and hoped no one would notice.

"I think it means that he's choosing to ignore what you said. He's lying in wait, planning his next move."

"Really? I just find that hard to believe. More likely, he just didn't care enough to respond." Which kind of really bummed her out. Not that she could go out with him, but it would be nice if he did actually want to.

Suzanne rolled her eyes. "Oh, Lord, we're going to have to dust off your boy radar, girl. Of course he cares. He would not have asked you out in the first place if he wasn't interested. And the number one rule of men is that if something happens or something is said that they don't like, they just ignore it, hoping it will go away."

Somehow she could believe that. "So what should I do?"

"Wait a minute. You canceled. He let it drop. You don't have to do anything now."

Shoot, Suz had a good point. "Right."

"Unless you want to see him again . . ." Suzanne raised her eyebrows and looked at her expectantly.

"No, no, of course not." Not really. She was pretty sure. Maybe. "I don't know. I have no clue what I'm doing and I just feel like crap."

"Wear a great dress tonight," Suz said. "That will make everything feel better, I promise."

That might work when you were five, but at thirty-two, it wasn't likely.

ELEC stood outside Ryder's condo sweating bullets. He had no idea if Tamara was there or not, and he was as nervous as a cat in a roomful of rocking chairs. Normally he slept late on Mondays, but after getting a call from Ryder the night before about a half hour after he'd talked to him saying the party was a go, and for the next night, Elec hadn't slept much. In fact, it was fair to say he hadn't slept at all.

He'd done a lot of tossing and turning trying to figure out what to say to Tamara and how exactly he could convince her that there was no sense in pulling the plug without at least a date or two. That seemed fair to him. Maybe after a few dates they would discover there wasn't anything between them except sexual attraction, and he wouldn't be stuck with a case of wondering "What if?" Though somehow he doubted he was going to lose interest in Tamara after a few dinners. But he might never get the chance to find out because there was nothing slick about him, and he was well known for keeping his mouth shut instead of using it to cajole anyone into anything.

There was no hope for it. If she didn't want to see him, she didn't want to see him. Wasn't a hell of a lot he could do about it.

It was that thought that had him sucking in a breath and ringing the doorbell. Maybe just showing up at Ryder's would speak volumes to her. And if it didn't, he'd deal with it. Life had dealt him tougher stuff than one sexy, intelligent woman turning him down.

But she was one *very* sexy, intelligent woman . . .

Suzanne Jefferson opened the door right then, which

surprised Elec. He could have sworn Ryder and Suzanne were divorced, last he heard.

"Hi!" she said brightly, wearing a green sundress and sandals, her blond hair up in some kind of twist or bun thing. "Ryder and I are so glad you could make it."

"Thanks for the invite," he said, feeling a little confused.

"Come on in," she said. "Ty's already here with his date, and my best friend Tammy Briggs is here, have you met her?"

Elec stopped with one foot on the threshold. Was Suzanne serious? She didn't know about him and Tamara? Elec thought women told their best friends everything about their sex lives. Yet Suzanne was just smiling at him calmly, and didn't look the least bit like she was lying. Which made him wonder if Tamara was regretting their night together if she hadn't mentioned it to Suzanne. Or worse, she thought he sucked in bed. There was a thought to bolster his already crappy confidence.

"I met her again just the other night," he said, following Suzanne down the hall. "But we also met years ago when I was a punk teenager. There was a barbeque incident involving me and a car with the keys in the ignition."

"Oh?" she said, glancing back over her shoulder. "That sounds like a good story."

"Not really." He would have elaborated, but they had arrived in Ryder's living room and kitchen area, and Tamara was sitting on the couch, a full glass of wine in her hand, and a forced smile on her face as she chatted with the very young, very skimpily dressed woman next to her.

Ryder noticed him and stood up to greet him with a "Hey, Elec, what's up? Glad you could make it."

"Thanks, Ryder. Glad to be here. Hey, Ty, how you doing?" He nodded to the other Hinder Motors' driver. "Congrats on being number two."

"Likewise, Rookie. And cheers to Ryder, man. You owned the final three laps."

"I didn't think I was going to do it," Ryder said. "My car was loose the entire race."

As much as he enjoyed race talk, Elec felt he needed to greet the other guests, so he turned to the couch. And he was full of shit if he thought for one minute that he would have done that if Tamara hadn't been the woman sitting there. His etiquette sucked and he was the first to admit it, but in this case, he wanted to make a decent impression. Not to mention see if she looked even remotely pleased about his presence.

Not really. The expression on her face was more akin to horror. Oh, boy. No one had told her he was going to be there. That was damned obvious. Good times ahead, clearly.

So Elec made eye contact with the other woman in order to give Tamara a second to compose herself. "Hi, I'm Elec Monroe, it's a pleasure to meet you."

"Hi, I'm Nikki," the blonde said in a high-pitched voice that immediately set his nerves further on edge. "Are you a driver, too?"

"Yes." Elec tried not to look at the cleavage spilling from her supertight red dress, but it was aiming right at him, like a couple of torpedoes about to fire, and he found it distracting.

"Do you win as many races as Ty?"

There was a snort behind him that he was fairly certain came from Suzanne.

"Oh, now, baby, that's not really a question you should be asking," Ty said, looking embarrassed.

But Elec figured there was no sense in denying the truth. "No, I'm sorry to say I don't. Maybe in a few years, but right now I'm just a rookie."

"Oh, so you probably don't have as much money either, do you?" Her plump lips had turned down.

Elec almost grinned, but he kept it at bay. "Well, I can't say as I've seen the bottom line on Ty's bank account, but I'm guessing you have the right of it."

"Nikki. Damn," Ty said.

"What?" She blinked innocently at her date.

"Come here a second, I need to talk to you."

"A little adult-to-child discussion?" Suzanne muttered behind Elec.

"Suz . . ." Ryder said, his voice sounding pained.

"What?" Suzanne said right back, her own voice razor sharp.

Okay. This was exactly how he wanted to spend his only day off. Not. Elec turned to Tamara to avoid getting sucked into either argument about to take place behind him. "Hi."

"Hi," she said, her fingernails digging into her thighs. She was wearing a fluffy yellow skirt that landed right at her knees, and a tight white T-shirt. Her hair was pulled back into a ponytail and she had on simple gold jewelry and gold sandals. She looked pretty and fresh and smart and sexy, and Elec wanted to own the right to sit down next to her. He wanted the ability to put his arm around her, to kiss her, to make her laugh, to make her come, to hold her all night, and to get to know every single thing about her.

Which scared the absolute shit out of him.

He had never felt this way about any woman after one night and it was damn crazy.

It was freaking nuts, he knew it, yet that didn't stop him from dropping his ass onto the couch right next to her and saying, "It's really good to see you, Tamara. I'm glad you came tonight."

"Congrats again on the great finish," she said, clearing her throat. "I didn't realize you'd be here tonight."

"Of course he is," Suzanne said, suddenly appearing in front of them and shoving a beer toward Elec. "Here's your beer, Elec."

Had he even asked for one? He just took it since he was afraid she might hit him with it if he didn't. There was some serious tension in Ryder's living room all the way around.

"You didn't mention it," Tamara said, locking eyes with Suzanne.

"Elec was right behind Ryder and Ty in the Six Hundred last night. This is a victory party. Of course he's here." Suzanne smiled brightly and the two women stared each other down, eyebrows rising, mouths pursing, heads tilted as they silently communicated.

Elec realized then that Suzanne knew exactly what had gone down between him and Tamara and she was a party to Ryder's plan to throw them into the same room together. And clearly Tamara hadn't known, and wasn't exactly thrilled with the whole situation.

Wonderful. He took a sip of his beer and wondered what the hell he was supposed to say. Him not knowing what to say? Now there was a shocker. God, he'd never wished for his sister or brother's big mouth so much in his entire life. They were never at a loss for words.

Nikki said, "Wait a minute. All three of you won the race? That's fun!"

Tamara watched Nikki beaming over her glass of wine, clearly unaware that not a single other person in the room was having an ounce of fun at the moment. She almost wished for that level of ignorant bliss herself. Because she was even not coming close to fun at the moment. She was about as comfortable as a turkey on Thanksgiving and she wanted to kill Suzanne for setting her up like this.

Suzanne should have warned her Elec was going to be there so she wouldn't be sitting on Ryder's leather couch gaping at him like a hooked trout. Of course, Suz knew her too well. If she had told her the truth, she would have bailed on the dinner party. No doubt about it.

Tamara knew Suzanne felt bad about initially reacting poorly to the news that Elec had asked her out, and Suz felt responsible for the fact that she had canceled on him. Suzanne was trying to right a wrong by throwing them together, and it was sweet, but deluded. Tamara hadn't canceled the date just because Suzanne had mentioned he was frequently in the company of blondes. There had been a lot of other reasons, too, all of which were damn hard to remember at the moment when he was staring at her with those rich brown eyes, looking like he wanted to take her into his arms and kiss the stuffing out of her.

Truth be told, she wanted him to kiss the stuffing out of her, and that was ludicrous. Her many reasons that she couldn't think of were all valid, she remembered that much, and she couldn't give in to a bad idea just because the man made her feel like she was the only woman on the planet. At least, she didn't think she should give in to him.

Elec didn't even turn away from her when Ty tried to explain to Nikki what had happened during the race. Tamara tried to ignore Elec, but she could feel his gaze pressing in on her as Ty said, "No, we didn't all win. We came in first, second, and third."

"Oh." Nikki frowned, then opened her mouth, then closed it again.

Lord. Where the heck had Ty picked this one up? Amoebas probably had more thought capacity than she did.

"Did you watch the race?" Elec asked Tamara in a low voice, leaning closer to her.

She turned to him, startled at the throaty tone. "Yes," she said, and dammit if her voice wasn't breathy. "Nice finish."

He grinned. "I'm known for that."

Oh, my. That was a sex reference, wasn't it? Her inner thighs seemed to think so, anyway.

"I couldn't say. I haven't followed racing the last few years."

"Did you enjoy it?"

Tamara felt her cheeks flush. "Enjoy what?"

"The race."

Right. The race. "Yeah, definitely. Your car looked a little tight early on, but your crew must have worked it out."

"So you actually do like the sport?"

He was doing that thing again, that intense stare he had where she felt like she was in danger of losing her clothes, her heart, or both. Good God, he was sexy, and she was kidding herself if she thought she could sit there and stay unaffected by him.

It was time to get off the couch and run away before she found herself begging him to take her to dinner after all.

"Of course I like racing," she said, and went to stand up. Only Ryder's couch was too low to stand up with a glass of wine in her hand and she only got a few inches up when she was in danger of sloshing Merlot onto her skirt. She froze, half standing, half sitting.

"Let me hold that for you," Elec said, taking the glass from her.

"I guess you'd rather not have another shirt ruined by my clumsiness, huh?" Tamara stood all the way up, arms across her chest, looking down at Elec.

"Depends. If it gets us both naked again, I'm willing to sacrifice a shirt." He didn't grin, but gave her a slow, naughty smile.

Yikes. Definitely time to retreat, because she was wearing a white T-shirt and there was no hiding the effect he was having on her nipples.

"I'm going to see if Suzanne needs some help."

"I don't," Suzanne said from right behind her. "You just visit with Elec, but thank you."

Tamara turned and glared at her. They were going to have a little chat later about how friends shouldn't throw friends in front of buses.

Ryder moved in next to his ex-wife, bless his heart. "How about feeding us, Suz, I'm starving."

Tamara half expected Suzanne to snap at Ryder again, but she just forced a smile and said, "Well, y'all better be starving because there's plenty of food. Nikki, I hope you like enchiladas. I went with a fiesta theme since Mexican is Ryder's favorite."

The blonde, who was perched on Ty's lap in a leather chair, said, "Oh, I don't eat."

Elec coughed behind Tamara to cover up a laugh as he stood, her wineglass still in his hand. Tamara blinked at Ty's date, not sure what to say.

Suzanne had no such problem. "What do you mean you don't eat?"

"I try to eat as little as possible. When I eat, I gain weight."

Oh my God. Was the woman even serious?

Nikki ran her eyes up and down Suzanne. "And I don't look good with the kind of weight on me that *some* people carry."

Uh-oh. Tamara moved forward on instinct, knowing Suzanne just might be inclined to throw whatever was handy in the girl's face. In fact, Tamara could swear Suzanne was eyeballing the wooden bowl with decorative glass balls in it resting on Ryder's coffee table. Ryder beat Tamara to Suzanne first, and he put his arm around his ex-wife and gave her shoulder a squeeze, whether in warning or reassurance Tamara wasn't sure.

Suzanne stepped out of Ryder's touch, eyes blazing, but she had a very sweet smile on her face. "Oh, honey, well that just explains a lot then. You have to eat something tonight, I absolutely insist, because given what I've seen so far, clearly you're starving your brain."

It didn't get any better when they were seated around the table together.

For being a victory party, the only thing anyone seemed to be celebrating was the opening of a fresh bottle of wine every half an hour.

Tamara was sitting next to Elec, and his leg kept accidentally brushing against hers, which was driving her to distraction. Keeping the conversation going was a strain, since the table was rife with tension, and every topic they tried to cover was derailed by the random remarks of Nikki.

A headache was throbbing behind Tamara's eyes, and the enchiladas were unpleasant lumps of flour and fat lying in her stomach, just churning. Finally she couldn't stand it anymore and leaned over to Ryder, who was sitting at the head of the table.

"Where's your aspirin? I have a slight headache and I think if I take a couple, I can get rid of it."

"They're in the cabinet in my bathroom." Ryder started to get up. "I'll get them for you."

"No, no, I can get them. You stay." She was actually looking forward to a moment of privacy away from the snarky barbs going back and forth, and the uncomfortable awareness of Elec sitting just inches to her right.

Tamara tried to walk, not run, down the hallway and into Ryder's bedroom. It was very classy and masculine, with lots of chocolate brown and very artistic black-and-white photos of various racetracks around the country, plus one of him winning the championship two years earlier. She wondered if Suzanne had decorated it, or if he had hired someone. She couldn't picture Ryder picking out duvet covers on his day off, but the end result was soothing and quiet, and she was grateful just to be alone for two minutes.

Ryder's bathroom was a mess like his coach had been, with dirty clothes lying on the floor and his shaving accoutrements scattered all over the counter. She stepped over a dirty towel and a pair of boxer shorts and opened the medicine cabinet. Ryder had four half-used tubes of toothpaste, a giant bottle of aspirin, dental floss, mouthwash, and three boxes of condoms. It appeared his goals in life were fresh breath and ensuring he never had the headache of children.

Tamara grabbed the aspirin and untwisted the cap.

"Tamara."

She jumped and let out a shriek. Good Lord, Elec was

standing in the doorway, watching her. "Geez, you scared me." And what the hell was he doing? There was a powder room in Ryder's front hallway, so if the beer was catching up with him, he could have used that bathroom.

"Sorry."

He didn't look sorry. He looked sexy, damn him. How any man could do nothing more than prop up a door frame with his shoulders and look that intense and hot was beyond her. And it was annoying.

"Did you need the bathroom? I'm leaving." She rolled two aspirin between her fingers and wondered how she could exit past him without touching any part of his body with hers.

"I don't need the bathroom. I came to talk to you privately."

The pain behind her eyes gave a throb of protest. She did not want to talk to him. Not now. Not tomorrow. Not ever until she could learn to be rational in his company and not want what she couldn't have, which was sex with him on a daily basis, twice on race days.

"What did you want to talk about?" Damn her mother for teaching her manners. She should have just told him they had nothing to talk about.

"You didn't know I was going to be here tonight, did you?"

She shook her head. "No."

"I knew you were going to be here. That's why I came. But I'm sorry if it's making you uncomfortable."

Well, that was nice enough. "It's not." Liar. "Why would I be uncomfortable?"

"Why would you cancel our date?"

Tamara had known that was coming. She cleared her throat and stared for a second at Ryder's dirty towel on the floor as she gathered an ounce of courage. "Because it's not a good idea. My kids, my in-laws—"

"Are not invited on our date."

That almost made her laugh. "I know that. But it's complicated, Elec. I am not free to just do whatever I want with no regard to other people's feelings."

"It's not a big deal, it's only dinner. I would just like to get to know you a little better." His eyes rolled over her body, all the way down and all the way up again. "Better than I already do."

Wincing as her head throbbed harder, Tamara rubbed her temples. She needed to explain—without sounding like a total bitch—that she didn't regret their night together but that she couldn't actually have a relationship with him. Even going into the whole thing with inhibitions thrown out the window, she had known enough to assume one night was all it was going to be, and she had still gone with it. It was flattering and nice to know that Elec was actually interested in her as more than a random hookup, but she just didn't see how in their reality of his crazy traveling schedule and her many responsibilities, they could manage anything resembling normalcy, and it was stressing her out, frankly.

"Your head really hurts, doesn't it?" he asked softly, moving into the bathroom.

She wasn't popping aspirin for the fun of it. "Yes," she said, knowing her face had to be sour and pouty.

"Turn around."

That sounded like a trick.

"I'll rub your head," he said when she didn't move.

Touched by the thoughtfulness of that, Tamara turned around as he came up behind her. His fingers touched her hair and gently undid the tie that was keeping her ponytail in place.

"This thing can't be helping. It's pulling all your hair back really tightly."

It did feel better the minute her hair fell loose. "You're probably right. Thanks."

His fingers were gliding into her hair, working the strands

free of the shape the ponytail had left it in, and Tamara shivered at the tactile sensation. She had always loved having someone touch her hair and it had been so long since she had felt that. Too long, just way too long. Her eyes drifted closed as he stroked, digging his fingertips into her scalp and rubbing away the tightness and tension.

"Does that feel good?" he murmured. "Or am I doing it too hard?"

"No, it feels great. Thank you."

Elec massaged up and down her scalp and down her neck with all of his fingers, his breath audible next to her ear, the scent of his aftershave drifting up into her nostrils. She felt her shoulders relaxing, and when he rubbed her temples with the pads of his thumbs in a deep circular motion, she sighed.

Shifting her hair to the side, Elec focused on her neck again, then kneading the tension out of her shoulders. He went up the sleeves of her T-shirt and pulled her bra straps down a little so they wouldn't impede his movements as he systematically worked her muscles. It occurred to her maybe she shouldn't let him take that kind of liberty with her clothing, but it felt too good to put a halt to it, and really, it wasn't like he hadn't already touched every inch of her.

She shouldn't have been surprised when his lips brushed against her ear, but she was. Sucking in a breath, she tried to shift forward, her eyes opening, but Elec pressed his hands into her forearms.

"Don't go anywhere. I'm not finished."

"Elec . . ." Yeah, that was really putting up a stellar protest. Especially since she was settling back into his grip.

"You're feeling better, aren't you? I can make you feel even better."

Oh, she just bet he could. The question was whether or not she should let him.

Now that his lips were strolling down her neck, his fin-

gers peeling back the neckline of her shirt so he could lick
along her shoulder, it seemed like a moot point. His tongue
felt so good and she wanted to stop him, she really did, but
it was relaxing and it was just a little kissing, and what difference did it make? Really.

Her fingers unfurled and the aspirin rolled out of her
hand onto the countertop.

"I don't know . . . we should go back to the party . . ."
Aware that she sounded more breathy than resolute as his
fingers wandered around the front of her T-shirt and brushed
over her nipples, Tamara wondered why she had even bothered to speak. She was full of grade-A horseshit and she
knew it.

Elec knew it, too, since he turned her around by her
shoulders and looked into her eyes, his own dark with desire. "Not until I do this."

CHAPTER
SEVEN

HE was going to kiss her, and she was going to let him. No doubt about it.

And when his mouth brushed over hers, then settled in for a nice, long, lovely worship of her lips, she decided she'd made the right choice. This was definitely a better way to spend the dinner party than watching Suzanne glop extra sour cream onto Nikki's plate while Ty squirmed in chronic embarrassment.

Letting go of the countertop she'd been clenching, Tamara wrapped her arms around Elec's neck and kissed him back. It was amazing how much she hadn't realized what she'd been missing until she had it again. The feel of a man's arms around her, the hitch and catch of their breathing as they both became aroused, the press of his leg against hers, the soft silkiness of his hair beneath her fingers as she stroked the back of his head. She had been touch deprived, she realized now. It had been something she'd taken for granted in her marriage, the soft and random brushes, the right to invade someone else's personal space, and the ease of having a man's strong hand on her waist.

"You taste good," he murmured as his hands went lower to grip her backside and his lips caressed her chin and neck.

"So kiss me again," she said, wanting his tongue inside her, wanting more.

"You got it," Elec returned, and this time, the minute he touched her mouth with his, desire exploded between them.

They were gripping each other, hands here, there, everywhere, digging into each other's hair in an effort to get closer, to meld their mouths completely, Elec's tongue doing amazing things to hers as he thrust into her. Tamara could feel his erection pressing against her thigh and she had a feeling she knew this was going to the point of no return, but she somehow couldn't bring herself to care.

When Elec broke away, panting, his hair sticking up, and leaned back and closed the bathroom door and locked it, she knew he was having the same thoughts.

"We shouldn't be doing this . . ." she said, trying to hold on to some vestige of respectability.

His answer was to bend over and suck her nipple through the fabric of her T-shirt and bra. It was exquisite torture, the sensation of pleasure intermingling with the need for more freedom, to have him touching and tasting her bare flesh. When he moved lower and did the same to her inner thighs, Tamara leaned back against the sink. She needed something to hold her up. Especially since before she could blink, he had her skirt lifted and was sliding his tongue along the front of her panties.

"Elec," she whispered, squirming at both the intimacy of the position and the fact that it just wasn't good enough. It was a tease for what she really wanted, and he obviously knew it.

He kissed her thighs, licking a wet trail across her bare flesh, causing goose bumps to appear as she shivered in anticipation. He sucked her clitoris through the satin of her panties and she couldn't prevent a soft moan from slipping out.

"Do you like that?"

"Yes." And she was wet to prove it if he cared to investigate that.

He did. Elec pulled her panties down to her knees and used his fingers to spread her folds. Tamara wanted to feel embarrassment, wanted to tell him that he really should stop, but she couldn't work up any sort of protest. Especially not when his tongue slid over her, again and again and again until she was spreading her legs wider, clutching at his hair with eyes half closed, and drowning in the wave after wave of tight hot pleasure he was creating.

Who the hell was she kidding? There was no putting the brakes on. She wasn't feeling worried or regretful or inhibited in the least. She wanted his mouth on her, she wanted him inside her, and she wanted it right now, rough and racy and raw.

"More," she said, yanking her skirt up so she could see him better. The fabric was blocking her view and she wanted to see his tongue dipping inside her, wanted to see his dark eyes clouded with desire.

"More what?"

Tamara wasn't sure what he meant, but damned if he hadn't stopped touching her to look up at her, and that just wasn't allowed. "More, *please*?" she said, thinking he was teasing her for being bossy.

But Elec just laughed softly, his breath tickling her thighs. "No, I meant what do you want more of? More of me licking you, or by more, are you saying you want me inside you? But I like the way you said that so politely. You really are a lady, you know. The kind my momma would like."

She didn't think there was anything particularly ladylike about being pressed against the vanity in a friend's apartment with a man's head in her crotch while she held her skirt up for him. "Somehow I doubt your momma would agree if she saw us right now."

"Well, I'm just going to say how grateful I am she isn't here. But you still haven't answered the question."

And all this talking wasn't getting her what she wanted. She wasn't sure if she had the courage to say it out loud, but she bit her lip when he gave a soft, teasing flick across her clitoris. She could say it after all. "More of you licking me."

Elec murmured into her thighs, "You got it, gorgeous."

He started doing the most amazing and delicious things to her, dipping inside her and stroking up and down, slow, then fast, until she lost the ability to speak or think or do anything other than moan in encouragement. When he sucked her clitoris softly, a finger inside her, she came, bucking forward, clamping her lips shut to hold back a sharp cry.

It was good and long and intense, her entire body shuddering in ecstasy. When she was finished, and she'd forced her eyes to refocus, Tamara loosened her grip on Elec's poor maligned hair and struggled to catch her breath.

"Good?" he asked.

"Oh, yes."

Elec stood up and yanked open the medicine cabinet. "Condoms." His movements were so jerky that he dropped two boxes of condoms into the sink and knocked Ryder's dental floss onto the counter. Tamara wanted to help, but she needed all of her strength to stay standing. Elec got a condom out and his pants unzipped while she felt her panties slide all the way to her ankles, giving in to gravity as she pulled her legs slightly together.

"I'm so glad Ryder is such a Boy Scout."

He slapped the condom on his erection with a speed that

impressed Tamara. If that wasn't evidence of quick driver reflexes, she didn't know what was.

"Turn around," Elec told Tamara, his hands at her waist, encouraging the movement. "I want you to see yourself in the mirror." He wanted her to see how beautiful she was, how flushed her cheeks were, how loose and free her hair was, and how dilated her eyes were. He wanted to look over her shoulder as he thrust inside her and see the pleasure on her face in the glass.

She didn't even hesitate. Tamara just turned around and placed her hands flat on the countertop. Elec felt his cock jump in anticipation. God, he wanted her. Like he had never wanted another woman ever. It amazed him all over again every time he realized that.

Elec drew up the bottom of her skirt slowly, sliding his hands along the softness of her thighs, her hips. The position did beautiful things to her ass, her legs spread slightly, her backside pushed out a little as she bent over. It was all tight and inviting and he swallowed the gallon of spit that had suddenly appeared in his mouth. Brushing his fingers across her smooth skin, he dipped between her legs and stroked inside her, making sure she was still wet for him. She was, no doubt about that, and she gave a soft moan of encouragement that made his whole body tense with tight, hot want.

When he settled himself against her, and thrust deep inside her, they both moaned. Oh, damn, she felt good surrounding him with her slick heat. The angle heightened sensation for him, letting him feel her tightness as he drove good and deep. He liked the way his abs and his thighs bumped into her curves as he pulled in and out of her. A glance in the mirror showed Tamara, her eyes half closed, her mouth open, lips moist and swollen from his kisses, her hair falling forward as she accepted him, as she enjoyed him inside her. It was sexy as hell, her nipples peaking against her T-shirt, her hands pressed rigidly onto the countertop.

He knew when he hit a good spot, because her eyes snapped open and rolled back, and her heavy breathing actually stopped, her mouth open on a silent cry of intense pleasure. Elec pulled back and repeated and was rewarded with an expulsion of air from her mouth followed by, "Oh, shit, yes."

When he did it a third time, she dipped her head, covering her face with her hair, and groaned loudly, the muscles inside her contracting on his cock. He thrust again and said, "Tamara, look in the mirror."

"No," she whispered, arching her hips backward as she came.

"Please . . . let me see you come," he said, moving faster and harder. God, he was so close, so ready to explode inside her.

She actually did look up, tossing her hair back, and meeting his gaze in the mirror as she finished her orgasm. Her teeth were tearing into her bottom lip and her eyes were dilated, cheeks pink with exertion and desire. It was all he needed. Elec gripped her hips and pumped his way to a hard, shattering orgasm that had him gritting his teeth and losing the power of speech.

When he finally could speak again, his movements slowing, his back itchy with sweat and his fingers releasing their rabid grip on her hips, the only thing he could think to say was, "Damn."

Tamara pressed her forehead against the mirror and she said breathlessly, "My thought exactly."

RYDER looked at his ex-wife in disbelief over the dinner table. "Suz, I don't think Tammy and Elec would appreciate me interrupting. They've been gone at least fifteen minutes, so clearly they are talking."

"More likely they're fighting. I should have never sprung this on Tammy. That was wrong of me. But I was hoping she would see that there's nothing wrong with a little fun, you know? I want her happy."

Suz was looking on the verge of tears and Ryder felt instantly horrible. "Alright, I'll go check on them." He'd feel like a giant jackass doing it, but he'd do it.

Excusing himself—not that Ty and Nikki looked like they gave a shit what he did, since they were clearly groping each other under the table—he stood up and went into his bedroom, expecting to find Elec and Tammy either talking or wrestling naked on his bed. It surprised him that they weren't in the room, but were in his bathroom with the door shut. Maybe Tammy really was sick or something.

Ryder went up to the closed door, ready to knock, when he heard the unmistakable sounds of sex coming from his bathroom, punctuated by Tammy moaning, "Oh, shit, yes."

Alrighty then. Guess he wasn't needed to smooth out a fight. They were just smoothing it all out themselves.

And damned if he wasn't a little bit jealous. He couldn't remember the last time he'd wanted a woman badly enough to nail her in the john at a dinner party.

It had probably been since Suzanne, which really made him cranky.

Suddenly horny and annoyed, he went back out and sat down hard in his chair, saying, "They're fine."

"Well, what are they doing?" Suzanne asked, her forehead creased with a heavy frown line.

To which he just raised an eyebrow and stared at her.

"Oh," she said, eyes going wide. "Ooohhh." Her fork was halfway to her mouth. "Really?"

"Yes, really."

Ty had heard the exchange and he looked at Ryder curiously. "Tammy and Elec? For real?"

"Apparently."

"What's going on?" Nikki asked. "Where are the other people?"

"In the other room," Ty told her.

"Well, why are they in there and we're in here? Is there something better in there?"

The poor girl looked so confused that Ryder almost felt sorry for her. Almost.

Suzanne clearly didn't. "Because Tammy is in there making like her feet hate each other, and they don't need us around for it."

Ty laughed and Ryder couldn't help but grin. Suzanne always had a crazy way with words.

It was too much for Nikki. She just frowned, then resumed chewing the plain iceberg lettuce she was eating. It was meant to serve as a topper for the fajitas, but she was just eating it all by itself and nothing else.

Ryder looked at Ty and said, "Dude."

Ty gave him a sheepish grin. "I'm not in it for the conversation, that's for sure."

"I hear ya."

"You're both pigs," Suzanne said.

Ryder was suddenly tired of the whole self-righteous act from his ex. "Why? Because we're just honest about it? And for the record, if a chick says she just wants sex, all you women are like, 'Woo hoo, you go girl, take what you want.' But we do it and we're pigs."

"I've never known a woman who will tolerate grating stupidity just for sex. When women go for sex only, usually they do find something intriguing about the guy besides his penis. And talk about double standards . . . when a woman just wants to get it on, everyone calls her a slut."

It was his fault for opening the door to the argument, but Ryder still didn't feel like backing down. This was supposed to be his victory party and Suzanne had been kind of mean to him all night. He didn't like feeling her bite when he hadn't done anything wrong. "So you're telling me that in between riding his jock, you found Carl intriguing? That's amazing, because I didn't think he could string two words together beyond 'pass me the chewin' tobacca.'"

Throwing out the name of the first guy Suzanne had dated post-divorce was asking for fajita innards tossed in his face, but Suzanne just turned an interesting shade of red and mutilated her paper napkin.

"Who's Carl?" Nikki asked.

"Just eat your damn lettuce," Suzanne said. Then her shoulders slumped when Nikki looked like she'd been slapped. Suzanne said, "I'm sorry, Nikki, I didn't mean to snap at you. Ryder has just made me furious. Men can be so stupid."

"Oh, that's so true," Nikki agreed, giving a frown in Ty's direction. "Men are *horrible*."

Ty sat back in his chair and held his hands up. "What? What did I do?"

"The question is, what haven't you done?" Nikki asked darkly.

The sunny and vacant blonde looked suddenly satanic. Ryder immediately felt better. The night was bound to get even more entertaining.

TAMARA bent over to retrieve her panties and tried to keep herself from smiling. She should be shocked, appalled at herself, ashamed really, that she had done something so completely tacky as to have a quickie with Elec in Ryder's bathroom in the middle of a dinner party. But it just felt too good to feel bad. That had been amazing sex, and she knew beyond a doubt that if Elec wanted to have a repeat performance, she would let him.

He was grinning at her as he tucked everything back in and rubbed his hand over the top of his head to flatten his hair. "Now that's the kind of victory celebration I'm talking about."

She couldn't help but smile back at him. "Congratulations."

"Why, thank you, darlin'."

"And a positive side effect is that my headache is gone." Tamara tried to smooth out her hair, which was probably a lost cause. She threw it back up into a lumpy ponytail and called it good. "Thank you for the massage."

"Oh, it was my pleasure. Whenever your head hurts, you just call me and I'll see what I can do."

Now there was the best form of pain relief she could imagine.

Tamara tugged the bottom of her T-shirt down and adjusted her skirt so everything was all back where it needed to be and wondered if she had blown it with Elec by canceling their date, then arguing with him about it. Because now that she had gone for round two with him, she couldn't even remember why it had made sense to cancel in the first place. What exactly was she so worried about?

They weren't talking long term or serious. It was just casual dating and, clearly, lots of really great sex. She wanted that, deserved that, needed that. As long as it didn't affect her children, why couldn't she enjoy herself instead of staying home every Saturday trying to make do with batteries?

"That's very thoughtful of you," she told him wryly.

"I'm that kind of guy." Elec pulled a loose hair off her lip and tossed it in the sink. "Guess we need to go back out there, huh?"

"Guess so." Tamara hesitated, annoyed with herself. Was she really going to go back out there without telling him she wanted to go out with him, on her terms?

Elec squeezed her hand and turned around.

She couldn't let him just walk out, nor could she blame him for not asking her out yet again. He probably didn't want to ruin the satisfying moment between them, and he had to be feeling a little rejected.

So she said, "Elec, if the offer still stands, I'll go to dinner with you."

He stopped and turned around, his mouth breaking out

into a crooked smile. "Really? Well, alright then. That's very cool."

Now she had to be clear about what she wanted, yet somehow tactful. "Can we go to your place?"

"We can go wherever you want."

"Can we be . . . discreet?" That didn't sound great, but she didn't know how else to put it.

She had thought he would question her further, but he didn't and she refused to analyze what that meant. Hopefully it just meant he understood her reasoning. Not that she'd given him any.

But Elec just said, "Okay. We can do that. You want me to cook dinner for you?"

"You cook?" Not that it mattered. She wasn't in this for the food, and if it meant they would not be seen in public together, she was definitely on board with that.

"I can handle myself in the kitchen. Nothing fancy, but I can manage."

"That would be nice." And now she suddenly felt shy for some stupid reason. "So Mondays probably work best for you, right?"

"Yep. Does early or later work better for you with getting a sitter?"

Yeah, her children. She needed to do something with them. "Can I let you know?"

"Of course." Elec gave her a soft kiss. "Now we really should get back."

This ought to be fun. Tamara tried really hard not to blush as they went back out through Ryder's bedroom and reappeared in the dining room. Four pairs of eyes looked at them curiously and it was obvious that everyone knew what had gone down. Well, everyone except for Nikki.

"You two have been gone forever. What were you doing?" the blonde asked.

"Umm. Well." Lord, Tamara was awful at lying.

"I gave Tamara a neck and shoulders massage and her headache is much better," Elec said, casually dropping into his empty chair next to Nikki.

"Yeah, it's much better." Tamara took her seat, feeling heat in her cheeks and the weight of Suzanne's curious stare.

"Can you pass me the wine?" Nikki asked Elec. "I want to see how many calories are in it."

"Sure." Elec handed her the bottle.

Nikki wrinkled her nose at Elec. "You smell like balloons. Like . . . what is that stuff they make balloons from?"

"Latex," Ty said, struggling to contain a grin.

"Yeah, you smell like latex. Why?"

Tamara was going to die. She was going to slide down off her chair and collapse in a puddle under Ryder's dining room table.

"They were practicing safe massage technique," Ryder said.

"Oh." Nikki's brow furrowed.

"Can I have that pie server sitting next to you, Elec?" Suzanne asked.

Tamara loved her best friend more at that moment than possibly any other. "You made pie? That's awesome, I can't wait to have a piece."

"I can't wait to have a piece of Suzanne's pie either," Ryder said, with a tone that made it clear he hadn't left the subject of sex behind.

"Sure, Suzanne," Elec said, looking like he intended to just ignore all the innuendos and brazen right through the party. He handed her the pie server.

"Did you wash your hands?" Ty asked, eyeing the server exchange.

Oh. My. God.

Elec glared at Ty. "Yes."

Tamara could vouch that he had since she'd seen him do

it post–condom removal, but if she said anything, it would be like confessing there was a reason he needed to wash his hands so she kept her lips clamped shut.

"Because you know, I'm just thinking that maybe you shouldn't be touching the utensils . . ." Ty said.

Suzanne dropped the pie server, leaned clear across the table, and picked up a knife that was lying unused next to Nikki's plate of lettuce.

"But now *you've* touched the pie server," Ryder pointed out to her.

To which Suzanne turned, picked up the pie, and slammed it straight into Ryder's face. "That's the last pie you're ever getting from me," she said, sounding thoroughly satisfied.

Tamara figured maybe it was time to call the victory properly celebrated and head on home.

"Well, thanks for a lovely evening," she said, shoving back her chair and standing, while Ty laughed hysterically and Ryder swiped chunks of apple and piecrust off his face. "Congrats again, boys, on a fabulous one-two-three finish.

"Call me," she said to the room at large, hoping Suzanne and Elec—the two she actually wanted to contact her—would figure out she meant them.

But of course it was Nikki who answered. "I don't have your number," she said.

"Well, Ty has it," Tamara said, not ever wanting to engage in any sort of phone conversation with Nikki, but not wanting to be rude either.

She gave a seething Suzanne a half hug, then got the hell out of there.

Tamara was in her car putting the key in the ignition when her cell phone beeped to indicate a text message.

It was from Elec.

I think we're the only two to walk away from this dinner satisfied.

Tamara laughed. He had a point. She texted him back.

I agree. ☺

She was pulling out when he responded so she paused at the bottom of the driveway and read it.

I'm glad you had a headache.

If that was the end result, she was going to be faking a lot of headaches in Elec's presence.

CHAPTER
EIGHT

BY the following Monday afternoon, Tamara didn't need to fake a headache. She had the real thing again.

The day after the dinner party, she'd gotten a call from Petey's school saying that he was running a fever, and by Wednesday, it had been clear he had the chicken pox. She had spent almost a week solid with a cranky, itchy kid who, while still unable to go back to school, was to the point of boredom. And now Hunter was in the fever phase, and Tamara expected pox to appear at any given second.

Tamara was exhausted, stir-crazy, and nervously eyeing the number of sick days she had left at work. Her mother-in-law had stayed with Petey three days the previous week, but she was serving jury duty this week and wasn't going to be able to watch the kids at all. Tamara had lined up her father-in-law for watching Hunter at the end of the week, hoping Petey would be back in school by then and Hunter would be past the worst of it. But until then, she was on her own, which meant actually missing two days of administering final exams at school, and she swore if she never had to clean the tub again after yet another gooey oatmeal bath, she would die a happy woman.

Calling Elec that morning to cancel had been depressing as hell, even if he had been understanding about it. She could really, really appreciate someone cooking her dinner at the moment since she was about to OD on peanut butter and jelly. Not to mention, she could use the neck and head massage, along with whatever might happen to come after that in the form of nudity and Elec's erection inside her.

But there was reality and there was reality. No room for anything else in her life at the moment, and while she was worn out and experiencing major cabin fever, she was grateful that she could be the one there comforting her kids and soothing their itching.

Even when they could turn whining into an art form.

"I'm bored," Petey said, lolling around on the couch and tangling himself up in his blankets. He had six DVDs scattered around him as he was trying to make a choice for a movie, but clearly none of them appealed in the slightest. He took a sip from the water bottle she'd given him and made a face. "I want the purple juice, not the red. This is gross!"

From the other couch, Hunter made little sounds of distress in her feverish sleep, then leaned over half-asleep and threw up onto the carpet, missing the basin set out for that purpose by a solid two feet.

Tamara loved her children. She wouldn't trade them for all of Bill Gates's assets. She wouldn't trade them for a perfect man, a perfect body, or eternal youth.

But was there really anything so wrong with mourning the loss of an hour of rip-roarin', boot stompin' good sex with a hot race car driver?

She didn't think so.

"ARE you even listening to me?" Eve asked Elec impatiently.

"Not really," he told her in all honesty, forcing himself to focus on his sister across the table.

His brother Evan laughed and took a swallow of his beer. "Nobody listens to you," he told Eve.

She stuck her tongue out at both of them.

Evan threw a balled-up paper napkin at her.

Their mother put down her salad fork and gave them a once-over with a stern look. "You know, at some point in my life, thirty years after becoming a mother, I thought maybe my children would actually stop behaving like children and start behaving like adults."

"He started it," Eve said, pointing to Elec.

"What did I do?" He'd only been half paying attention, too busy mourning the loss of his date with Tamara. What could he have done?

"You're not paying attention. This isn't chitchat. It's a business meeting to discuss your schedule for next week at Pocono." Eve sipped her soda. "You two fail to appreciate that I rep both of you. Double the work. I need you to co-operate." She tapped the schedule on hard copy she had handed Elec. "Do you have any questions?"

He glanced over it. It was all standard appearances, and his sister was a master at booking him for sponsor events and interviews around meetings with his team, engine checks, and practice runs. "No. Looks good. Thanks, Eve."

"You're welcome." She turned to Evan. "What about you?"

Evan was making a face at his paper. "I don't want to go to this party on the fifth," he said. "I have plans that night."

"So cancel."

"I don't want to cancel."

They descended into an argument and Elec zoned out. He felt really bad that Tamara was stuck in the house with a couple of sick kids. She had sounded tired when she'd called him and said her son had been sick almost a whole week with the chicken pox. He wanted to do something for her, but he didn't know what.

His mother touched his knee. "What's got you so preoccupied?" she asked him, her expression curious.

His siblings were still bantering on the opposite side of the table, so Elec asked his mother in a low voice, "Is it hard to be at home with a couple of kids who have the chicken pox?"

Though the question clearly startled her, she didn't hesitate. "Oh, Lord, yes. It's like hell on earth. Everyone's scratching and whiny and oozing. The three of you fell one right after the other with it, so all told, it was three weeks of sick kids. Why do you ask?"

"A, uh, friend of mine is at home with her two kids who have the pox, and she's going on a week stuck in the house. I was wondering if maybe there was something I could do to help her."

"Where is her husband?" his mother asked baldly. "He could be giving her a break."

"He's dead."

His mother lost her wariness. "Oh, my. Poor thing."

"Her in-laws seem to be helpful, but I'm guessing it's not the same thing as having a husband in the house." Elec had been thinking about that a lot, about how much responsibility Tamara really did have on her shoulders. It was no wonder she had hesitated to go out with him. Between both of their insane schedules, how often were they really going to see each other?

But Elec figured once a week was a hell of a lot better than nothing, though this week they weren't even going to get that.

"No, it's not the same. What kind of friend is she, Elec?" His mother was studying him in a way that made him uncomfortable.

He just stared back at her.

His mother smiled. "My little eyeball. So she's *that* kind of friend, huh? I get it."

Elec cleared his throat. "We had plans to go to dinner tonight, you know, without the kids, and I feel bad. She sounds exhausted. So I was wondering if maybe there was something I could do to help her out, you know what I mean?" He didn't know what he meant exactly, but his mother must have understood what he was getting at because she nodded.

"I'm sure she would appreciate that. Why don't you drop off some dinner for her? And maybe get a little something for the kids. They get bored with the chicken pox because after the first two days they don't feel sick, so a new book or toy goes a long way."

"Really? You think that it would be okay to go over there?" Elec had been pondering doing that very thing since Tamara had called, but he had talked himself out of it.

"Of course. She's got to be desperate for company, and giving her kids a distraction will be totally appreciated. And I bet she's sick to death of eating soup and Jell-O for every meal."

"So I should bring her dinner?" Elec sat back in his chair, ignoring his own lunch. He wanted to do that for Tamara. She didn't have it easy being a single parent, and he liked her, damn it. He wanted to give her a break, and he wanted to see her.

"Absolutely." His mother smiled and said, "You're such a good boy, Elec."

He rolled his eyes. "Thanks, Mom."

"But I have a serious question for you. How do you feel about dating a woman who has children already and no father? Are you sure you want to take that on?"

"We're just seeing each other casually. It's not a big deal."

"Yeah, but every relationship starts out casually then

grows into something more. Are you okay with the possibility of having a hand in raising another man's children?"

Since it was the only way he was ever going to raise children, either through stepchildren or adoption, he was going to have to be okay with it. He had come to terms with not having his own kids for the most part. But he had to admit he wanted children in his life in some capacity or another. He liked kids, and enjoyed their energy and sense of wonder.

"I'm very okay with it, Mom. But let's not go jumping ahead, alright?" Sometimes, in the back of his mind, he'd done some jumping in the past week or so, but he tried to ignore it. That was crazy talk and he knew it.

"Okay, fine, I just wanted to make sure you had thought this all through. I think this woman is lucky to have you around. But just make sure you're still planning to give me my own grandbabies someday."

Ouch.

His mother smiled at him, smoothing down her sleek, brown bob haircut, with no idea that she had just stabbed him in the heart.

So maybe he still wasn't totally okay with it. But it was the way it was. And he had never told his mother the truth. At eighteen it hadn't seemed like a conversation he'd wanted to have with her, and in the meantime, it had just never come up.

Eve, the only one who knew the truth, had heard their mother and she shot him a look of sympathy. "Elec's too smart to have any rug rats."

"Good plan," Evan told him. "I'm not having kids either. Too much crying and drooling and crapping."

Their mother swatted Evan on the arm. "Those are not good reasons not to have children. What if I had said I wasn't going to have you because you were going to fill your diaper one too many times?"

Elec laughed as Evan made a face.

Then their mother went for the jugular. "I've gotten so much joy from the three of you that I would have changed a thousand more diapers to have you in my life."

His brother put up his hand. "Alright, point made. But I guess I'm saying I'm not ready for kids right now, and I don't see that changing anytime soon."

Elec wondered if he would feel the same way if he knew that he *could* have kids. While he'd always loved kids, chances were he would have wanted to wait until thirty or so himself if his boys could still swim. Strange that knowing he couldn't have offspring ever made him ache for them earlier than he probably would have.

It wasn't often that he allowed himself a bit of melancholy over the stupidity that had landed him in his current position but at the moment he felt washed in it. What the hell had he known at eighteen about the consequences of sex? He'd been excited and enthusiastic and the girl he'd been seeing had assured him she was on the pill. That had seemed like a huge bonus—not only did he get to dip his toe in the water, he got to do it without a condom. Only he had not been her first partner and she had been completely unaware that she had a common STD, which got passed right along to him. When he'd been told he'd had it a year later, he had been shocked to learn that 50 percent of sexually active adults who had STDs didn't even know it. The one he'd gotten had been easily cleared up with a course of antibiotics and could never return without additional exposure, but since he'd had it for a year without realizing it, the result was sterility, rare, but possible.

Maybe he should have told Evan and his parents, but how exactly did you go about explaining that? It had been stupid and pointless, and while he'd learned his lesson and never went without a condom now, it was still a hell of a price to pay.

Which was why he had been dating women like Crystal, casual, no strings attached. They didn't want children, but ultimately it seemed every one of them wanted fame and money more than they actually wanted him, and it had left him feeling incredibly empty.

Then he'd met Tamara.

And he was going to drop by her place and cheer her up, showing her that he understood what she was going through raising her kids on her own, and that he wanted more than just a casual hookup. He wanted a real relationship.

TAMARA wondered how it was that six o'clock had arrived and she still wasn't dressed. But somehow between loads of laundry trying to combat all the dirty sheets, towels, and pajamas, entertaining the troops with card games and movies, and trying to find something that Petey would eat, she had never managed a shower. Her hair was back in a ponytail, her skin felt like she'd slathered Crisco on it since she hadn't cleansed it and had been running around all day in the house, and she was still wearing her Tinker Bell pajama pants with a pink T-shirt, sans bra. At least she could say she had brushed her teeth. That had to count for something.

Eating a piece of bread with peanut butter slathered on it, Tamara was debating stripping Hunter out of her sweat-soaked pajamas yet one more time and ruing the day she had passed on the varicella vaccine for her kids, when the doorbell rang.

Fabulous.

Licking crumbs off her bottom lip, Tamara went through the family room to the front door.

"Doorbell's ringing," Petey said, stating the obvious as kids so often did.

"Thanks, I've got it."

Tamara hoped it was a package being delivered, though she hadn't ordered anything. But she didn't really want to face anyone. A check through the peephole had her rubbing her shiny nose on her sleeve and trying to stick stray hairs back in her ponytail.

Oh, Lord, it was Elec.

What the hell was he doing standing on her front porch? And could she look any worse?

She debated not answering, but he'd have to be a moron to believe she wasn't at home, and she just couldn't be that rude.

Plus, he had a bag in his hands, and she was curious as to why he was there.

So she tugged at her T-shirt to make sure it wasn't clinging too much to her breasts, and opened the door. "Elec. Hi."

He smiled. "Hey, Tamara. Are you hanging in there?"

She was hanging on the door, is what she was, hoping somehow he wouldn't notice she looked like she'd been rode hard and put away wet. "I'm okay. How are you?"

"Good, even though I was disappointed we couldn't go to dinner. So I got to thinking, maybe you could use some company. And some good food." He lifted the bag.

It took her a second to process what he was saying. He had brought her dinner? Real food? Her stomach growled, clearly not impressed with the peanut butter and bread.

"My mom said that it's tough to be stuck in the house with sick kids, especially the chicken pox because they're well enough to complain, but too sick to go to school."

That was true. But he had discussed her with his mother? That set a certain amount of panic off in her. "Wow, that's very thoughtful of you." But broke every single rule about how they were supposed to be seeing each other.

It was a secret, damn it. They were supposed to get together privately, talk, laugh, have great sex. Not discuss each other with their parents or hang out all cozy-like with her kids. It crossed all sorts of boundaries that she wasn't prepared to cross. Apparently she hadn't made that clear enough to Elec because he was standing there smiling at her with dinner and adult conversation she sorely needed, yet really, really shouldn't accept.

"Who's at the door?" Petey yelled from the family room.

"A friend," she called back, anxiety creeping over her. This was a bad idea.

"Can I come in?" Elec asked.

But there was no way around it. Rude wouldn't even begin to cover it if she suggested he leave. Besides, she liked Elec, she wanted to see him again, even if she was annoyed that he had sprung this on her, and annoyed with herself for not being more clear on what she was asking for.

"Oh, God, of course you can come in, I'm sorry. My brain is foggy." She stood back to let him in. "Thanks so much for stopping by."

"I understand you're sleep-deprived. Well, not totally, since I don't have any kids, but I can only imagine." He walked inside and glanced around her foyer.

"Do you want kids?" Tamara asked, then wondered why she would ask such a personal question. Blame it on the lack of sleep.

"Yes," he said simply. "I do."

Something about the serious look on her face set off alarms, but before she could respond, he smiled.

"This is a beautiful house. It really reflects your personality."

"What? Disorganized?" she asked, kicking aside a basketful of clean towels that she'd left at the bottom of the stairs.

"No. It's not all fussy or pretentious. It's put together and elegant, yet comfortable." He leaned over and looked at the pictures of the kids she'd hung behind the glass panes of an old window and had centered above a black table. "Very cool. And you have cute kids."

"Thanks." Yet another thing to blame on lack of sleep, but she had a lump in her throat from his compliments.

"Well, here, let's get that into the kitchen." She tried to take the bag of food from him, but he refused to surrender it.

"I've got it. I didn't come over here so you could wait on me. Have a seat and I'll serve you."

It was an innocuous statement, but she knew the minute they both realized a possible second meaning. Elec's eyes went dark, and her heart rate jumped a dozen beats per minute. She had a sudden image of him on his knees between her legs . . .

Tamara tried to shut down the thought. Her babies were fifteen feet away and she was getting turned on. That was just completely wrong. Flustered, she crossed her arms over her chest to cover her nipples. "I'm sorry I look so awful. It's been one of those days."

He glanced at her breasts—she didn't imagine it.

"You look fabulous. And just point me in the right direction of the kitchen," he said, his voice a bit rough around the edges. He cleared his throat. "Though do you mind if I say hi to your kids first? If I remember anything about being a kid, they're probably dying of curiosity about who's in their house."

Tamara hesitated even though she knew there was no way around it really. Her kids would bring their itchy bodies into the foyer in the next two minutes if she didn't introduce him. But that didn't mean she was at all comfortable with it.

Elec gave her a grin. "Don't worry, I know my role. Just a friend."

"Okay," she said. "I'm sure they'll appreciate the distraction. They're definitely bored. Well, at least Petey is. Hunter still has a fever." She started back toward the family room, then glanced at him over her shoulder. "You did have the chicken pox, didn't you? I don't want to be responsible for you catching it and missing the next three weeks of the season."

"Oh, yeah, I had it as a baby. Caught it from my brother and sister."

"Alright then." Tamara went into the family room and found her son sitting up craning his neck to see into the foyer. "We have company, Petey."

Petey eyed Elec with curiosity and a fair amount of suspicion.

"This is Elec Monroe, a friend of mine and Ryder and Ty."

"Hey, Petey, it's nice to meet you," Elec said as he strolled into the room, looking way more comfortable with the whole thing than Tamara.

She felt like it was more than obvious that Elec was not just a friend, but then again, her son was a child and hopefully wouldn't think anything of her having a male friend stop over. Not that she'd ever had one do that before.

Lord, she felt like slapping her hand on her forehead.

"Hi," Petey said. "What's in that bag?"

Leave it to a nine-year-old to not worry about relationship details when there might be something in it for him.

"Just dinner for me," she told him. "Elec was nice enough to bring it by since I haven't been able to get to the grocery."

"If he's up for eating, I did bring spaghetti and meatballs for the kids."

Petey's eyes lit up. "Cool."

"Thanks, that was nice of you." Tamara was actually touched by that. Needing a distraction, afraid if she looked at Elec he would see too much in her eyes, she sat down on the couch next to Hunter and checked on her daughter.

Hunter was awake, glassy-eyed and clutching the blanket around her, but she whispered to Tamara, "He's a driver. He finished third behind Uncle Ryder and Uncle Ty in the Six Hundred. His brother's a driver, too. Will he sign my program?"

Trust that her race enthusiast daughter would know exactly who Elec was. "I'm sure he will if you say hello and ask him politely." She smoothed Hunter's hair back off her forehead.

Elec felt his throat constrict just a little as he watched the tenderness with which Tamara touched her daughter. His mother had a point. It was a little more complicated dating a woman with kids. But at the same time, it was incredibly appealing. Elec thought that if a woman was a good mother, it said wonderful things about her as a human being. It said she was caring, compassionate, loyal, strong. All things he wanted in a woman he would give his heart to.

Not that he would—should—be giving out his heart. Just yet.

They were whispering, heads bent together, so he took the opportunity to set his bag down and pull something out. "I figured you must be getting bored," he told Petey. "So I brought this for you. Your mom told me you like bugs."

"What is it?" Tamara's son actually got off the couch and peered into the bag. "Whoa. Cool! Mom, it's an ant farm!"

"An ant farm?" Tamara's voice rose in alarm.

Elec shot her a sheepish look. Maybe he hadn't thought about that from a mother's perspective. He'd been thinking in nine-year-old-boy terms and the idea of ants tunneling through bio-gel had seemed really cool to him. "It's all contained," he told her. "I promise."

Petey pulled out the box. "It's glow-in-the-dark gel! Sweet. Thank you!"

"The ants are in that other container." Elec pointed to the plastic cone. "This one. The other one is your dinner."

"You have the ants in the same bag as our food?" Tamara was looking at him like he'd suggested they eat on the bathroom floor.

"Umm, yes. They're all sealed." Losing points fast. "Maybe we should add the ants into the farm out on the front porch."

"Good idea," Tamara said, her cheeks pale.

But first Elec wanted to say hello to Tamara's daughter, who was struggling to sit up on the couch. Squatting down, he smiled at her and said, "You must be Hunter. I'm Elec."

"Hi. Will you sign my program?"

"It would be my pleasure." Elec took her little hand and kissed the back of it, amazed at how smooth her skin felt, and how much she looked like a miniversion of Tamara. "You're as pretty as your mother."

Hunter's eyes went wide, than she gave him a grin, complete with two missing front teeth. She turned to Tamara. "Mom, he's sexy."

Elec choked back a laugh.

"Hunter!" Tamara looked at her daughter in horror. "How do you know what sexy is?"

"That's what Suzanne says whenever a man kisses her hand."

"Well . . ." Tamara looked like she was struggling with how to address the subject, but Hunter was pushing the blanket off herself.

"I have to go get my program and my Sharpie."

"I'll get it, baby," Tamara said. "Elec can take Petey out on the porch to put the ants in and I'll find your program. You stay put and rest."

"Sounds good," Elec said. "Come on, Petey. Let's get these ants settled in their new home."

"I'll put the food in the kitchen," Tamara said, giving him a look that gave her opinion yet again on his putting dinner and ants in the same sack.

Elec just gave her a sheepish smile.

Since Petey was wearing sweatpants and a T-shirt as pajamas, he didn't seem to care about going out on the front porch, and while he had scabs all over his arms and face, he didn't look to Elec like he felt sick at all. Petey ran to the door and bounded through it, skidding to a halt on his knees and looking back at Elec.

"Are there directions?" he asked. "I'll read them to you."

"Okay." Elec got everything settled on the porch floor

and handed the direction sheet to Petey. It didn't look complicated, but he could appreciate a kid who wanted to follow the rules and didn't want to skimp on details. He'd been that kind of kid himself, unlike his siblings, who had just dove in without looking.

While Petey studied the directions, Elec glanced around at Tamara's property. Her house was a raised-roof cottage with a big sweeping front porch, which she had filled with wicker chairs and a sofa, hanging ferns, and colorful pillows. There were pots of red and yellow flowers spilling down the front stairs.

It wasn't a huge house, but it was very comfortable, and everywhere Elec turned, it exuded a sense of home. This was a great place for these kids to be growing up, giving them stability and comfort.

Elec wasn't surprised Tamara had provided this for her children, but at the same time, it did funny things to his innards again. He was starting to ache for things he couldn't have, at a time when he should be thrilled with the way his life was going. He was driving in the cup series, he was doing damn well, he'd taken third at the Six Hundred, and yet he was suddenly pining for the babies he'd never have.

His phone beeped in his pocket, so he pulled it out and glanced at it. It was yet another text message from Crystal. That girl didn't know when to quit. Not bothering to even read it, he deleted it.

"Okay, so here's what we do," Petey said. "We just open the top and shake the ants in."

"That's it?"

"That's it. This is a self-contained environment. They don't need to be fed and this doesn't need to be cleaned."

"Cool." Thank God it was easy. Tamara was already less than thrilled with his gift. "I'll open the lid and you pour the ants in, okay?"

"Yep."

Petey bit his lip in concentration as he carefully poured the ants into the farm, and Elec could see Tamara in the boy's features, though not as clearly as with Hunter. But Petey did that same furrowing of his brow that his mother did, and he shared her petite nose. Elec enjoyed watching him, and felt sorrow for Petey that he no longer had his father. Elec had a lot of special memories with his own dad, and this boy wouldn't have any more of those.

"Put the lid back on," Petey said anxiously, once the last ant was in.

Elec clicked it into place. "It's on." Then he and Petey lay flat on their stomachs on the porch floor in companionable silence, chins resting on their arms, and watched the ants get busy tunneling their way through the gel. They seemed to have a preplanned architectural strategy and it was fascinating to watch.

"So you like bugs, huh?" Elec asked, ignoring his cell phone beeping again.

"Yep."

"More than car racing?" Elec said it casually, staring straight ahead at the ant farm. He wasn't sure why, but he got the feeling Petey wasn't so into racing and he wanted to let him know that was perfectly acceptable.

"Yeah," Petey said slowly, shooting Elec an anxious look. "More than racing. But don't tell Ryder that. He's my godfather and my dad's best friend, and it might hurt his feelings."

"I won't tell anybody anything if you don't want me to. But you know your mom and Ryder just want you to be happy. It's cool if you're more into bugs than racing. Everybody's got their own thing."

"Hunter's thing is racing. And she's a girl."

Ah. So Petey was already feeling the pressure of testosterone. "But Hunter's younger than you . . . don't you think maybe some of that love of racing is a way for her to hold on to your daddy?"

"She wasn't even five when he died. She doesn't really remember him much, not him being at home, I mean. She remembers seeing him more on the TV than with us. I remember him better." Petey stared into the plastic of the ant farm and chewed his lip industriously. "He used to throw me up in the air and run around the house with me under his arm like a football. And he used to toss me onto my bed at bedtime, then tuck me in and tell me he'd crossed the finish line in first place when I was born."

There was a lump in Elec's throat as he listened to the matter-of-fact tone in the boy's voice, and he fought to keep his own tone casual. "You're lucky to have those memories. I'm guessing Hunter doesn't have those."

In his pocket, his phone beeped again. Lord, Crystal had lousy timing. Elec pulled it out to silence it.

"Who keeps calling you?" Petey asked, glancing over curiously.

"It's a girl who likes me."

"Do you like her?"

"Not that way. And I told her we couldn't be anything but friends, and she won't take the hint. She's been calling me every day."

"So she's stalking you?" he asked with the morbid curiosity of a nine-year-old.

"You know, it just might be considered that, Petey."

"Could you call me Pete?" he asked. "I don't like being Petey anymore, but my mom won't stop."

"Sure. No problem." Elec nudged Pete with his elbow, knocking him off balance and making the boy grin. The kid was clearly experiencing some growing pains and Elec wanted to reassure him. "If you promise not to tell your mom I'm being stalked."

"Sure." Pete glanced over at him. "Do you like my mom?"

"Yeah. I like her a lot."

"Like *like* her, like her?"

They were heading into dicey territory with that question.

Elec knew Tamara didn't want her kids to know they were in any way dating. "How would you feel about that?"

"That would be cool." Pete tapped the plastic side of the ant farm. "Geoffrey was gross. I met him at the Christmas thing at my mom's work and he was old and bossy. I know my mom thinks I didn't know she was going on dates with him, but I'm not *stupid*."

"No, you're clearly not that. So where are you going to keep this ant farm?"

"In my room. Want to see it?"

"Sure." Elec couldn't resist. He reached over and ruffled Pete's short brown hair. "Next time I'll get you a tarantula."

Pete laughed. "My mom would freak out."

"Might be kind of funny, huh?" The image of Tamara's face if he strolled in with a giant fuzzy spider made Elec laugh, too. Probably not the best strategy to convince her they should be spending more time together.

When Elec laughed, Pete laughed harder, and Elec lay on the porch floor and just enjoyed the moment.

TAMARA opened the front door to let Elec know she had Hunter's race program and her daughter was anxiously waiting for him to sign it. What she saw when she put one foot outside and looked down literally ripped the breath right out of her lungs.

Her son was lying on his stomach next to Elec, who was similarly sprawled out on the wooden floorboards, and they were laughing together. The ant farm was set up in front of them and they were watching it as they cracked up to whatever private joke they'd just shared. It was so normal, so masculine, so casual, that damned if she didn't have tears in her eyes.

This was what her son had lost when Pete had spun out and hit the wall at Talladega. Easy, comfortable moments like this. Rolling around on the floor. Bugs. Guy stuff. Something she could never give him no matter how much she wanted to. Partly because, well, she wasn't a guy, but also because there was only so much time in a day, and she was responsible for everything. There just hadn't been a lot of spare time for lolling around and enjoying the moment.

Petey spotted her, and he nudged Elec. "Shhh," he said in a stage whisper. "Mom's here."

That brought an unexpected stab of pain. Her son was cutting her out, preferring Elec's company over hers. Maybe that wasn't entirely rational, because Petey had just spent an entire week at home with her, but it still tweaked her.

Elec nodded to Petey then gave Tamara a sheepish smile. "We're going to check out Pete's room and give the ants a permanent home there."

And now Elec had taken it upon himself to shorten her son's name. Pete was her husband, Petey was her son, and it bothered her, but she wasn't about to say something in front of Petey.

"Petey, hold up a minute on taking Elec to your room. Hunter wants her program signed, and I'm not sure how much longer she can stay awake. The fever is wearing her out." She addressed Elec. "Do you mind?"

"No, of course not." He had stood up and was holding the ant farm carefully in one hand. When he walked past her, he murmured in her ear, "You changed."

Tamara blushed. "No, I didn't." It was still the same pajama pants and pink T-shirt.

"You added something to the outfit," he said, pulling the racing program out of her hand and continuing on to the family room.

Yeah, a bra, and damn him for noticing. Though of course he had noticed she wasn't wearing one before. They had both been aware of that fact, which was why she'd been walking around with her arms crossed. When she'd dashed upstairs for the program, she'd tossed a bra on since her arm muscles were tired from the effort to cover her nipples jutting out in the cotton shirt.

Mixing her kids and Elec and all her sexual wants was not at all enjoyable. She really wanted him to just go home and she would catch up with him later, alone, when she was feeling at least marginally sexy.

But there was no hope for him leaving anytime soon. Hunter was chatting his ear off while he signed her program, asking him questions about his driving history and where he hoped to place for the season. Sometimes it was downright frightening to listen to her daughter—she was like a miniature female version of her grandfather, Pete's father. Even Hunter's hand gestures were straight from Johnny, the way her index finger came out to tick off points she was making.

It was interesting that Petey was more her child, with her interests in science and sociology, and Hunter was a Briggs through and through.

Hunter held up her program, with Elec's sprawling signature across the front. "He signed it!"

"I see that. That's awesome. Did you say thank you?"

"Yeah," Hunter said, with eye-rolling annoyance.

"She was very polite about it," Elec said. "And I'm sure she'll be equally polite when I show her what I brought for her."

Her daughter's eyes lit up. "You brought something for me?"

"Of course. I brought Pete an ant farm. You didn't think I'd leave you out in the cold, did you?"

"I don't know," Hunter said with the honesty of a seven-year-old. "I didn't even know you until today."

"True. But the answer is yes, I brought something for you, too."

Tamara watched Elec pull a box out of the bag and hand it to Hunter. Even from where she was standing, Tamara knew it was a die-cast stock car.

"Whoa!" Hunter said, turning the box around and around. "It's your fifty-six car! Thank you!"

"Yep. Can't get these in stores because, well, I'm a rookie, and I ain't all that yet." Elec grinned at Hunter. "But my father had a few of these made as a gift right before I hit the track in Daytona for my first cup race."

"Your dad gave this to you?" Hunter said. "I should give it back then," she added, even as she clutched it to her chest.

It did a mother proud to have Hunter say the right thing, even though she looked like she wanted to die at the mere thought of having to return it.

"He gave me ten. I don't need ten of my own car lying around. One for my condo, one for my coach, and one for my office, then I'm out of display places. So I'm happy to give one to you."

"Thanks." Hunter studied the minicar. "I like your colors. Red and silver are good colors."

"Yeah, I like them just fine. I lucked out with my sponsor." He pointed to the car in Hunter's hand. "The hood and trunk open and the engine has manufacturer specific details."

"Cool."

The doorbell rang again and Tamara went to answer it, wondering if she was ever going to get to eat the food Elec had brought for her. But all the distractions had certainly eliminated the whining. From the kids and from her.

The phone was ringing in the kitchen, but Tamara ignored it, figuring if it was important they'd leave a message. A quick glance through the peephole showed Ty and Ryder standing on her porch. Now that surprised her. They weren't known for randomly showing up without a phone call. Actually, she couldn't remember the last time they'd been over. They were both good guys, remembering her kids' birthdays, and sending her gifts or flowers from time to time to let her know they were thinking of her. Ty had even sent her roses on the first Valentine's Day after Pete's death with a card that had said, "Because Pete would have sent these if he could."

They were definitely good guys, but they just didn't show up at her house on a Monday, and being a worrier, she started to panic. Throwing the door open, she demanded, "Okay, what's wrong?"

But they both looked startled. "Nothing, why would anything be wrong?" Ryder asked.

"Nice outfit," Ty commented, gesturing to her pajamas.

"I just thought since you were both here . . . maybe Suzanne . . . I don't know." Tamara clutched her chest and let her heart rate return to normal.

"Nothing's wrong with Suzanne that a little sex couldn't fix," Ty said with a grin.

"Hey, that's my ex-wife you're talking about," Ryder said, giving Ty a punch on the bicep.

"That's my point . . . I think she'd be a lot happier if you two were still sharing a bed. Why are you divorced anyway?"

Tamara figured that was an uncomfortable subject for Ryder, given that his face was turning a vivid eggplant shade.

"Well, I'm glad everything is fine and it's so good to see you both. Come on in. Did you drop by for a specific reason or were you in the neighborhood?"

"We heard the kids have the chicken pox and that you've been stuck in the house, so we brought a crap-load of sugary candy." Ty held up a large bag that definitely had more candy in it than Tamara ever wanted in her house at one time.

"Wow, well, that was sweet of you guys. The kids will be so glad to see you." Tamara led them down the hallway to the family room. "They're getting quite a lot of company today," she said, willing herself not to blush, unable to say Elec's name out loud, knowing that Ty and Ryder both knew exactly what she had done at the dinner party.

"Look who's here," she said cheerfully to the room at large, noting that Hunter had now climbed onto Elec's lap and was taking her car out of the box. Trust her daughter to not be even remotely shy.

Tamara knew the minute Ty and Ryder spotted Elec because Ty muttered, "Well, well, check out the rookie," and Ryder responded right back, "Guess no grass grows under his feet."

They were both grinning at her when she turned around and glared at them.

The men greeted each other. "Hey, guys, what's up?" Elec said, Hunter snuggled into his arms.

"We brought candy for the kids." Ty held up the potentially eight-pound bag of sugar and told Elec, "Maybe if you're good, we'll let you have a piece."

"I'm always good," Elec said.

"That true, Tammy?" Ryder asked her with a grin.

She refused to respond to that. Her kids were jittery with excitement at all the company and Hunter was already begging for candy. "Tomorrow, Hunter, when your fever breaks."

Her daughter pouted, but got distracted by the tattoo she found on Elec's inner wrist. She traced the numbers of his car over and over with her finger and he let her, clearly amused. "What if you change cars?" Hunter asked. "Then this is stuck here."

"Doesn't matter. Fifty-six will always be my first cup car, so it's special."

And what Tamara was learning was that so was Elec. He was thoughtful, sentimental, loyal. She appreciated all those things about him, even at the same time it scared the hell out of her. Watching her daughter with him was equal parts exhilarating and heartbreaking.

Petey came over and showed off both his ant farm and his various pox.

"That's a good one right there," Ryder said, pointing to a pock on Petey's forearm. "It's oozing like crazy."

"Oh, Ryder," Tamara said, grossed out by the glee with which he said it.

"What? It's true. It will probably scar, kid, and you can tell all the chicks you got scratched wrestling a bear."

"Yeah," Petey said. "I'll say I took him down with my bare hands and had him pinned when he swiped me."

The words were accompanied by a visual demonstration by Petey, which Ryder took as an invitation to act out the part of the bear, and in the blink of an eye, Petey was upside down laughing, his T-shirt over his face.

The doorbell rang yet again and Tamara went for it, warning Ryder, "If he pukes, you're cleaning it up."

Wondering if it was her in-laws or Suzanne, because she couldn't imagine who else would show up at seven o'clock on a Monday, and praying it was Suzanne, Tamara opened the door. It was neither of her guesses, but was her teaching assistant, grad student Imogen Wilson, who had become a friend since she'd joined the program. Imogen was from New York and somehow managed to look like she was pounding the pavement in Manhattan even standing on Tamara's front porch in North Carolina. Imogen had dark brown hair pulled back in a sleek ponytail, stylish designer glasses, a black pencil skirt and ivory sweater set, and an expensive handbag that she was pulling a stack of papers out of.

"Imogen, hi, how are you?"

"Hi, Tamara, I'm sorry for dropping by unannounced."

Tamara noted Imogen was the only one who had bothered to apologize for that.

"I tried to call you but you didn't pick up and I figured I'd chance it and stop by anyway. I brought you . . ." She held up the stack of papers with a flourish. "Final exams to grade. I'm sure you're thrilled."

Tamara laughed. "Oh yeah, ecstatic. Come on in. I tell you, I'm kicking myself for not doing the chicken pox vaccine."

"Isn't it mandatory for kids now?" Imogen asked.

"Not if your kids were born before a certain date. And

since it's two doses, and both kids would have to get the vaccine at the same time, I never quite got around to it. I figured what were the odds they would be exposed to it?" Tamara shrugged. "Serves me right, I guess."

"Well, I'm sorry it's such bad timing with exams."

"Me, too. Do you have a minute?" Tamara asked. "I wanted to discuss how we're going to handle the summer classes."

"Sure, I have a minute." Imogen rolled her eyes and gave a sheepish shrug. "I have a lot of minutes actually, since I have zero social life."

"Now why is that? Too busy studying?"

"It's been hard to meet people. I'm a bit of a fish out of water here."

Tamara could see how that might be an issue. Imogen was more likely to eat sushi than barbeque and she probably didn't know a single verse of "Redneck Woman," which was a requirement if you were going to go out dancing or sing karaoke.

"You should come out with my friend Suzanne and I sometime. We're older than you, but we're not totally awful company."

"Thanks, I'd like that."

Tamara kicked the same laundry basket out of the way yet again. Why wouldn't those damn towels just fold themselves? "I have some friends over visiting my kids, so don't be startled. The level of testosterone in my family room is at an all-time high right now."

"Oh, okay, no problem."

Though Imogen did look startled when they entered the family room. Petey was on Ryder's back going for a gallop around the room, while Ty was juggling dime-sized pieces of candy in the air in front of him, occasionally leaning over and catching one with his mouth. Elec was still on the couch, but Hunter had moved around to his back and was on her knees, her arms around his neck, leaning over his shoulder as she informed him she was going to be the first girl to win the cup series championship.

Tamara was about to call attention when Petey slid, Ryder lost his balance, and Petey's foot kicked over the ant farm on the coffee table. And the lid popped off.

"No!" Petey shrieked.

"Oh, shit," Ryder said, sliding Petey to the floor.

"It's alright," Elec said calmly, dropping to the carpet and righting the farm.

"Holy crap!" Hunter said.

"Hunter Danielle Briggs!" Tamara said, absolutely horrified. "You do not use that kind of language. Ever."

"But that's what Suzanne says when she's upset. And Ryder just said sh—"

Tamara cut her off. "That doesn't give you the right to say it. When you're an adult, you can speak however you want, but for now, you follow my rules and there is no swearing in this house."

"Sorry," Ryder said, joining Elec and Petey on the floor.

"Are there ants crawling all over my family room?" Tamara asked, a little fearfully. She did not want to have to call an exterminator over this.

"Nope." Elec shook his hand over the open farm. "Just a few and we're getting them picked up. Most of them stayed in the tunnels when it tipped."

"Good." Tamara turned to Imogen. "Anyway, let me introduce you to the madness. The man who had my son on his back is Ryder Jefferson, Petey's godfather, and a professional race car driver. That boy is my son Petey. The monkey on the couch is my daughter Hunter. The other man crawling on the floor is Elec Monroe, also a race car driver. And standing here eating candy instead of scooping up ants is Ty McCordle, Hunter's godfather, and yet one more race car driver. Everyone, this is Imogen Wilson, my TA at the university."

"It's nice to meet all of you," Imogen said with a nervous smile, pushing her glasses up on her nose.

"I'm sorry, what did Tammy say your name is?" Ty asked Imogen, tossing the colored candy discs back and forth in his hands. "I didn't quite catch it."

"It's Imogen," she said, fussing with the buttons on her sweater set.

"Come again?" Ty tilted his head like he couldn't figure out why he wasn't quite getting it.

"Imogen."

"Oh." It was clear Ty still had no idea what the hell she had said and he wasn't willing to ask her a third time. "It's a pleasure."

"So you work with Tammy?" Ryder asked from the floor, giving up on ant retrieval and falling onto his back. Petey took the opportunity to launch himself onto Ryder's gut and a playful wrestling match ensued.

"Um . . ." Imogen said, because clearly the person who had asked her the question was now engaged in horseplay and wasn't going to hear her answer.

Before Tamara could save her, Elec did, still calmly picking up ants one by one. "So you're a grad student, Imogen?"

And bless his heart, he'd actually gotten the poor girl's name right.

"Yes. I have one more year. I need to start working on my thesis but I haven't found a topic that appeals to me yet."

"Masters in sociology? Maybe you should do a thesis on the culture of stock car racing." Elec grinned at her. "Plenty of material there."

Tamara was fairly certain he meant it as a joke, but Imogen looked thoughtful.

"There might be something there . . . huh."

"You can interview me," Ty said, holding his bag out to Imogen. "Candy?" Ty actually looked annoyed that he couldn't figure out what the grad student's name was, like

Imogen had intentionally taken a difficult moniker just to trip him up.

"No, thank you." Imogen shook her head. "I'm allergic to red dye."

"Oh. Sorry. Wasn't trying to kill you or anything." Ty turned and Tamara saw him roll his eyes at Ryder.

Hoping Imogen hadn't seen the rude gesture, Tamara said, "Well, we're heading into the kitchen for a few minutes to discuss some school business. Can you all try not to burn the house down or destroy anything for five minutes?"

"Actually, Tammy, we'll head on out of here," Ryder said, peeling himself off the floor. "We just wanted to say hi to the sick rug rats."

"Yep." Ty dropped the bag of candy on the coffee table. "Don't eat all of that tonight," he said with a wink at the kids. "We'll talk to you soon, Tammy. See ya, Elec." Then he said to Imogen, "Nice to meet you, Emma Jean."

Tamara sighed. "Her name is—"

But Imogen just shook her head. "Don't worry about it."

"What?" Ty said. "Look, I'm sorry, I admit it, I can't figure your name out. I've never heard that name before and I can't wrap my brain around it. But that doesn't mean I shouldn't try or that you shouldn't expect me to learn it."

Before either of them could say anything to his speech, he added, "It's really not Emma Jean?"

Imogen actually pressed her lips together to contain a grin. "No, it's not. It's Imogen. I-m-o-g-e-n. It's Shakespearean, and I'm very aware it's a difficult name for the average person, so I appreciate you trying to learn it."

Ty grinned at her. "You calling me average?"

Imogen blushed. "No, no, of course not."

Ryder leaned in to Tamara. "So, uh, what exactly is going on with you and number fifty-six over there?"

Tamara looked at Ryder, not sure what his reaction to her dating Elec would be, knowing how close he had been to Pete. "I don't know," she told him in all honesty.

"Well, just so you know, I'm all out of properties for you two to get it on in, unless you want to do it in my car."

Yep, that was a blush flooding her cheeks. "I'm sorry, I know I'm being tacky . . ."

"Hey, sometimes you just can't wait and I can appreciate that. I think it's great that you're having fun. Just be careful. Be sure of what you're doing, you know? What you want."

That was the problem. She had no clue what she really wanted. "Thanks, Ryder. Now will you take Ty out of here before he has my TA running back to Manhattan with her hands over her ears?"

"Sure." Ryder gave a whistle. "Hey, McCordle, train's leaving. I'm in need of a cold one. Let's hit the bar."

"I'm there with ya," Ty said, giving a wave to Imogen.

They said good-bye to the kids, then they were gone, slamming the front door behind them. Tamara looked at Elec. "Do you mind if I talk to Imogen for a minute?"

"No, not at all."

"Are you okay with them?" she asked nervously. She didn't want to foist the responsibility of watching her kids onto him.

"We're fine. Aren't we?" he asked Hunter, who was still hanging on his back.

"Yep," her daughter said.

"Okay, we'll be in my office." Tamara led Imogen down the hall. "I'm really sorry about Ty . . . he wasn't trying to be rude. He just honestly didn't understand what your name was."

"I know." Imogen shrugged. "I'm used to it. When I was a kid, I wished desperately that if my parents had wanted a Shakespearean name, they could have chosen Paris or Portia or even Juliet, but I've grown into it. I hear it's a very popular baby name in Britain now, which strikes me as amusing. I'm never quite in the right place at the right time. And it definitely could have been worse. They could have named me after a piece of fruit."

Tamara laughed. "That's true. Hey, for what it's worth, I love your name. Try having everyone call you Tammy. It's so ordinary. And virtually no one outside of my professional environment calls me by my full name."

"I noticed Ryder and Ty call you Tammy. It surprised me."

"I ask them to call me Tamara, but they never do." Tamara stepped into her office, which was her kid-free haven. It had an abundance of turquoise, pink, and splashes of black on a completely white backdrop. "Have a seat."

"Ty is, um, quite attractive," Imogen said, settling into a faux Louis IV chair that Tamara had painted turquoise and reupholstered in a zebra print, and resting her bag in her lap.

"Yeah, he is," Tamara said, somewhat surprised. Ty didn't seem like the type Imogen would find good-looking, especially after he'd butchered her name twelve times.

"Very . . . masculine."

Uh-oh. Tamara knew that tone and that look and she figured she might as well nip this one in the bud. Ty and Imogen would be about as good together as bacteria and penicillin. And she wasn't sure who would destroy who, but it wouldn't be pretty.

"He's definitely a true driver—great reflexes, competitive . . . and interested in young bimbos. You should see the latest he's been dating. If that one could string three words together, I'd be stunned."

"Oh, really?" Imogen looked disappointed. "Why do men do that?"

"I don't know. Because it's easy? No danger of hurt feelings? I have no idea."

The wheels in Imogen's very intelligent head seemed to be turning, so Tamara changed the subject back to work. "So about the summer . . . I'm scheduled to teach three courses."

Ten minutes later, she had shown Imogen out the front door, satisfied that they could continue their mutually beneficial working relationship over the summer. No one was in the family room, so trying not to worry, Tamara went into the kitchen.

Petey was sitting at the table eating spaghetti. Elec was putting an aluminum dish into the oven, his behind looking mighty nice in his jeans when he bent over.

"Wow, you're eating," she said to Petey, feeling a little flustered at the domestic scene laid out in front of her. Her husband had never put anything in the oven, ever, and the fact that Elec did so easily was a little unnerving. "Where's your sister?"

"I'm hungry," Petey said, like that was an obvious reason for eating, which she supposed it was. He slurped up a noodle. "This is good."

"Hunter's in bed," Elec said. "She was worn out and wanted to lie down, so I figured this time of night, might as well put her in her bed so you don't have to move her later."

"She let you put her to bed?" Tamara was amazed. Hunter wasn't an easy kid to settle down at night.

"Yep. She was just about asleep by the time I left the room."

"Oh. Wow. Thanks." Tamara rubbed her temples. "I'll just run up and check on her."

"Dinner should be ready by the time you get back," Elec said with a smile.

Tamara walked out of the room, fighting the urge to run. She didn't understand the chaos of feelings she was experiencing. Anxiety, anger, longing, pleasure . . . they were all swirling around inside her and she didn't know how to deal with any of them.

When she got to Hunter's bedroom, her daughter was indeed already asleep under her checkered flag comforter.

Inhaling the lingering scent of rubber, Tamara stared in the dark at her baby, her mouth open on a silent snore, and wondered what the hell she was doing.

This wasn't supposed to be like this. She was supposed to keep her relationship with Elec, which was supposed to revolve solely around sex, separate from her children. In one night, he had shattered that compartmentalization and questioned her very ability to have that kind of secretive affair anyway. She was too apt to get attached to think that she could have a sex-only fling and not be affected. Already she was feeling jealous of women like Crystal.

In the hallway she heard Petey coming up the stairs loudly, telling Elec some kind of fact about cockroaches being able to survive a nuclear war. Tamara leaned on the door frame of Hunter's room, glancing over her shoulder as they walked past her to Petey's room. Elec reached out and brushed his hand across her waist and the small of her back and she clenched her fists in her armpits, fighting back tears that had suddenly popped into her eyes.

This was too much. This was too much a reminder of what she'd lost. Hell, it was a reminder of what she'd never *had*. Pete had been a great guy who had loved his family, but by no means had he been hands-on. She could count on her hand the number of times he had tucked his children into bed. Which was why it always struck her as interesting that doing so was one of Petey's primary memories of his father.

"Meet you in the kitchen, okay?" Elec whispered to her.

"Okay. Good night, Petey," she called to her son.

"Night. Love you." He waved from the door of his room, popping his head in and out and grinning. Clearly he was bouncing right back from being sick.

"Love you, too."

When Petey disappeared into his room, she was left

standing alone with Elec, his intense stare on her in the moonlit hall.

"I'll be down in a minute," he said in a gravelly voice.

"Good."

Because they clearly needed to talk.

After he kissed her.

CHAPTER
TEN

ELEC walked into the kitchen, not sure what his reception was going to be. Tamara had pulled the lasagna out of the oven and put it on two plates on the table. She had opened a bottle of red wine and poured one glass. Next to the other plate was a bottle of beer, which stupidly touched him. She remembered that he didn't drink wine.

God, he was in way too deep and they were only ten days into this thing. Being in her house, with her and her kids, was comfortable and satisfying, just as much as being in bed with her was, though in a totally different way. Making love to Tamara satisfied him physically and as a man, a lover. It was hot and sexy and emotional, intimate and intense. Sharing an evening at home with her satisfied his need for a friend, for companionship, for the need he had to protect and take care of someone.

Together, it was dragging him under quick and he wasn't at all sure how she felt.

"I broke the rules, didn't I?" he said when she turned around, napkins clutched in her hand.

She nodded. "Yeah, you did."

"I'm sorry, that really wasn't my intention. I wasn't trying to push or manipulate you. When you told me about being stuck in the house, I just thought that it would be a help if I stopped by with dinner. That's all."

"I know. I can see that." She set the pink napkins down on the table. "It's just that the minute you walked in the door, it changed. It's not just you and I hooking up for fun."

"Were we really going to be able to do that?" he asked. "I know we fell into this impulsively, but at least on my part, there is a deeper attraction than that. I agreed to keep it quiet and casual because that's what you wanted. It's never been what I wanted."

Tamara didn't answer his question. She just chewed her lip and fretted. "My kids are going to ask about you. Hunter will root for you on the track. They'll wonder why you don't come over."

"Ty and Ryder don't come over all the time, do they?"

"No."

"So chalk it up to them getting special visitors because they were sick. We don't have to involve them if you don't want, I promise." Even though he could honestly say he would enjoy spending more time with her kids. "But don't shut me out. I want to see you, Tamara."

She gave a little laugh. "Funny how you're the only person outside of work who calls me Tamara."

He wasn't sure if that was a good thing or a bad thing. "That's how you introduced yourself to me," he said, baffled. "Would you rather I call you Tammy?" Hell, he'd call her whatever she wanted as long as he got to see her again.

"No. I like Tamara." She looked at him over the table with those big blue eyes, wide with uncertainty. "I like you, I mean really like . . . and I'm so confused. I don't know what we're doing, I don't know how to date. I haven't dated since I was eighteen years old, Elec."

"Do you honestly think anyone knows what the hell they're doing when they start a relationship? I don't know what I'm doing either. Do you think I meant to come over here and make you upset? I was just thinking it would be a nice thing to do, and now I'm regretting that I ever met your kids because it's going to be damn hard to promise you I won't get involved in their lives. I like them. I like you." Elec jammed his hands in the pockets of his jeans. "Being here with you . . . it feels so good. But I know we can't fool around with this, that protecting Pete and Hunter is the most important thing. I swear to you I'll make that my number one priority."

"Thank you." Tamara fiddled with a fork next to her plate. "I think maybe you got more than you were expecting with me. I'm a bit of a mess."

"No, you're not. You're just trying to do the right thing for your kids at the same time you're trying to respect the fact that you're a woman with a woman's needs."

She gave a slight smile. "I do have a woman's needs."

Elec moved closer to Tamara, wanting to taste her lips so bad he ached. "For which I am very grateful. As a matter of fact, I'd like to respect those womanly needs right now if you'll let me."

Tamara looked at him suspiciously. "What are we talking about here?"

"Just a kiss. That's all."

"Then I'll let you."

He already had her in his arms before she even finished speaking. Elec breathed in the scent of her, running his lips over her neck.

"Oh, God, I'll let you," she said, her head falling back.

That sensuous capitulation nearly did him in. Elec pulled her closer to him, burying his hands in her hair. Then he kissed her, feverishly, urgently, desperately. He wanted her to understand how much he desired her, how beautiful he thought she was, how much he wanted to bury his body between her soft, wet thighs. How much he wanted to make her come over and over until she was limp from pleasure, begging him to stop.

She kissed him back with the same furiousness, her tongue meeting his, her hands running over his shoulders, and landing low, down on his ass.

"Oh, shit," he told her, pulling back breathlessly, bumping his cock into her thighs one last time. "We've got to stop."

Nodding and panting, she whispered, "This is going to be a problem."

"We can get creative. You get a lunch break, right?"

"Yes."

"I'm usually free on Mondays. We can meet for lunch, if you know what I mean."

Tamara looked a little shocked, but she did nod. "I could do that."

"What time?"

"One thirty would work. I'm actually done for the day at one on Mondays. I guess we could meet . . . here." Her face had lost some color and her voice had dropped to a whisper, but she was in agreement and making plans.

Good enough for him. Now he figured he should retreat before she changed her mind. "Perfect, I'll be here. Now should we eat or what? My stomach is digesting itself."

"Oh, right, dinner." Tamara pulled her chair out abruptly and sat down. "Just ignore the fact that I'm eating dinner in my pajamas."

"I won't tell if you won't."

She gave him an earnest look. "I do appreciate all of this. Please don't think that I don't. I'm really grateful that you'd go to all this trouble for me."

"I'm not looking for gratitude," he told her as he took a seat in front of the beer. "Just your friendship."

"That you have," she said with a small smile. Then she took a deep breath, like she was digging into her reserves for fortitude. "Now tell me how things are looking for Pocono."

"I'd love to. If you will then explain to me what courses you teach."

"Deal."

They talked as they ate, and Elec was enjoying their easy conversation so much, he lingered way past when he should have left. A glance at the clock on her oven showed it was ten already and he knew Tamara had to be tired. They had cleaned up the dinner dishes together and Elec was itching to touch her again. But he knew if he started, he wouldn't want to stop.

She looked to be thinking the same thing. The dish towel in her hand, she kept leaning forward, then swaying back on her feet. "Wow, I didn't realize how late it was."

"Yeah, I should shove off."

Neither one of them moved an inch.

There was no telling how long they might have stood there gazing at each other with sexual longing flying between them, but Elec's cell phone chimed in his pocket. He was going to throw the damn thing off a bridge if it didn't stop making that noise when he got a text. The minute he was alone, he was going to change the setting to silent.

"Do you need to answer that?" she asked.

"No, it's just a text."

"Don't you want to read it?"

"Not really." What he wanted was to taste Tamara's mouth again, and to slide his hand up under her T-shirt and undo the bra she had put on. He wanted to lay her back across her round white table, peel her pink pajama pants off, and flick his tongue over her clit.

Not read his stupid text that he could almost guarantee was from Crystal.

"It's that girl again, isn't it?" she asked, her lip curling up.

He shrugged.

"Go ahead and see."

"I don't want to. I want to ignore her and hope she'll go away."

Tamara laughed. "It doesn't work that way. Just read it."

"Fine." He pulled his phone out of his pocket and pushed the buttons to read the text. Only it was a picture text, the image speaking louder than he imagined any words ever would. "Oh my God."

He actually felt himself recoil away from his phone and the picture of Crystal's naked chest, his car number somehow attached to her nipples. He wasn't sure if she'd used tape or what, but her right breast had a large 5 on her nipple, and the left had a 6, creating a 3-D effect.

"What?"

"Nothing." Damn, that was disturbing. He wasn't sure if he was supposed to be flattered or what, but it just left him feeling like he wanted to reach into his phone and snatch his numbers off her nipples. It felt sacrilegious.

"Oh, come on, you can't turn white as a sheet and grimace like that and then not tell me. Or show me."

"I don't think you want to . . ." Too late. Tamara had turned his phone toward her.

"Oh, my. Well, there's nothing subtle about that, is there?"

"Not really." Elec hit Erase with a fair amount of disgust. "I don't think ignoring her is working."

"Guess not." Tamara looked at him curiously. "How long did you date her?"

"For about a minute." Elec stuck his phone back in his pocket. "We went out three times! That's it." And even though Tamara wasn't asking, he felt it was important to point out, "And I didn't sleep with her. Not even close. These texts are showing me way more of her than I ever saw on our three very casual dates."

He couldn't tell if Tamara believed him or not.

But she said, "Clearly she is determined to show you what you missed out on."

"I don't want it," he insisted.

Tamara laughed. "Okay, I can see that. You look genuinely horrified. But what I can't figure out is why you'd want saggy old me when you can have that perky perfection."

She didn't get it, and he didn't know how to explain it to her. And he was afraid that no matter what he said, it would be misinterpreted. Maybe later he would try to explain what made her so gorgeous to him and why Crystal was artificial and empty. But for now he just settled for, "I think you're beautiful. I want you. No one else."

Her eyes softened. "Thank you. Now go home before I do something I'll regret, like rip your clothes off."

Elec grinned. "And how is that supposed to send me running to the door? I'd like to stick around for that."

"Except that you respect me and know I'll regret it, so you're going to be stronger than me and leave."

Damn. "Alright, alright." Elec gave her a soft kiss on her forehead. "I'll be on the road, but call me if you want. And let me know if the kids aren't back in school next Monday and we can reschedule."

"Okay. Good luck in Pocono."

"Thanks." And Elec got the hell out of there before he let her down and ravaged her on her kitchen table.

"HOW could you say something like that? Oh my God, this is a disaster!" Eve threw her messenger bag onto the sofa in Evan's coach and glared at him, and Elec almost felt sorry for him.

Almost. Eve was furious at Evan for creating a PR nightmare. Elec was furious for more personal reasons.

"I didn't mean it the way it sounded! You know what it's like . . . I had just climbed out of the car and they're hitting me with questions. I didn't mean it the way they made it sound."

Eve, who had ripped her sandals off, grabbed the TV

remote and whirled in the pink summer skirt and white top she'd been wearing at the track. "Listen to yourself, Evan, just listen."

Oh, Lord, she was going to make them suffer through it again on DVR. There was Evan, grinning and victorious from his win at Pocono, climbing out of his car. Elec glanced back and forth between his brother sitting next to him, his elbows on his knees, his hands holding his head up, a grimace on his face, and the elated guy on the TV screen. Yeah, Elec almost felt sorry for him.

Microphones were shoved in Evan's face and he answered a few questions, inserting his sponsor and car owner in at appropriate intervals. Then the reporter, a cute twenty-something who didn't look like she'd know squat about stock car racing, said, "With this win today at Pocono, you just surpassed Pete Briggs's record for the most victories at this track."

"Really?" Evan said, looking startled.

Elec wouldn't have known that either. Monroes weren't ones to chase records. What mattered to them was climbing in the car week after week and making it count.

"Yes, he had four victories here and this is your fifth. How do you feel about that?"

"Well, that's a fun bit of news, Theresa, thank you for sharing." Evan gave her a big, charming smile and she smiled back. It was a little on-camera flirting that wasn't necessarily appropriate but wouldn't have been all that noteworthy, except that Evan opened his mouth again. And said, "And I guess all I can say about passing Pete's record is that clearly things have turned out better for me than they have for him."

Which probably wouldn't have been a terrible thing to say except the man Evan was referring to was dead.

The reporter, who had been a flirty little sweetheart two seconds earlier, turned into a story shark and sank her teeth into Evan. "I guess they have turned out better for you since you're standing here collecting another victory and he hit the wall at Talladega. Do you think that's skill or just the luck of the driver?"

Evan's grin had fallen off his face and he stammered a bit, before saying, "Everyone knows Pete Briggs was a great driver. His death was a huge loss to his family, fans, and to racing."

Elec nudged his brother's leg. "That was a good save, but dude."

"I know, I know . . . but admit it, it just as easily could have been you."

"No, it wouldn't have," Eve snapped. "Because Elec doesn't get distracted by perky little reporters. The problem with Elec is that he never says enough. You, on the other hand, could stand to zip it once in a while."

"Hey, now. I don't see you having to do these interviews, Eve!" Evan dropped his hands and glared at her. "You think it's so easy, but you try climbing out of a car that's a hundred and ten degrees that you've been strapped into for four hours, dehydrated and still vibrating from the engine. You see how sharp on your toes you are."

"I know what it's like to drive a car! I was the quarter midget champion at fifteen, if you're too blindsided by blond reporters to remember."

"Midget cars ain't stock cars, sweetheart."

Oh, Lord, here they went. It was descending into something uglier than it already was. Elec could see both of their sides. It wasn't easy to climb out of a car and answer tricky questions. But Eve was right—what Evan had said sounded just awful given that Pete was dead.

"Can we just focus on damage control here?" Elec asked. "Do you think Evan should offer an apology or maybe he can go to one of those events as a gesture . . . don't Pete's parents have a charity in his name?"

Image was important in racing, and Elec didn't want this misstep to affect Evan's career. Sponsors wanted to know they could count on a driver to stand behind their name and their product with integrity.

"That's a good idea. You should go with him, Elec. Present a united front."

"Oh . . . I don't know." Elec panicked at the thought of being at an event with the Briggses and possibly Tamara and not being able to acknowledge the relationship they had.

"Why not? It will look better than Evan going alone."

"Don't abandon me, man," Evan said, and his eyes were pleading.

"Shit, I don't know if it's a good idea for me to be there because . . ." Elec cleared his throat. "I'm kind of, well, dating Pete Briggs's widow."

"*What?*" Eve shrieked. "What does that mean? Like you go for coffee occasionally, or that you're dating, dating, meaning you're sleeping with her?"

Elec didn't answer, just stared at his sister. She'd figure it out.

She did. "Oh my God, you're sleeping with her . . . between you and Evan I'm going to have a heart attack. I will be dead at the age of thirty from stress."

"When did you start sleeping with Tammy Briggs?" Evan asked, looking baffled as hell. "I didn't even know you knew her."

Then Eve slapped her forehead. "This is who you were talking to Mom about at lunch . . . this is the woman with the sick kids. Oh my God, you went over there with dinner and toys for her kids, didn't you?"

"Yes. So what?" he said defensively.

Evan was looking at him like he'd grown a second head since they'd walked in the door.

"This is a good thing actually." Eve paced back and forth, her skirt twirling when she turned. "We'll have you do some PR with her kids . . . and make it obvious that you're dating. That will deflect attention from Evan's gaffe onto you. Everyone will be thrilled to dissect a race car romance. What a great story . . . the noble widow finds love again."

Sweat was breaking out all over Elec's body. "No. No, no, no. Stop, halt, do not pass Go, Eve. No one is going to be telling anyone about my relationship with Tamara. I am dead serious on this one. What we are doing is private. End of story." Tamara would never, ever forgive him if he splashed their relationship all over the media. And hell, he didn't want that himself. What they were sharing was special and needed to be just between the two of them. He wouldn't have even told his family if he hadn't had to.

"Why not? It's not like you can keep it a secret forever."

"But we can keep it a secret until Tamara decides she wants people to know, and then we'll do it her way. Not with a media blitz. Pete's parents are her in-laws and she's still close to them."

"Well, you know Johnny Briggs and Dad hate each other."

"I know. And the reason is ridiculous as far as I can tell. Something about a stolen trophy and a fistfight. They're grown men and they need to get over it."

"You tell that to Dad," Evan said, biting his fingernail. "I'd like to see that one go down. He'll actually be madder at you than at me then."

Now Elec was starting to feel as stressed out as Eve. His relationship with Tamara was complicated enough already. Why did everyone else have to keep sticking their finger in the pot and stirring things up? "I'm not going to say anything. All we need is Dad making an issue of their feud and we'll have a PR nightmare on our hands. They'll say you took a swipe at Pete intentionally."

Eve stopped paced. "Oh, no. Oh, no. And then suddenly your blossoming romance will be seen as a maneuver on the part of the Monroes to get back at the Briggs family."

Elec sat back in shock. "No one would believe that." He looked up at Eve. "Would they?"

"Doesn't matter if they believe it or not if the media chooses to make an issue out of it." Eve stuck her finger out at him. "Don't let anyone know what you're doing with Tamara Briggs. Keep your little romps a secret or I will duct tape you to this coach when you're not on the road."

"I told you I wanted to keep it a secret!" he said in annoyance. "Don't go threatening me, Eve Alexandra. I don't want to hear it."

"He's pissed if he's bringing out the middle name," Evan said. "Let it go, Eve."

Their sister didn't look at all concerned with his stern voice. She was back to pacing. "Okay, here's what we do. Elec keeps his diddling on the sly and Evan makes a better apology and goes to a Briggs Foundation charity event."

Though Elec took a hell of an exception to the term *diddling*, he couldn't disagree. "Fine."

"I can do that," Evan said.

Eve gave a massive sigh and headed for the kitchen. "Thank God. Now if you don't have chocolate in here, I'm going to go bat shit crazy on you."

Elec prayed he did, because neither he nor Evan wanted to see Eve's head explode.

TAMARA picked at her dinner and tried to ignore the fact that her father-in-law was ranting about the comment Evan Monroe had made about Pete after his win at Pocono.

"I mean, who the hell does he think he is? That was just damn rude, tossing that remark out there so casually."

"I'm sure he didn't mean it the way it sounded," Beth said. "Do you want more mashed potatoes, dear?"

"No," Johnny said. "I don't. What I want is an apology

from that punk kid for insulting my son, who in his four short years in the cup series has a list of accomplishments longer than my arm."

Tamara had seen the clip of Evan speaking, and she agreed with Beth. It had sounded a little rude, but she didn't think it was that big of a deal. He was clearly elated from his victory, hot and sweaty, and being forced to answer questions before he could even have a drink or hit the bathroom. And when he'd realized how his response had sounded, he'd given a very respectful follow-up comment.

It hadn't offended her in the least, but then she hadn't lived her entire life active in the sport like Johnny had, where personalities clashed, tempers ran hot, and men died. As much as she loved racing, it wasn't her career, her livelihood, her legacy.

"Evan did seem surprised that he'd passed Pete's record. He didn't seem to even know that until the reporter mentioned it," Tamara commented.

"Well, he should have!" Johnny said, destroying his dinner roll by tearing chunks out of it and dunking them in gravy.

Clearly, there was no talking to Johnny until he had calmed down. Even Petey and Hunter were quiet as they ate, picking up on the fact that their grandfather was hopping mad.

"I'm sure he'll apologize," Beth said.

"I don't want to see or hear anything from either of those Monroe boys. Ever."

Tamara couldn't swallow. All she needed was for her kids to find their voices and mention that Elec Monroe had been at their house for hours the Monday before.

But they must have figured out that mentioning a little fact like that might turn Grandpa's anger on them, because they both sat with wide eyes and opened their mouths only to shovel more food in.

"And why do they all have names that start with an *E* anyway? It's stupid. That Elliot's an arrogant SOB."

"Johnny." His wife gave him a stern look. "Now there is no reason to be insulting the names that man gave his children. He can name his offspring whatever he wants, and I happen to think they all have attractive names. And watch the language in front of your grandchildren."

That was enough for her father-in-law. He slapped his napkin down on the table and stood up. "I'm going out. Don't wait up for me, Beth."

Her mother-in-law watched him go then sighed. "Don't mind him. It's just days like this it hits him hard that Pete is gone forever."

"I miss Daddy," Hunter said, her eyes filled with tears.

Tamara thought it was probably just an emotional reaction to the tension at the table, and Hunter seeing her normally jovial grandfather cranky as hell, but she still had to deal with it.

"I know, baby girl, we all do," she told her. "Come sit on Momma's lap."

Tamara rocked her daughter and wondered how she could possibly justify leaving the university the next day and speeding home to have a clandestine meeting with Elec, who her father-in-law deemed the enemy.

She should cancel.

It was all too damn complicated.

But somehow she just couldn't bring herself to do that.

CHAPTER
ELEVEN

TAMARA popped a third breath mint into her mouth and wiped her sweaty palms down the front of her skirt. Elec was supposed to be there in ten minutes and she was nervous as hell. It was one thing to spontaneously have sex with him, it was another to know he was showing up at her house at one thirty for that precise reason.

Never in her life had she made these kind of plans and she was so worked up she actually inhaled the breath mint whole and started coughing. Where were they supposed to go when he got there? Was she supposed to offer him a drink? Lead him upstairs? Do it on the couch?

Glancing at the clock in her kitchen for the nineteenth time, she wondered if she had enough time for a shower. The car had been about ninety degrees when she'd left school and she felt hot and sweaty, especially in places she would really like him to linger. If she was self-conscious about perspiration, she wasn't going to be able to enjoy herself.

So whether or not she had enough time, she really needed a shower.

Of course, if he arrived while she was in the shower, she wouldn't hear him, and what if he left? That would seriously be horrible, after all this work and anxiety and desperate anticipation.

Running up the stairs, she debated putting a note for Elec on her unlocked front door, but dismissed that idea. Any crazy who happened onto her porch could just stroll on in then and murder her like poor Janet Leigh in *Psycho*. She would send him a text message instead and tell him to come in if she didn't answer the door. That would work.

Texting while walking, Tamara started the shower and kicked off her shoes and skirt. After hitting Send, she tossed her phone on the bed and grabbed a towel. Cranking up her iPod in the speaker in her bedroom, hoping a little music would distract her from being nervous, she put her hair up in a knot and got in the shower.

She had five minutes to shave, buff, and refresh the hell out of her body, and maybe figure out how to extract her heart from her throat in the meantime.

It was a lot to ask of five minutes, hot water, and apricot shaving cream, but she was determined to try.

ELEC was nervous as hell as he strode onto Tamara's front porch, feeling sort of like a kid cutting school. He even found himself glancing around at the neighbors' houses to see if anyone was watching, but the street was sleepy and quiet at that time of day. There was one mother pushing a stroller and walking her dog, but she didn't even glance his way.

He had gotten Tamara's text so he knew he was supposed to walk on in, but he wasn't sure what he was supposed to do after that, nor did he understand why she couldn't answer the door. For half a second he had thought that maybe Tamara had planned a seduction for him, and that he was going to wander through a house strewn with rose petals or something, and at the end of the line, Tamara would be waiting for him in sexy lingerie.

But the thought had barely popped into his mind when he dismissed it again. Rose petals, slinky underwear, and artful posing on the bed just weren't Tamara.

He sent her a text that read, "Where are you?"

But after an agonizing minute or two, he had no reply, so he cautiously opened the front door and stepped into her foyer, listening for a clue as to where she was. Elec didn't really hear much of anything, just a clock ticking and the air-conditioning humming. A quick stroll around the downstairs revealed nothing but empty rooms, so he sucked in a breath and started up the stairs, hoping this was what she wanted him to do. If not, next time she needed to give him better instructions.

There was music playing in what he knew was her bedroom, so he knocked on the door frame, even though the door was open. "Tamara?" he called, glancing in.

She wasn't naked on the bed, which was a little disappointing. In fact, she wasn't even in the room as far as he could tell. But when he leaned his head in, he realized her bathroom door was open and he could hear the shower running.

That realization produced an instant erection. Knowing she was ten feet away, with no doors or locks between, naked and wet in a steamy shower, made him appreciate how long it had actually been since they had last had sex.

Fourteen days. It had been two very long weeks, with one torturously pleasurable make-out session in the meantime. That was clearly way too long, because his body ached with want from head to goddamn toe.

And she was in for a surprise if she thought he was just going to sit down on her pretty little pink bedroom chair and wait for her to finish up. Yanking his T-shirt off over his head, Elec strode toward the bathroom. He was feeling a little dirty, and he was going to join her.

Her bathroom was like the rest of her house, clean and free of clutter, and he was downright thrilled to see that her shower wasn't hidden by a curtain. It was just steamy glass doors, and while the view was a little distorted, it wasn't by much. He could see Tamara in all her glory, perky little backside facing him as she . . . Oh my God. She bent over to grab her razor.

Elec's vision blurred as every last drop of blood in his body rushed straight to his cock. Women just had absolutely no idea what that particular position did to a man. It made him a speechless, drooling mass of stupidity, and Elec demonstrated that very thing by standing there in the doorway and drinking in the sight of Tamara, water sluicing down her back, suds collecting on her breasts and nipples as she turned and let the stream hit her shoulder blades. Her skin was pink from the heat, wisps of her hair were curling damply on her cheeks, and she was humming along to the music. Her dark curls between her thighs were dripping water and he wanted more than anything to lean below her legs and capture those droplets into his mouth.

He really should warn her he was there.

In a minute or two.

For the moment, he was perfectly content to just watch her hands roaming around her slick body, washing and scrubbing with a foaming shower gel and a big puffy sponge.

KNOWING she had to be pushing her luck on time, Tamara wiped the steam off the door hoping to catch a glimpse of the clock on the nightstand in her bedroom. Elec was probably sitting in her family room . . .

Tamara let out a shriek when she realized that no, he wasn't sitting on her sofa downstairs. He was standing in her freaking bathroom door three feet away from her, his chest bare, and his jeans riding low on his hips as he stared at her.

"What are you doing?" she said, covering her breasts with her arm. "You scared me half to death!"

"Sorry," he said, but he didn't look the least bit sorry. Nor did he leave.

Trying to figure out what was the best way to stand so he could see the absolute least of her possible under the harsh fluorescent lighting of the bathroom, Tamara squeezed the life out of her sponge and wondered how she could miraculously wrap a towel around her without opening the shower door.

There was no way to camouflage any of her nudity, damn it, and she said, "Just give me a second. I'll meet you downstairs in two minutes."

"I'm not leaving," he said. "And you have no reason to hide your body from me."

"I'm not entitled to some modesty?" She glared at him through the steamy glass.

"No. And if it will make you more comfortable, I can get naked, too." Without even waiting for an answer, Elec dropped his jeans to the floor.

Even as she swallowed a bucketful of spit and felt a surge of moisture between her thighs at the sight of him in his tight black boxer briefs, she was still annoyed. "It's easy for you to get naked. You didn't squeeze two babies out of your body and wind up with a stomach that has more lines than Charlotte has people."

Elec was right in front of the shower and Tamara was starting to get a little scared as to what that meant. She pressed back against the tiles, wincing when her butt made contact with the cold ceramic. "You're starting to make me mad," she told him, but she was more nervous than angry.

He didn't understand how hard it was to forget about those flaws, for her to appreciate the beauty of his hard, young body at the same time she was painfully aware of how many laps her own body had done around the track.

The shower door yanked open and Elec stood in front of her. "You're making *me* mad."

"What am I doing?" Sponge clutched in front of her jiggly stomach, she blinked as the water bounced off the side of her face.

Elec took the sponge out of her hand—just grabbed it—and tossed it on the floor of the shower.

"What the hell?" she demanded.

"Do you know how frustrating it is to me to hear you be so hard on yourself? To hear you criticize your body when there is absolutely nothing wrong with you? You have a gorgeous figure. You have a woman's body, with a woman's curves, and yes, you have a few stretch marks on your stomach, but do you honestly think that makes you one bit less attractive?" Elec's voice was louder than she had ever heard him speak and he was ignoring the fact that he, too, was being pelted by shower spray, which bounced off his chest. She stared at him uncertainly as he lifted his knee and jabbed a finger at it. "I have a scar on my knee from surgery. It's purple and raw and a good four inches long. Does that make me any less attractive when I'm naked? Did you even notice it until I pointed it out?"

Tamara glanced at the scar he was tapping. It was a significant scar, and no, she'd never noticed it. "No, I didn't see it, but that's because it's on your knee. It's not an erogenous zone. You can't avoid my stretch marks."

"The hell it isn't. If you touch anything on me, it becomes an erogenous zone. Period. That's how much I want you. You could touch my freaking eyebrow and I would get turned on. And I'll have you know that I happen to like your stretch marks. I look at those and I'm reminded of what a good woman you are, how you sacrifice every day for your children."

Tamara's heart was racing, and she wanted to believe him, she did, but she had been too self-conscious for too long. The marks on her could be ignored, she could agree with that, but there was no way he could actually like them.

"You're insane," she said, because she really didn't know what else to say and she wanted to get out of the shower and cover herself with the biggest towel known to man.

"Yes, I am," he said, leaning in and kissing her hard and with a thrusting, possessive tongue. "Insane from the fact that it has been fourteen long days since I've been inside you."

That was kind of hot. Okay, a lot hot. Tamara was trying to formulate a response, really, any words whatsoever, when Elec turned around and bent over to dig into his pants pocket. Then back still to her, he shoved his underwear off and she caught a glorious, divine view of his tight butt. That was almost worth the embarrassing discomfort she was feeling at the moment. He really had a quite perfect man body, from the broad shoulders, to the defined biceps and abs, down to the rock-solid thighs and, of course, that fine, fine ass. When he turned back around to face her, he had an impressive erection, which he had already covered with a condom.

Clearly he was getting in this shower with her. "Don't you want to go to the bed?" she asked tentatively. The whole wet thing, standing up, cold tile . . . it all seemed a little dubious to her. She and Pete had abandoned the idea of sex in the shower early in their marriage because she'd never been able to get wet enough to make it work, and Pete would have taken it as an insult to his manhood if she had suggested a lubricant. So they had just ignored the subject and found other places to have sex.

"No, I don't want to go to the bed," Elec said and stepped into the shower, thoroughly invading all of her personal space.

Wow, that was a lot of hard man pressing against her. Tamara had nowhere to go, and he was warm and the tile behind her was cold, so she moved closer to him, gasping in pleasure as her nipples brushed against his skin, and his erection nudged her while the hot water rained down on them.

"I want you," he said, kissing her mouth, her jaw, her shoulder, "so freaking bad."

"Take me," she said, feeling all her inhibitions evaporate the way they always did whenever Elec touched her. He had the most amazing way of touching her *right there* and making every nerve ending in her body stand up and do a happy dance.

"Hot and wet," he said as he stroked his finger inside her.

"The shower?" she asked breathlessly, clinging to his shoulders and moving her knee out so he could go deeper.

"The shower . . . you . . . everything between us."

She knew exactly what he meant.

Making little sounds of encouragement, Tamara closed her eyes against the water spray and rested her forehead on his shoulder as he stroked inside her at the perfect angle with the perfect pressure. She should do something, she should participate, she should at least stroke him in return, but he was hitting that place that made her lose all thought, all breath, all speech.

"Don't come," he whispered in her ear.

"Why not?" she managed to say into his slick, damp flesh. And if he objected to her having an orgasm, he needed to stop hooking his finger like that inside her.

"Because I want you to come with me inside you," he said, pulling his finger out of her.

Damn it, that was disappointing. "I can come both ways," she assured him.

Elec pressed her against the tiles and she gave a yelp at how cold they were, but she was immediately distracted by Elec's pushing her feet apart with his. He was kissing her neck, lapping the water off her chin, sucking her nipples so hard that she felt the sting of pain intermingling with plea-sure. Assaulted by sensation, Tamara shook her hair, which had fallen out of its knot, out of her face, and ran her hands over his hard, muscular back. She was covered in goose bumps, from the mix of hot and cold, from the light, shimmering touches of his fingers, to the damp trail he left across her skin with his tongue, and she shivered.

"Cold?" he asked her.

"A little."

Elec reached up and adjusted the spray so it was running down her shoulders and back, then he said, "This should help, too."

And with no warning whatsoever, he pushed his erection inside her.

Tamara sucked in a breath hard, then forgot to release it. She just held on to a lungful of air, silent and immobile, eyes rolling back in her head as she felt his hardness thrust into her deeper than she would have thought possible. It felt amazing, like an erotic mixture of hot and cold, hard and soft, and she threw her arms back against the tiles to grab something, anything, to hold her up. When he'd entered her, she had gone up on her tiptoes on instinct and from impact, and she realized that her toes were tingling so she dropped back down onto the balls of her feet.

Which sent him so deep inside her that they both groaned out loud.

"Holy shit," he said.

Her thoughts exactly.

"Oh my God," Elec said, gripping her waist hard. "Do that again."

It hadn't been her intention to do anything other than release the pressure in her toes and arches, but let him think she had some tricks up her sleeve. Tamara went up on her toes, which pulled her up off of him slightly. She flattened her feet again, and dropped down hard onto his erection a second time.

Even expecting it this time, it still shot aching tremors throughout her midsection. Wow.

"You move on me," Elec told her, and she could hear the excitement in his voice, hear that he was spinning out of control.

The idea that she had gotten him to that point was so titillating that she didn't even hesitate. Squeezing his shoulders for leverage, Tamara pumped up and down on him, without thought or any particular skill, just with enthusiasm and desperation. The sudden orgasm rocked her, and she moved harder as the waves of pleasure rolled over her, her muscles contracting over and over. Her foot slipped on the wet floor, but she didn't stop until she had eked every last second of ecstasy from that orgasm.

When she slowed down a little and remembered that breathing was essential to life, Elec didn't give her a chance to rest. He slammed her back up against the tiles and pinned her there, thrusting with such a single-minded ferocity that Tamara came again, so overwhelmed by sensation that she whimpered as it rushed over her. If he hadn't been nailing her to the wall, she would have slid straight on down it.

"Elec," she said for no apparent reason.

"What, baby?" he asked, leaning forward and kissing her, his lips damp and warm from the shower stream.

"I . . . I . . ." She had no idea what she had intended to say. But she recognized that feeling building inside her as he stroked in and out, his finger sneaking between their bodies to tweak her clitoris. She knew that feeling, but she couldn't quite believe it. Never, ever in her entire life had she had three orgasms in one sex session and she couldn't possibly be going to do that again.

His erection buried inside her, his finger on her clitoris, Elec flicked his tongue across her nipple and Tamara couldn't believe it, but it was actually happening.

"Oh my God," she moaned. "I'm coming again!"

"And it's the most beautiful thing I've ever seen," he said.

Then he paused and she felt his orgasm join hers.

Together they held on and moaned and pulsed in harmony, and Tamara thought it was quite possible that she had stopped existing for any purpose other than to feel this way every second of every day.

When Elec finally stopped moving, she was a gelatinous mass of sexual nerves, replete and satisfied, and upright only because he was holding her that way with both his arms and his penis.

Gradually she became aware of the fact that her skin was wrinkled from the constant water stream, that her hair was stuck to her cheek and neck in saturated hunks, and that her calf was in spasms from being forced to tense repeatedly.

But she didn't care one whit. She was just going to lie there against that tile for the rest of her life.

Or until Elec moved, which he rather unfortunately did before she was ready. When he backed up, she was certain she was going to drop to the floor and get a closer view of her less than stellar housekeeping, but Elec startled her by sliding a hand under her thighs and picking her up.

"Ack!" she said, flapping her arms around with zero grace as she struggled to find her balance. "What are you doing?"

"I'm ready to go to the bed now."

"What are we going to do there?" she asked. He couldn't possibility be capable of a repeat performance so soon, and there was no way that she could be touched by finger, tongue, or penis without leaping ten feet in the air. All that water and all those orgasms had left her hypersensitive and she suspected it would just be downright painful if he tried anything. But she kept all those thoughts to herself, because she tended to be a worrier, and maybe for once, she should sit back and see how it all played out.

Elec shot her an intense look. "We're going to do whatever you want." He stepped out of the shower and walked across the bathroom.

She couldn't believe he was carrying her so easily. That was incredibly sexy, but she was still enough of a priss that she heard herself say, "Don't we need a towel?" They were dripping a whole heck of a lot of water all over her ceramic tile. The carpet would be even worse.

"No. The bed will dry us off. And what it doesn't dry on you, I'll lick dry."

"Oh." My. Goodness. Did that mean she was supposed to lick him in kind? Because while it sounded shocking, she thought she could get into a thorough exploration of that hard body.

In the bedroom, Elec set her down on top of her fluffy white down duvet, and didn't drop her or look like he was gasping for air. Tamara grabbed the pillow and plopped it down over her stomach and various other important parts. She couldn't help it, it was just instinctive, and she still wasn't comfortable with giving him a big old look-see in the bright afternoon light.

Elec made a sound of impatience. "Move the pillow," he said.

"No."

"Don't you trust me?"

He almost sounded wounded and that relaxed her enough to release some of the tension in her shoulders. "Of course I do."

"Then why won't you let me see you?"

"This is my problem, not yours, Elec. It has nothing to do with me not trusting you. I just need time to get over it."

"I can be patient."

"Thanks." Tamara sucked in a breath, gathered all her courage, and tossed the pillow off. "Is that better? Are you happy?"

Elec ran his finger down her cheek as he leaned over the bed. "I'll be happy when you can walk across the room naked in front of me and not even think about it. I'll be happy when you finally believe that I think you're beautiful, every inch of you."

"It may take a while for that," she told him with all honesty.

Elec climbed onto the bed and settled in beside her. He pulled her so that they were spooning, her backside resting against his stomach. His hand rested on her hip and his lips brushed her temple.

"What did he tell you about your body?" Elec asked softly.

"What? Who?" she asked, startled.

"Your husband. What did he say about the stretch marks, about your breasts?"

Tamara swallowed hard, fighting the urge to suddenly cry. She had no idea why she would be tearing up, but Elec was being so gentle and understanding with her that it was overwhelming her. "Pete wasn't a mean guy."

"I never said he was. But maybe he was insensitive in that he never reassured you that you looked just as good after the babies as you did before."

"No, he never told me that." Tamara closed her eyes. "He'd joke that he guessed he wouldn't be looking all that hot after pushing out a couple of basketballs either. And he'd tease me that it was all good—that he had mental airbrush."

"Those are really shitty things to say." Elec had stiffened behind her, and he sounded quietly angry.

"Yeah, they are. But to be fair, I never told him those things upset me. Maybe at the time I didn't realize how much they did. It was when I decided I was ready to maybe start dating again, that I realized how awful I feel about how I look naked."

"I guess that's a lot of years of worry facing you all at once, isn't it?"

It definitely was. "I do appreciate how wonderful you've been, Elec. You've said all the right things."

"I haven't said anything that wasn't true."

Tamara relaxed onto her pillow. "My hair is soaking wet."

"It will dry."

"You going to lick it?" she asked with a laugh.

"No, that only applies to skin. Which I'll get to in a minute. Right now just lying here feels good."

It did. It was another reminder of how much she had missed the constant closeness of being in a relationship, the right to touch someone casually or intimately, the ability to rest her head on a man's shoulder or chest and know it was welcome, that she belonged there. It would be dangerous to enjoy those things too much with Elec because she didn't want to be devastated when she had to give them up, and she would eventually. Either when their relationship became too complicated from time constraints on both their parts, from media and family responsibilities, or when Elec figured out that a twenty-five-year-old hottie had more options available to him than a thirty-two-year-old widow with a couple of kids.

"It would feel even better with a blanket over us. The air-conditioning is cold."

Elec touched her hard nipple.

She jumped. "Hey!"

"Wow, you are cold."

Tamara couldn't help but laugh. That was such a guy thing to do.

Elec reached down and yanked the duvet up, folding it in half over them.

It only came to her waist, but it helped and she gave a yawn. "I'm tired."

"Me, too." Elec shifted his hand from her hip to her stomach and gave his own yawn in her ear.

The spot he was touching was her major jiggle spot, and

Tamara felt herself tense, felt something akin to a panic attack that he would be residing right on top of her major flaw, and that with his hand there, there was no hiding it. But it clearly wasn't bothering him, and she needed to get a grip, let it go. Closing her eyes, she used the technique of relaxing from her head down to her toes, one muscle group at a time. By the time she reached her feet, Elec was asleep, his even breathing rushing past her ear.

She dozed off, too, going in and out as the sun warmed her from her bedroom window and Elec's body heat created a warm cocoon under the duvet.

Snapping awake for no obvious reason, Tamara had the sudden realization that between the shower sex and the talking and the napping, a fair amount of time must have gone by and her kids came home at three o'clock. Craning to see over Elec, she eyeballed the clock. Two forty-seven.

Oh, Lord. She could only be eternally grateful that her kids hadn't discovered her exactly the way she was at the moment. They still had time but it was cutting it close.

"Elec," she whispered.

He just sighed in his sleep.

"Elec." Panicking a little, she shoved him and threw back the blanket. "Get up."

"Why?" he muttered, his eyes still closed.

"The school bus gets here in ten minutes."

"Oh, shit," he said, eyes popping open. With a dexterity that both impressed and reared envy in her, he leaped off the bed and ran into the bathroom.

She was still struggling to disengage herself from the damn blanket, but she was grateful that he immediately understood the importance of the school bus arriving and how he couldn't be there when it did. Her kids would find it weird that she was in her bathroom showering on a Monday at three o'clock, but she could explain that one away. Elec naked in the bed next to her? Not so easy to get around.

When she managed to get herself out of the bed, she

yanked open a dresser drawer and pulled on some panties
and a T-shirt, forgoing a bra for the moment. Dashing into
her closet, she found a pair of jeans conveniently on the
floor next to the hamper and she shoved herself into them.
Then she went to find Elec, who was still in the bathroom.
He was on his knees in his black underwear wiping puddles
of water up off the floor with a towel.

"What are you doing?" And why was he still mostly
naked?

"We made a mess, and it's my fault, so I'm cleaning it up."

While the movement did wonderful things to his butt
muscles, she didn't have time to drool over it. "Don't worry
about it. Get your pants on!"

"Done." He tossed the towel aside and stood up with his
jeans in his hand. He stepped into them, then jumped a
little to get them into place.

Tamara tried to move around him to shoot her hair with
the blow-dryer really quick and she misjudged and bumped
him. Elec lost his balance since he was only half in his
pants and he crashed into the wall.

"Oh, sorry!" she said, reaching out like somehow that
was going to help him.

He started laughing as he finished pulling his jeans on.
"This will be really funny if we don't get caught."

She grinned back, despite having one ear trained for the
school bus roaring up the street. "The key here is not to get
caught."

"Should I climb out the window and shimmy down the
trellis?" He pulled his shirt on and ran his hand through his
hair.

"I don't have a trellis." Tamara dragged a hairbrush
through her hair, towel dried it, and called it good. "And
since your car is in the driveway, I don't imagine going out
the window will throw anyone off the scent."

"Good point." He looked around the bathroom. "I had
shoes around here somewhere."

"Here." Tamara found them under her vanity and shoved them at him. "At least get downstairs. I can explain you in the family room. I can't explain you in the bedroom."

"I don't think you can explain the wet hair, since it's probably not at all believable that we just happened to go swimming. Don't worry, I'm out of here." Elec grabbed his shoes, kissed her hard. "Next Monday?"

She nodded, which was insane. They were on the verge of being severely busted by her children and she was agreeing to continue this madness?

"I'll call you!" he said, and took off running.

He was across the bedroom in two seconds and she could hear his bare feet pounding down the steps. The front door flew open and a car door did likewise before she was even halfway down the stairs. Picking up her own pace, she made it to the front window in time to see him back up out of her driveway and head down the street. He passed the school bus three houses down the cul-de-sac.

She could only hope her kids weren't the least bit observant.

Or that a major spit-wad fight had ensued on the bus right when Elec had driven by so they would not notice that a certain race car driver had just left their house.

Tamara twisted her wet hair around and around and rested her head on the windowpane.

Wasn't she too old to be sneaking a boy out of her bed?

CHAPTER
TWELVE

ELEC couldn't get Tamara out of his mind all week, and knowing it was probably going to annoy her, he still couldn't stop himself from calling her on Friday from his coach. Evan wasn't back yet and he was feeling a little lonely.

"Hello?" she said, sounding breathless and surprised.

"Hi," he said eloquently, settling back into his couch and trying not to smile in the empty room. It was a sign of how far gone he was that just the sound of her voice cheered him right up. "How are you doing?"

"I'm fine. Just put the kids to bed. How is Michigan?"

"Cold. It's the first of June and I don't think it got to be more than sixty-five degrees today at practice. Makes for an easier time in the car on the track, but tonight it makes me want to build a bonfire. Roast me some marshmallows."

"You know I have a fire pit in my backyard but I've never used it. I'm not exactly firewood savvy. I grew up in Seattle, you know."

"No, I didn't know that. How'd you end up in Charlotte?"

"I came for the sociology program at the University of North Carolina and because I wanted an adventure. Considering how shy I was, that's kind of a joke in retrospect, but I was proud of myself for moving all the way across the country."

"You should be proud of that. That's a big deal. So you came to school, and then you met Pete."

"Yeah. So I stayed."

Elec propped his feet up on the coffee table and crossed his free arm over his chest. He was glad that Tamara was willing to talk to him, that she hadn't even questioned why he was calling. "So how long have you had the fire pit?"

"It was here when we bought the house, which was the year Petey was born, so nine years."

"And you've never used it?"

"Well, at first the kids were babies, so it wasn't safe. But like I said, I don't see myself building a fire, and Pete's schedule was intense. You know that schedule, you live it."

"Yeah, I do." The season ran thirty-six weeks a year and during those weeks he spent Thursdays flying to the next track. When he and Evan arrived, their coach was waiting for them, driven to the compound by their driver. Friday was for practices and last-minute adjustments to the car with his team, Saturday was qualifying, Sunday was racing. He flew back to Charlotte late Sunday night after the race and usually slept in on Mondays, his only real day off each week. Tuesdays and Wednesdays he had sponsor events, business meetings with his team and crew, discussions over the car he would be driving in the weeks ahead, and various other odds and ends to take care of. Then Thursday he started it all over again.

But he would still find time to light a bonfire for Tamara.

"Well, hell, it's time we made that fire pit work for its keep. We'll get a big old blaze going and have s'mores and beer, and when you're giddy from alcohol and chocolate, I'll take advantage of you."

She laughed softly. "And where might my children be when we're doing this?"

Good question. "I don't know." He wanted to say they could go to a sitter's or her in-laws but that would sound like he was trying to farm her kids out, and he didn't want her to think that he didn't want them around, or that he didn't appreciate her responsibilities.

Tamara sighed. "You know, Tuesday is the kids' last day of school. Monday will be our last chance to meet during the day."

He hadn't even thought about that. "Damn, and we just got started on that."

"I know, I wasn't even thinking of that. But the school year is just about done. My students have already taken their final exams, and after Tuesday I'm spending two weeks at home with the kids, then I start summer classes, which are only part-time. And while I'm at summer classes, my kids stay at my house with my mother-in-law."

Their schedules did seem damn near impossible. But Elec thought it would all go a hell of a lot easier if she didn't insist their relationship be kept a secret.

"I guess we'll have to make the most of this Monday and then see what we can do to sneak some time together." Elec heard the door of the coach opening, but he had a point to make, and he didn't care if Evan heard him or not. "I will be with you, Tamara. You can count on that."

There was a pause, then she said softly, "What do you mean?"

"It means that no matter how complicated it is, I intend for us to be together." He meant that, damn it. Maybe it was rushing things to tell her that, but he wanted to be honest about his feelings, and he had a lot of them when it came to Tamara.

His brother looked over at him, eyebrow raised in curiosity as he dropped his keys on the coffee table.

"Elec . . ."

She sounded like she was about to give him a laundry list of reasons why they wouldn't work together and he didn't want to hear them. "Tamara, my brother just walked in and he's clearly got something he needs to talk about. I'll see you on Monday, alright, gorgeous?"

Evan stopped on his way to the kitchen and scoffed.

"Okay."

He dropped his voice to a whisper. "I can't wait to see you."

"Yeah," she said, and her voice was a little raspy. "I feel the same way."

"Good night."

She said the same, and Elec hung up the phone and met the stare of his brother. "What?"

"I don't have anything I want to talk about. Why are you using me as an excuse to get off the phone with your girlfriend?"

Girlfriend. He liked the sound of that. "Because she was about to give me a whole bunch of practical reasons why we shouldn't be together and I didn't feel like listening to them."

"Like what reasons?"

"Oh, let's see. Johnny Briggs hates our father, and now you, too, I'm sure, since you inadvertently insulted his dead son. Her two kids that she doesn't want hurt if things don't work out between us. Her work schedule. My work schedule. Our age difference. And I'm guessing she has a healthy dose of fear about being with a driver again since she lost Pete on the track."

"How old is she?" Evan asked, like that was the only conflict in all those Elec had listed that really mattered.

"Thirty-two."

"Oh, okay. I thought you were going to say she was

pushing forty and I was going to be like, dude. Fifteen years is a bit much."

"She doesn't look forty." Elec frowned at his brother.

"I don't know what she looks like. I haven't seen her since Pete's funeral, and she looked terrible that day, with good reason. I didn't think she was that old, but what do I know?"

"Obviously nothing." Elec eyed a hole in the toe of his sock. "It's friggin' cold here," he complained.

"And you're a whiny ass. Just because you're 'in love' doesn't mean you own the right to sit on the couch and pout. You've been annoying as hell all week." Evan rolled his eyes for emphasis as he made air quotation marks.

Elec dropped his feet to the floor. Evan's words, joking or not, hit him hard, right in the chest, and he felt a little bit like he couldn't breathe. "What makes you think I'm in love?"

"Dude." Evan shot him a look of sympathy. "You are so gone. I hope you have a spare ten grand lying around."

"What would I need ten grand for?" Was he in love? Elec pondered that thought. He couldn't honestly say he'd ever been in love before, but he was fairly certain he wasn't quite there yet. Almost. Falling hard and fast. But not quite yet.

"Mark my words, little brother. You'll be forking over major cash for an engagement ring by Christmas." Evan burped to punctuate his point.

"You're disgusting. And why would I buy an engagement ring?" Though he had to admit, the thought had a weird and sudden appeal. Yellow gold was totally Tamara, classic and elegant. Elec frowned. He needed to halt those kinds of thoughts right there. It was ludicrous. "I just got done telling you all the reasons why she doesn't even want to date me. There is no way she'd ever agree to marry me. And I never said I wanted to marry her."

"I'm telling ya. Listen to your big brother. I see it all going down, not a doubt in my mind."

"When have you ever known what the hell you were talking about?"

"Who has predicted the winners of the last four World Series? The last three winners of the Kentucky Derby? Not to mention the latest *American Idol* and the *Dancing with the Stars* winning couple?" Evan did a mock Samba move and finished up with a flourish.

Elec stared at his hip-shaking brother and just missed Tamara all that much more.

TAMARA knew she shouldn't be looking forward to Monday, but she couldn't deny it—she totally was. All weekend she fought the urge to stare off into space and fantasize about Elec and all the things they'd done and all the things they could still do.

She was like a kid at Christmas, a dog with a new stuffed toy, an addict with a fresh fix. She was ridiculously, obnoxiously, offensively giddy when one o'clock rolled around and she was on her way home.

It was just so *bad* to be behaving the way she was. There was a big long list of reasons why she should call this relationship, or whatever she was doing with Elec, to a halt. There was only so far they could take this without someone finding out what they were doing, and that was a scary proposition. Her in-laws, her kids, his family, the media. Members of two stock car racing dynasties dating would be big news on the circuit, and given that she was a widow of a driver, it would garner even more attention.

Really, even beyond all of that, it wasn't like she and Elec could be *together* long term. He had an insane schedule that didn't jive with hers. He was six years younger than her and would want to have his own children someday, something she didn't think she was prepared to do. Hunter was already finishing up first grade, and the thought of going back to sleepless nights and diaper changes wasn't all that appealing. Not to mention she was not willing to risk finding herself alone again with yet another child to raise.

Of course, it wasn't like thinking about kids wasn't a giant leap ahead anyway, but it seemed like something they should consider before they could ever be more serious than they were at the moment.

Not that she really understood what they were at the moment. She kept trying to adhere to the sex-only idea, but Elec kept disregarding that. He called her, he texted, he brought her dinner and gifts for her kids. He clearly had mentioned her to his brother since Evan had been standing in the room when they'd been talking on the phone.

Parking in the garage, Tamara went in through the kitchen and tossed her keys in the basket by the phone. None of what she was doing made a whole lot of sense, but she was doing it. And excited to be doing it.

And Elec was early. She was starting up the steps to change into jeans when the doorbell rang. He must have pulled in right behind her, which was both good and bad. Good, because it meant he was enthusiastic and she wouldn't have that awkward waiting period, sitting around her house trying to figure out if she should put on sexy underwear—not that she owned any—and getting nervous. It was bad because there was no time to shower or change or fix her hair or makeup. Half of her face had probably slid off in the car, but there was no time to do anything about it.

She ran back down the stairs and opened the door with a smile. Elec was standing there, one hand in his back pocket, the other holding a hot pink rose that he had clearly snapped off her rosebush next to the porch steps.

"Hi," he said, and held it out for her. "It's almost as beautiful as you."

Yeah, the giddiness wasn't going to go away anytime soon if he kept saying things like that. Tamara took the rose and said, "Thank you. It's good to see you."

She felt oddly shy again, and she realized it was because she wanted Elec to keep wanting her. She wanted him to want to continue what they were doing, and while it was stressful and unnerving sometimes, she wanted him to want more, to want to date her. It felt fabulous to have the interest of someone as thoughtful and intense as Elec. She liked him, damn it, and knew that the reason she was giddy was because she wanted to share more of these moments with him, she wanted to enjoy their time together.

She wanted to be a couple.

Lord help her.

ELEC only listened with half an ear to Tamara's apologies for the state of her house, the state of her work clothes, the state of her makeup and hair. He thought she looked fabulous, tousled and real, with a pink flush on her cheeks, and he wanted to see if she was dewy and pink anywhere else.

"Tamara," he said, taking her hand and pulling her to the stairs.

"Yes?"

"I've missed you."

Her eyes went wide as she let him lead her up the stairs. "It has been a long week."

"And I'm not going to be fit for normal conversation until after I've buried myself deep inside you." No sense in beating around the bush.

"Oh." She blinked at him, clearly shocked, but he could also see how her eyes had darkened, and her nipples had hardened. "I guess you should do that then."

"It's kind of you to indulge me," he said with a small smile as they reached the top of the stairs. He walked to her bedroom, but glanced at her over his shoulder.

She was giving him a flirty little toss of her hair, her eyes looking up at him from under the luscious mink-colored eyelashes. "It's a huge sacrifice, but I'm willing to take one for the team."

"You do realize you've done great things for my driving."

"I don't think it has anything to do with me, but I did see you finished ninth yesterday. That's awesome."

"You watched the race?" He was stupidly touched, knowing that she hadn't been watching racing since Pete's death.

"Yeah. I watched."

Her lips had parted, her eyes wide, and the effect was so sultry, so seductive, that Elec leaned over and gave her a hard, long kiss. It was on his lips to say, "God, I love you," but he stopped himself just in time. He wasn't sure what he meant by love, or why he felt like he wanted to say it, or what she would do if he laid something like that on her. So he kept his mouth shut.

He would let his body do his talking.

Tamara was breathing hard as they entered her bedroom, just from his kiss and anticipation, and that was the hottest goddamn thing he had seen. Elec brought her to the bed and took her mouth again, slower this time, savoring the softness of her lips, the tangy taste of her mouth. Her arms wrapped around him, and he heard the sigh of pleasure, of abandonment, in her voice. He loved that moment with Tamara, the sound that let him know she wasn't going to express worry or fear or insecurities anymore, that she was deep enough into the pleasure, the passion that flared so readily between them, that she was letting it all go, and just enjoying herself.

Elec kissed her slowly, worshipfully, undoing the buttons on the white sweater she was wearing. He pulled it off and dropped it on the floor, then tugged the matching tank top off over her head. Her hair sprung up and Elec smoothed it back down, staring into her eyes and feeling like he was drowning in that intensity, that sweetness, that desire. For him. All for him.

She was wearing girl pants that he didn't know the name for, the kind that stopped above her ankles and were a soft, silky fabric that just slipped off her when he undid the hook and zipper. The bra and panties she was wearing were just a plain white lace, but she looked so sexy just standing there, the picture of the perfect lady, a professor and mother, who did and said all the proper things, yet when touched just right, became a writhing, enthusiastic lover. His lover.

Yanking off his shirt and throwing it on the carpet, he pulled a condom out of his pocket and tossed it onto the bed so he'd have easy access to it. Undoing his jeans, he shoved them to the floor before gently pushing her back onto the bed. He didn't want anything fancy or rough, just him, over her, enjoying that she spread her legs for him, and only him.

He brushed his hands over her skin, across her shoulders, between her breasts, down her hips, avoiding the area of her stomach that she was so sensitive about, over the mound of her pelvis, to her inner thighs and the backsides of her knees. Goose bumps rose on her flesh and her eyes fluttered shut.

He'd never have the words to tell her how amazing he thought she looked, how classy and sensual, and he didn't even try. He just traced with his lips the same path his hands had taken, spending extra time brushing back and forth over her panties, breathing in the subtle scent of her arousal. Elec put a little pressure behind his movement, dipping into the depression between her folds with a kiss, and was rewarded by a damp spot on her panties when he pulled back.

Then Tamara surprised him, in a good way, by reaching down and shucking her panties so that her sexy, damp curls were inches from his mouth. He couldn't resist that kind of invitation, and he opened her and slid his thumbs down the interior of her pink folds, loving the little shiver of pleasure she gave. He loved seeing her open for him, loved that he could satisfy her with his tongue, and make her squirm in ecstasy.

Elec replaced his fingers with his tongue, moving up one side and down the other, detouring off the main road to lick first one thigh and then the other just to tease and heighten her arousal. If the lift of her hips was any indication, it worked, and after a pause where he just exhaled onto her clitoris, he slipped his tongue inside her and was rewarded with a healthy moan. Her fingers found their way into his hair, which was always a telltale sign she was getting worked up nice and good.

But her fingers were gone as quickly as they'd appeared, and stroking in and out, Elec tried to glance up the length of her to see what she was doing. Tamara was half raised and was taking off her bra. Score. She was all sorts of hot and bothered if she was doing that all on her own, and Elec refocused on what he was doing before he went cross-eyed.

He only lasted a minute, though, before curiosity got the better of him and he looked up again. Tamara's palms were spread over her bare breasts, lightly rubbing her nipples. Elec swallowed hard, his cock throbbing against the bed between her knees, the sweetness of her vagina only an inch from his mouth. That was honestly one of the sexiest things he had ever seen, given the inhibitions Tamara sometimes showed.

Knowing if he stopped tasting her, she would stop touching, Elec flicked his tongue slowly over her again, trying to glance up now and again to catch the sight of her fingers caressing her full breasts. She was breathing heavily, not moaning, just exhaling hard, panting out her pleasure, and now that Elec knew her body, recognized the signs of her arousal, he knew when she was getting close to having an orgasm. Her thighs always tensed, and she got quiet, her fingers, her body all pausing before she went over the edge, and Elec knew she was reaching that point, so he pulled back.

Instead of rushing to fill her with his erection, he took his time, wiping his mouth and enjoying the pink flush on her cheeks, the dilated desire in her eyes, the way she mewled in disappointment. It was an act of supreme will-power to not drive himself into her, but Elec wanted to show her the tenderness he felt for her, wanted some way to convey that this was more than sex for him, that it had been more from day one, and had grown each minute he had spent with her.

So he pushed against her slowly, feeling her open and accept him, her body surrounding his inch by delicious inch. Elec paused halfway to close his eyes, to collect himself, to savor the moment.

"Elec . . ." she said, legs moving restlessly beneath him. "Please."

"Just feel how good that is," he told her, forcing his eyes open so he could stare down at her. "Us together."

Her blue eyes snapped open. She looked at him, her mouth open slightly, her expression one of vulnerability and surprise. She knew what he was really saying.

So he started to move inside her, deep, slow strokes that took all of her and made him feel like he was claiming her as his.

There was nothing casual about what they were doing, there never had been, and he didn't ever want to leave.

Elec moved inside her until they were both slick with sweat and Tamara's nails dug deep grooves into his back, and their moans of pleasure came in unison, and he had no thought other than the feel of her beneath him.

When Tamara came, she arched her back, and Elec leaned down and captured her cry, her pleasure, with a kiss, and let his own release take him under.

They moved and shattered together, holding each other, mouths and bodies and minds melded in passion. Elec hovered over Tamara long after their last shudders had passed, over-whelmed. He just stared down at her, and she stared up at him, and he knew that they had entered a new level of intimacy that they couldn't retreat from.

Nor did he want to.

Neither of them spoke, but eventually Elec pulled out of her and settled in beside her on the bed. She rested her head on his chest and he slid his arm around her shoulders.

They lay still and he stroked the soft skin above her elbow while Tamara's fingers trailed across his biceps.

Damn if his brother wasn't right.

He was in love with her.

TAMARA was lying on Elec's chest listening to his racing heart, her own still pounding furiously from exertion and emotion. That had been something more than she had been expecting. The look on Elec's face had seemed, well, like he cared about her. A lot.

She was starting to admit to herself that she felt the same way about him, whatever way that may be. But this wasn't just sex for sex's sake.

The phone ringing on her nightstand startled her. Rarely did anyone call her house phone and she leaned over Elec to check the caller ID.

"Oh, no, it's the school calling," Tamara said, instantly worried. Stretching, she grabbed the phone and said, "Hello?"

"Hi, Mrs. Briggs, this is Judith Anderson, the secretary at Westwood Elementary. Your son missed the bus this afternoon."

Tamara expelled the breath she'd been holding. No one was bleeding. "Oh, okay, thank you. Do you know if his sister made the bus?"

"Well, she's not here in the office, so I'm sure she got in her line and got on the bus like she normally would. Pete went down to get his art project and missed the bus."

"Okay." Tamara chewed her nail and sat up straighter,

pulling a pillow in front of her. It was a little disconcerting to talk to the school secretary naked. "I guess I'll have to wait until Hunter gets home off the bus. She'll panic if I'm not here, and I can't leave the house unlocked either."

"I can stay here," Elec said.

"Can you have a neighbor get Hunter off the bus?" Judith asked. "Everyone leaves here in the next twenty minutes."

"Let me see if I can arrange something and I'll call you right back," she said, hanging up and turning back to Elec. "Ugh. Why is nothing ever easy?"

"I can do whatever you need me to do," Elec said, already sitting up and reaching for his jeans on the floor. "I can stay here or I can go get Pete."

She hadn't intended to impose on him like that, but he was being nice enough to offer and she wasn't sure what else to do. None of her immediate neighbors were home at that time in the afternoon, and if she called her mother-in-law, it would be iffy if she could get to the house before Hunter got off the bus.

"Thanks, I really appreciate it. Maybe it would be better if you went and picked up Petey. I think it might freak Hunter out a little if she gets home and I'm not here but you are. And I'll just call the school back and tell them you're picking up Petey, and that way I can tell him, too, so he won't be upset."

"Sounds good." Elec pulled on his T-shirt as he sat on the edge on the bed. "Just tell me where the school is."

After throwing her own clothes on, Tamara called the school back and explained the plan to the secretary and asked to speak to Pete.

"Hello?"

Her son always sounded so adorably young on the phone. It made her smile. "I hear you missed the bus."

"I'm sorry, it was an accident. Are you mad at me?"

"No, I'm not mad at you, I just have to stay here to get Hunter off the bus. She's too little to stay by herself and she'll be scared if she comes home to an empty house. So Elec is coming to pick you up. You remember Elec Monroe, right?"

"Duh, Mom, of course I do. Why is he picking me up?"

"Because he happened to stop by right when I got the phone call from Mrs. Anderson so he offered to make my life easier and pick you up." "Happened to stop by" was a bit inaccurate, but that was all she was willing to offer up at the moment.

"Oh. Cool. Okay. Is he going to stay and play? I want to show him my new video game."

"You can certainly ask him."

"Okay. Bye, Mom." Petey hung up.

Thank God kids were too narcissistic to give anyone else's relationships much thought. She raised an eyebrow at Elec. "He's cool with it."

Elec laughed. "So what is he going to ask me?"

"If you want to stay and play video games."

"That's up to you. Do you mind if I stay?"

She should, but she didn't. "No, I don't mind." In fact, she liked the idea of her son having some guy time. She liked the idea of Elec lingering in her house.

"Good." He gave her a kiss, the kind that made her toes curl, the kind that made her feel feminine and beautiful and loved.

Not that he loved her.

God, he would croak if he knew that had even popped into her head.

"See you in a few minutes. The school is right down the road. Just go out of the neighborhood, turn right on the main road, and once you pass through the stoplight, it's Westwood Elementary on the left-hand side."

"The school is that close yet it takes them thirty minutes to get home on the bus?" Elec made a face. "It makes me carsick just thinking about it."

Tamara laughed. "You're a race car driver! You don't get carsick."

"I just might if I had to ride that yellow bus for half an hour." Elec pulled his shoes on and stood up. "Be back in ten. Five if I open up my engine and see what it can do."

"Very funny. Make Petey sit in the back. He'll angle for the front, but I'm sure you have an air bag and it's not safe for him to sit there. And make him buckle his seat belt, which he should do automatically because I've never let him ride without one."

"Okay and okay. I've got it covered."

"Okay, and thank you. I really do appreciate this." It was hard not to worry, but she forced herself to relax. She just wasn't used to having help, and she wasn't used to not being the one who had to handle everything. It felt strange. Nice, but a little unnerving.

"I'm happy to," Elec said.

Tamara believed him. She should be feeling guilty that this was further involving Elec in her children's lives, but it was just a ride, and she needed help.

It was fortuitous that he was there to help her.

Almost like it was meant to be.

CHAPTER
THIRTEEN

ELEC drove up the road, seriously glad that Tamara had allowed him to help. He knew that wasn't easy for her, giving up control, and it showed that she trusted him implicitly. Which made him all sorts of giddy.

He was definitely falling fast and hard, and while he wanted to be involved in all facets of her life, he didn't want to push her. But this opportunity had fallen into his lap and he intended to use it to spend more time with her and her kids.

It was odd walking into an elementary school for the first time in fifteen years, bringing back memories of disgusting cafeteria food, pulling pigtails, and sweating his way through timed math tests. He had only been an average student, and he had been quiet. No chicks had been digging on him in the fourth grade, and he remembered a particularly painful crush on a girl named Katie Sweeney who had dark brown hair and dimples. It had gotten around that he had the grade school hots for her, and she had walked up to him and informed him, in front of a whole crowd of his buddies, that she'd rather eat dead worms covered in snot than kiss him.

Everyone else had seemed to find that hilarious, but he had pretty much wanted to die. He'd actually faked a stomachache for two days to get out of school before his mom caught on and sent him back.

Elec rubbed his stomach as he pulled open the office door. He almost had an imaginary pain in his gut just from remembering the incident.

Petey was sitting on a chair talking to a brunette in her twenties who was wearing a badge dangling from her neck that indicated she was a staff member. Giving him a wave, Petey bent over and started to gather up his backpack and an awkward green-painted tube.

Elec said, "Hey, Pete, what's up?"

"I'm sorry I missed the bus."

"That's okay. It happens." Elec turned to the woman. "Hi, I'm Elec Monroe, I'm here to pick Pete up. Do I need to do anything or can I just grab him and go?"

The brunette's mouth dropped open. "Elec Monroe? Oh, my gosh! We went to grade school together. Do you remember me? I'm Katie Sweeney."

Well, no shit. How was that for a coincidence? Elec eyed Katie Sweeney and saw a faint resemblance to the little girl he'd fancied himself in love with. She was attractive enough, he supposed, but he thought her face looked a little pinched and she was a bit skinny for his taste. Then again, his taste seemed to be Tamara and no one else at the moment.

"Wow, no kidding? Good to see you again, Katie," he said mildly, wondering if it was petty to still hate her.

He decided it wasn't. Nine-year-old egos were a fragile thing and she had crushed his.

"I hear you're a driver now," she said, smiling and flipping her hair back.

"Yep. And you're a teacher?"

"Yes." Another smile, and this time she leaned into him. "So you're picking Pete up? Is he your nephew?"

"No." Elec took the green tube Pete was shoving at him and said, "Hey, buddy, what's this? It's very cool."

"My art project. It's supposed to be our ant farm with the glowing gel." He pointed to the black spots. "Those are the ants."

"Hey, that's awesome." And Elec was oddly touched.

"So what have you been up to these days?" Katie Sweeney asked. "You're making a splash in racing, but how is everything else? You ever get married?"

"No." And he'd be damned if he'd ask her the same in return. He was getting the "nail a driver" vibe from good old Katie Sweeney and he wanted no part of that.

"He's dating my mom," Pete said, not so subtly inserting himself between them. "We're going home to play video games while my mom cooks us dinner."

Elec grinned. He liked the way the kid thought. It was clear Pete was feeling territorial and that pleased Elec a whole hell of a lot. "Yep," he said to both Pete and Katie Sweeney. "That's what we're going to do."

"Oh. That's nice." Katie Sweeney faked a smile.

It wasn't quite telling her to eat a snot-covered worm, but it still left Elec feeling mighty satisfied.

TAMARA wasn't sure how she had wound up cooking dinner for both her children and Elec, or how the man who was supposed to be her sexual fling managed to fit so readily into her household, but she was and he did. Elec and Petey were playing video games in the family room while Hunter sat behind them on the couch and gave advice whenever she looked up from her race car coloring book. Tamara was in the kitchen whipping up some chicken and a salad, after being informed by her son that he had invited Elec to dinner.

To be fair to Elec, he had taken her aside and offered to go home if she wasn't comfortable with it, but Tamara couldn't bring herself to do that to Petey, nor did she really want Elec to go home. It was good, really good, to have him around. He was easy, and entertaining, and their dynamic was comfortable. It made everything just a little less stressful, a little better, to have another adult to talk to, to exchange a look with, or seek advice from, especially one as calm and pleasant as Elec. Nothing rattled him, and he seemed to genuinely enjoy her kids' company.

He had offered to help her with dinner, but she was content to let him keep the chattering kids out of the kitchen. She could accomplish amazing feats in short periods of time when she wasn't answering Hunter's endless questions or fielding Petey's requests for different meals.

When she called them in to eat, and Elec matter-of-factly had the kids wash their hands before sitting down, she knew she was strolling into some dangerous territory. Sometimes, Elec quite literally stole her breath away. It was getting harder and harder to remember why they couldn't do this.

Tamara turned and placed the salad bowl on the table.

There was their age difference.

Elec handed Hunter her napkin with a flourish. "Your napkin, my lady."

Her daughter giggled.

Despite what his age on his driver's license might indicate, there was nothing immature about Elec. He was hardworking, responsible, caring.

Yet there was still her concern over her kids' being upset by her relationship with Elec.

Petey turned to Elec. "Next time you're here, will you bring your Wii?"

"And your brother's autograph?" Hunter added.

Yeah, they didn't exactly seem stressed out by the whole thing. They were both assuming Elec would be back.

But even with those two concerns out of the way, though,

for the most part, that didn't resolve the big doozies. Her in-laws. Her and Elec's insane schedules. Her fear for his safety. And the concern over what it would do to her children if she and Elec couldn't make a go of it.

Those were all big enough to make her wonder what the hell she was doing.

She had a platterful of chicken and Elec stood up and took it from her and set it on the table.

He smiled at her and kissed her forehead. "Have a seat, gorgeous."

That was why she was doing what she was doing. He was making her feel absolutely and utterly wonderful.

When he took her kids outside after dinner and played Frisbee with them, Tamara sat on the porch in a rocker and just watched, all sorts of conflicting emotions running through her. It was fabulous to see her babies enjoying themselves so much, and it was doing all sorts of interesting things to her heart to see Elec laughing and smiling and proving himself just an all-around great guy, but it also scared her.

It would be worse to gain this again, only to lose it.

She wasn't sure she could survive that.

"Tamara, come on and join us," Elec called from the backyard. He grinned. "Show us your moves."

"Mom doesn't have any moves," Petey said, clearly astonished.

"Oh, I think she does," Elec said with a wink that only she could see.

"No, you all keep playing. I'm better off watching." She wasn't known for her athleticism and most likely she'd break her ankle in front of Elec.

"Aww, come on, Mom." Hunter put her hands on her little hips. "Don't be a stick up the butt."

"Hunter!" Good Lord. Tamara instinctively stood up from her chair, like getting closer could alter what her child had just spouted.

"What? That's what Suzanne always says."

Of course it was.

"The expression is a stick in the mud. Suzanne likes to change the words into a version that is not at all polite, which I do not want to hear coming from you again." Tamara moved on to the grass and kicked off her flip-flops. "Alright, someone throw me the Frisbee."

She wasn't sure what had possessed her to, but suddenly she wanted in on the game. It was inevitable she'd make a fool out of herself, but she decided she didn't care. She wanted to have fun, to laugh with her kids and Elec.

"Mom's in!" Petey looked astonished.

"Whoop, whoop," Hunter said, clapping her hands and rolling her hips in a way that made Tamara frightened for the teen years. "Go, Mom. Go, Mom."

Elec smiled. "We're glad you're joining us."

"You won't be in a minute when I halt the game by dropping it or tossing it into a tree."

But to her amazement, when Elec tossed the disc to her, she actually caught it. Maybe it was because he didn't whip it at her, but just let it gently glide straight toward her. Pleased, Tamara threw it back to him and impressed herself that he only had to shoot his arm out a little to the right to catch it. Maybe she didn't totally suck after all.

After a few minutes, she was feeling confident and enjoying herself.

"Hey, Pete," Elec called. "Throw it as far as you can, and your mom and I will run for it. We'll see who can catch it."

"It will be you," Petey said.

"Hey!" Not that Tamara was truly insulted. While she was holding her own with Hunter, she wasn't exactly ready for tricks.

"You never know," Elec said. He moved alongside of Tamara and whispered, "If you catch it, I'll give you another massage. All over this time."

"Really?" Now that was highly motivating. "You're on."

"What do I get if I catch it?" he asked.

Good question. "What do you like?"

His eyebrows went up. "You know what I like."

"Everything?" she asked with a laugh.

"Pretty much." He grinned. "But if I win, I want you on top. You've never done that."

That was because while she didn't in any way dislike it, it wasn't her favorite position. It always made her feel a little self-conscious, all up there in front of him, but in the spirit of the bet, she was willing to go for it. "Okay."

"I'm throwing it," Petey yelled. "Go long!"

Elec started running across the grass, his arms pumping as he spotted over his shoulder, so Tamara took off after him in her bare feet. Fortunately, despite her slow start, she wound up directly under the descending Frisbee when the wind caught the disc and Petey's throw didn't go as far as Elec had expected. She was standing there, staring up at it, hands out, convinced it was going to hit her in the eye, when Elec dashed up behind her, put his arms around her, and snagged the Frisbee from right in front of her.

"Hey!" She was sure that constituted cheating somehow.

"What?" He was bumping into her, legs against hers, arms crowding around her, and Tamara lost her balance and stumbled a foot forward.

Elec grabbed her arm with one hand to steady her. "Whoa." He kissed the back of her head.

"Good catch!" Petey called to Elec.

"Thanks, that was an awesome throw."

"Even if you cheated," Tamara told him, though she didn't really mean it. She was just enjoying the opportunity to spar with him.

"I didn't cheat. I came behind you and caught it over your head. That's fair and square." Elec lowered his voice. "But I think we both should get our prizes, don't you think? Call it a draw?"

Tamara felt her response to that between her thighs. She was suddenly hot and it wasn't from running across the yard. "Sounds good to me."

He wasn't moving away from her and it was very tempting to just lean back against his chest, but Tamara resisted the urge. She wasn't sure if her kids were ready for that. Hell, she wasn't sure if she was ready to do that in front of her kids.

Fortunately, Petey yelled, "Throw it back."

So Elec stepped back and did that.

Hunter came up to him. "You should go swimming with us," she said.

"I think it's a little late for swimming on a school night," he said.

"No, silly. Not tonight. Another day. We have a pool pass."

"I . . ." Elec bent over and picked Hunter up, pumping her up and down like a barbell while she laughed. "Would love that."

He met Tamara's gaze over her daughter's head, even though he was talking to Hunter. "And I want to have that fire in the fire pit I mentioned to your mom. Roast marshmallows."

"Cool," Hunter said, still dangling in the air.

Elec set her down. "Next Monday?" he asked Tamara, his eyes dark. "If you're not busy."

"Next Monday," she agreed, because she didn't want to say no.

In fact, she wanted to say yes to everything his intense eyes were asking.

CHAPTER
FOURTEEN

IT occurred to Tamara that she couldn't handle three margaritas anymore, given how infrequently she drank alcohol. Actually, she had never been able to handle three margaritas and she knew she was in danger of getting sloppy on Suzanne and Imogen in the bar they had decided to go to Friday night.

The kids were with her in-laws for the night, which struck her as a cruel irony. She had an empty house at her disposal and Elec was in New Hampshire. That was something she had to remember and be prepared to accept if she moved forward in this relationship. He was going to be gone a whole hell of a lot. He was going to miss birthdays and important events, and if she wanted to be with him, she had to accept it.

Who was she kidding? She wanted to be with him.

Which was why she was licking salt off the rim of her glass and trying to smile for her friends, who looked as morose as she felt. Suzanne looked morose and impatient, her foot tapping on the floor, repeated sighs emerging as she darted her gaze around the room. Imogen looked morose and uncomfortable, pushing her glasses up on her nose over and over as she fiddled with the charm bracelet she wore.

It was something of a dive bar, with sticky wooden tables and a pervasive grease scent clinging to the walls. They were sitting at a table, but there were at least ten men lined up at the bar, some alone, some in groups, and Tamara noticed the three of them were getting a lot of curious looks, especially Imogen.

The men seemed puzzled by Imogen. They leered at Suzanne, who was wearing a red cleavage-bearing top. And basically, they ignored Tamara. Which was fine with her.

"I thought it would be a little more happening," Suzanne complained. "It's a Friday night and no one is even dancing."

"That's okay," Imogen said. "I don't dance."

"Why not?" Suzanne looked both amazed and horrified by that statement.

"I have no rhythm."

"Everyone has rhythm. You have to. We're born with it."

"I don't. I'm serious." Imogen was sipping her second margarita, and her eyes were getting a little glassy.

"We're going to get you dancing before the night is out," Suzanne vowed.

Tamara somehow doubted that, but it could be entertaining to see Suzanne try.

"So have you talked to Ryder?" she asked Suzanne. Then she explained to Imogen, "I know I told you Suz and Ryder are divorced, but Suz had a victory party for him a few weeks ago and it didn't go so well."

"No, I haven't talked to him. It's his turn to apologize." Suzanne's jaw was set and she took a gulp of her drink.

Tamara wasn't sure what Ryder was supposed to apologize for, exactly, but she would trust Suz on this one. "I'm sorry the party was such a disaster."

"Hey, it got you laid, didn't it? I call it a success."

Tamara blushed. She said to Imogen, "Elec and I, are, uh, dating."

"I figured as much. He seems nice."

"He is." Tamara felt warm all over and she thought it was only partially the alcohol.

"Look at your face," Suzanne said with delight. "Girl, you are gone. It's so cute."

A trio of men approached their table. "Can we buy you all a drink?" the leader of the pack asked.

"No, thanks," Suzanne said. "Girls night out."

"Are you sure?"

"Yes, thanks, but we're just not interested."

The men nodded in acknowledgment and sauntered back to the bar.

"Oh, my God," Suzanne said to them, her jaw dropping.

"What?"

"I just realized I said we weren't interested and I actually really meant it. I mean, normally if I was out with my girlfriends, I would say I wasn't interested because, you know, you don't blow your girls off for men, even if I was interested in a little flirting. But I said that to these guys because we're hanging out together, and well, Tammy, you're all into Elec, but the truth of the matter is, those guys were cute and I really *wasn't* interested. What the hell is the matter with me?"

Tamara wasn't going to touch that one with a ten-foot pole.

But Imogen had no such reservations. "Can I make an observation?"

"Sure." Suzanne raised her glass to Imogen.

"It's been my experience that if a woman isn't looking around with an open eye for eligible men, it's because she is taken, whether in actuality or just emotionally."

"What do you mean?"

"I mean, you already have someone in mind you want to

be with, so you are no longer looking for a potential mate. In fact, I'm surprised that those men even approached us, because generally speaking, when women aren't available, they exude a friendly but closed demeanor that men pick up on. If you feel that way, and Tamara is smitten with Elec, then I'm surprised that they thought we were approachable."

"Maybe it was you," Suzanne said. "Though I can honestly say I don't have anyone in mind I want to be with."

Tamara gave her best friend a sidelong glance. "I'm only saying this because I've had too much to drink, but, sweetie, don't you think maybe you and Ryder have unresolved business?"

"That could be," Suzanne admitted, which showed Tamara she'd had just as much to drink to say those words out loud. "But I don't really think I want to do anything about it."

"Fair enough."

"Imogen, did you want me to go get those guys? I just sent them away without asking if you were interested," Suzanne said. "If you thought they were cute, I'll go haul their asses back over here."

"Oh, no, that's okay. I'm not interested. I am stupidly intrigued by someone I shouldn't be."

"A professor?" Suzanne asked. "Please tell me he dresses better than Geoffrey."

"Oh, it's not a professor."

Oh, Lord, Tamara knew exactly who it was. "It's Ty, isn't it?" She shifted in her hard seat, and wiggled her toes in her flip-flops. Imogen dangling for Ty had all the makings of a disaster.

But unfortunately, Imogen nodded. "He's really quite attractive."

"Ty! What?" Suzanne slapped her glass down so hard, her margarita sloshed over the side. "How the hell do you know Ty?"

"I just met him briefly at Tamara's house. It was no big deal."

"He called her Emma Jean because he couldn't figure her name out," Tamara told Suzanne.

"Well, I could see how that would get you excited," Suzanne said, looking extremely puzzled.

"Oh, trust me, it's a purely physical reaction on my part to his appearance. I know it's ludicrous." Imogen shrugged. "But the body wants what the body wants."

"Truer words were never spoken," Tamara said, feeling the weight of that statement all the way down to her inner thighs.

"Amen," Suzanne said and raised her glass. "I'll drink to that."

They all raised their drinks and clinked them together before taking a healthy swallow. Tamara still had a swig in her mouth when Suzanne choked a little and dropped her voice.

"Oh, shit, oh, shit, the pit lizard is here. Don't make eye contact!"

"What pit lizard?" Tamara asked, wanting to turn around but knowing Suz would smack her if she did.

"Crystal," she hissed in a whisper. "The chick you said Elec is getting texts from."

Naked texts. Now Tamara couldn't resist the urge to turn around. She wanted to see Crystal in the flesh. Apparently so did every man in the bar. When she turned, she saw the busty blonde sashaying across the bar in a miniskirt and high heels, her breasts spilling out of her yellow tank top, every male in the place following her with drooling interest. Ugh. Tamara knew that Elec didn't appreciate the texts he got from Crystal, but she couldn't help but look at this woman and wonder why he'd even been interested in three dates with her.

It didn't seem like him at all, and it bothered her. Why did Elec have a history of dating bimbos when he so clearly wasn't that type?

Crystal spotted them and beelined for their table.

"Oh, damn," Suzanne whispered.

"Hey, y'all," she said with a bright smile. "How are you doing, Suzanne?"

"Fine, thanks. You?"

"Great." Crystal plunked down in the fourth chair at their table. "I'm so glad to see you. I took a chance coming out by myself so it's great that I have someone to hang out with. Who are your friends?"

"This is Imogen Wilson, and this is Tammy Briggs."

"Are you in racing?" Crystal asked Imogen.

Imogen shook her head and Crystal promptly lost interest. "Are you Pete Briggs's widow?" she asked Tamara.

"Yes."

"And now she's dating another driver," Suzanne said with a touch of triumph in her voice.

Tamara glared at Suzanne. She did not want this woman poking into her business.

"Oh, really? Who?"

"It's a bit of a secret right now, so I'd rather not say."

"Uh-huh." Crystal said that like she didn't believe for one minute that Tamara actually was dating a driver.

Which was irritating, but not enough to make her tell the truth.

"Well, I'm dating a driver," Crystal said. "And it's not a secret."

Oh, no, why did she have the horrible feeling that Crystal was going to say . . .

"It's Elec Monroe."

Imogen gasped.

Tamara felt her blood pressure rise. She knew beyond a shadow of a doubt that Elec was not dating this woman, but it irritated her no end that Crystal would just sit there and lie about it.

"Oh, really?" Suzanne said. "That surprises me."

Recognizing that glint in her friend's eye, Tamara kicked

her under the table. Suzanne shot her a look that she interpreted as "put this bitch in her place," but it wasn't worth it. The whole thing would just escalate into some juvenile catfight.

She refused to fight over a man she knew was hers. Elec was. There was no doubt in her mind. If she said she wanted to take their relationship public, he would. She just wasn't sure she was ready to go there, three margaritas or not.

"Why would that surprise you?" Crystal said, her voice sour. "He likes beautiful women."

Before Suzanne could say whatever brutal thing was on her lips, they were approached by two men in golf shirts, who, to the astonishment of Imogen, asked her and Suzanne to dance.

"No, thank you," Imogen said, shaking her head a little violently.

"It's just a line dance, nothing too personal," the one assured her with a friendly smile.

"I wouldn't mind dancing," Suzanne said. "You come, too, Tammy."

"No, I'm fine here." Despite her conviction that Crystal was a liar, she was feeling a little nauseous from both the drinks and the conversation, and she needed a minute before she could try to follow the patterns of the dance.

"Are you okay?" Suzanne asked her as she stood up and Imogen nervously followed suit.

"I'm fine."

Suzanne stared at her for a second then decided she was telling the truth and went on to the dance floor. Crystal leaned over to Tamara and whispered, "Oh, my God, I'm so embarrassed."

Fighting the urge to roll her eyes, Tamara asked, "Why?"

"Because I slept with Suzanne's ex-husband and I just feel really uncomfortable about it. She's clearly not over him and he is so over her."

That was it. Tamara had intended to keep her mouth

shut, but when this chick started slinging barbs at her best friend, she drew the line. She happened to know for a fact that Ryder still had a tremendous amount of feelings for Suzanne. So she turned to the blonde and said, "Oh, really? Sort of like how you're sleeping with Elec?"

Crystal frowned, her plump lips pressing together. "What do you mean?"

"I mean, I happen to know for a fact that you're not dating Elec and you're not having sex with him, so I'm just wondering if you're lying about Ryder the same way you are about Elec."

Her eyes narrowed. "I am not lying about either one of them."

"Then why would Elec tell me the only time he's seen you naked is when you send him trashy text messages?"

It was a hit. Crystal flushed red. "I have no idea what you're talking about. Elec is my boyfriend. Of course I've slept with him."

"How can you, when every night he's not working, he spends with me?" Okay, so that was a lie, but Tamara was buzzed on tequila and hopping mad.

"What?" Crystal's red face drained entirely of color. "Are you trying to claim you're dating Elec Monroe?"

"I'm not claiming anything. It's a fact."

"Whatever." Crystal flagged the waiter down. "I don't believe for a minute that he would be interested in someone like you. All plain and mom-ish. God, you probably have stretch marks."

There was a buzzing in Tamara's ears that was not alcohol related. Crystal had just hit on her insecurities and it hurt at the same time it made her furious. Without thinking through the consequences, she pulled her cell phone out of her purse and went into her in-box. She pulled up the last text she'd gotten from Elec, at two o'clock that day, and opened it. It read, "Long day. Wish you were here."

She shoved her phone over to Crystal. "Read it."

There was a flicker in Crystal's eye, but she waved her hand in dismissal. "How do I know that's from Elec?"

"Look at the number." *You stupid twit.*

Crystal did. "Well, that isn't a very romantic text message."

"How about this one?" She couldn't believe she was stooping to this level, but Crystal pushed every button she had. She found one from the night before that read, "Can't wait to see you Monday."

"I would write that to a friend," Crystal said.

She pulled her own phone out and Tamara had a sudden horrible feeling that this was going to get ugly.

Crystal scrolled through and turned the phone to her. It was a text from Elec that read, "you do look hot." Even though it smacked her in the face, she took a breath and willed herself to be calm about it. It was lacking in capitalization and punctuation, which said to Tamara that he was rushing, because he always used proper English in his texts to her. It also sounded like he was answering a prompted question, and when she studied the data below the message, she saw it was dated two months earlier. Nothing inconsistent with what Elec had told her.

"That was in response to when I sent him this picture," Crystal said, punching buttons. She turned her phone to Tamara.

It was Crystal naked, which Tamara was familiar with, only this time she had a tiny die-cast car driving into her . . . eew. Tamara felt her mouth drop open and her eyes bug out. That was just beyond anything she would have ever thought made sense.

"You know, those cars rust when they get wet," she told Crystal, suddenly feeling the desperate urge to laugh.

Crystal made a cluck of impatience. "Let's both text him right now and see who he answers."

Was she really going to engage in such a juvenile battle for male attention?

Apparently she was, because her fingers were already flying across her keyboard. "You're on."

They both typed furiously and hit Send right about the same time. Tamara's was probably riddled with typos but the gist of it was that she was looking forward to making good on their bet.

Their phones sat on the table, next to each other, Tamara's plain black and silver, Crystal's pimped out in rhinestones. She glanced over at the dance floor and saw Imogen moving awkwardly and Suzanne getting into it, clapping her hands and smiling.

How long did it take to answer a text? She stared at her phone and willed it to chime.

It did.

Yes.

She opened it and read the message from Elec. "I can't wait either. Been thinking about you riding me all day, Cowgirl. xoxo."

Wow. He'd put hugs and kisses on the end. That made her feel all sorts of excited, as did the thought of being on top of him. The message was so personal, so beyond anything he'd ever written before, that she was almost reluctant to share it with Crystal. It was private.

But the other women yanked her phone out of her hands and read it. Her expression soured. But she rallied when her own phone buzzed. "It's Elec," she said smugly.

Then her face fell as she read it and Tamara decided she wasn't even going to ask what it said. She didn't like Crystal but she had no interest in rubbing Elec in her face. Not any more than she had, anyway.

"Aren't you going to ask what it says?"

"No."

Crystal shoved her phone at her. Tamara glanced down at it. It said, "Please don't text me anymore. I've told you, I'm seeing someone else."

"I'm sorry," she said, and she meant it. It hurt to be rejected, she understood that.

Crystal stood up. "Fuck you, bitch."

Well, alrighty then.

ON Monday, long after the margaritas had worn off, Tamara wondered if she should mention the little incident with Crystal to Elec.

But when he showed up at four o'clock looking sleepy-eyed and sexy and greeted her with, "I haven't been able to stop thinking about your text from Friday," she just smiled and kept her mouth shut.

Elec kissed her cheek, which she assumed was for the benefit of her kids, who were tearing around the family room. He said, "I think that's the first time you got sexy in a text with me. I liked it. A lot."

Yeah, she so wasn't telling him what had motivated that.

She did confess, "I was out with Imogen and Suzanne. I had a little too much to drink."

"I don't care what brought it on, as long as you keep doing it."

There were all sorts of things she wanted to keep doing.

So she leaned closer and whispered in his ear precisely that. "I plan to keep doing lots of things."

"That is the best news I've heard in *days*," he said.

"Rough weekend, huh?" she asked him sympathetically. He had a disappointing finish the day before when he'd blown a tire.

He nodded.

Hunter bounced up to him and grabbed his hands. "New Hampshire sucked," she announced as she crawled up his legs with her feet. "You can make it up next week, though."

Tamara was really going to have to sit her daughter down and have a stern talk about her language.

"Thanks, kid. I'll try." He held Hunter firmly while she finished her shimmy all the way to his upper thighs then dropped back down to the floor.

Hunter rolled her eyes and made a raspberry sound with her lips. "Don't try. Just do it."

Elec laughed. "Good point. Now should we go outside and fill up these water balloons I brought?"

"Yeah!" her kids both shrieked, running for the back door, flinging it open and tearing into the yard, leaving the door wide open for bugs to take advantage.

Elec shot her a bemused look. "Guess they like the idea of water balloons. Come on out and let's see if I can hit you in the chest with one."

"Elec!" Tamara smacked his arm. "I'm not having a wet T-shirt contest with my children around."

"Like they'd think anything of it. They'd just figure you didn't duck fast enough."

He was wearing tattered jeans and sandals with a beer T-shirt, his hair flat under a ball cap, and he was so damn cute she was having a hard time not reaching out and squeezing the daylights out of his butt. Not to mention other things.

"You can hit me back," he offered. "Make me look like I wet my pants."

She laughed. "You're crazy."

"Crazy for you." Elec leaned over and gave her a long, delicious kiss. "Mmm. Been waiting awhile to do that."

"Are you coming?" Hunter called loudly from the patio.

Elec gave her a look, and Tamara laughed. "Don't say it, not even under your breath."

"What?" he said, all innocence, like he hadn't heard the word *coming* and reached the same conclusion she had.

Knowing that she was pushing it, but unable to resist,

Tamara leaned in and whispered in his ear, "I wish I was coming. On top of you."

Elec moaned and squeezed her waist. "You're torturing me."

Torturing both of them. But she just smiled and said, "Yep," and headed out the back door.

ELEC sat in front of the fire he had built, Hunter wiggling on his lap, and held his stick over the flame, watching his marshmallow turn a nice golden brown. Tamara was sitting next to him, her feet crossed at the ankles, her hair up in a ponytail, the firelight dancing across her beautiful face whenever she glanced over at him, a smile showing off her teeth.

Pete was on the other side of the fire, tossing marshmallows directly into the fire to watch them catch and implode in the dark.

Elec could honestly say that he had never been quite so content and relaxed in his whole life. They'd had ribs on the grill, corn on the cob, and potato salad for dinner, and they'd gotten soaking wet running around and slamming water balloons into each other.

He liked hanging out with Tamara and her children. A lot. Like to the point where he thought he would get a lot of pleasure out of making this situation permanent. About being able to be at home with them whenever he wasn't traveling and having the right to call this amazing woman his wife, this fire pit his fire pit, these kids his stepkids.

Damn, he was in trouble.

And he was hopelessly, head over heels in love with Tamara.

"Your marshmallow's burning!" Hunter yelled, because almost everything Hunter said was in the form of yelling.

"Whoops." Elec pulled it back out of the flame and blew on it.

"Eew," Hunter said, licking sticky goo off of her fingers. "It's all burnded."

"Burnded?"

"Yeah. Really burnded."

He laughed. "It is burnded. But it still tastes good." He slid it off the stick and popped it into his mouth. It was good. It was all good. "Now let me up, baby doll, I'm going to help Pete catch some fireflies."

They had already found a frog earlier, down at the edge of Tamara's property, and now the fireflies were out in full force. He thought Pete would get a kick out of capturing a few and watching them flit around in the jar for a minute before releasing them.

"Tamara, do you have a jar we could use?"

"Sure," she said, tucking a stray hair back into her ponytail. "I'll go grab one."

"I'll come with you." He turned to Hunter. "Go on and play in the grass with your brother away from the fire until we get back, alright, baby doll?" He didn't want a log rolling out and hitting her leg.

"Okay." Hunter held out her arms to be picked up, so he did, figuring he'd just carry her to the grass himself.

Hunter gave him a sticky marshmallow kiss on the cheek and Elec felt his heart squeeze. Oh, yeah, he was in trouble. But it was an amazingly good kind of trouble.

He followed Tamara into the kitchen and watched her bend over at the sink and fish out a glass jar. The angle did great things to her ass in her plaid shorts, and he wanted to run his fingers across her thighs and backside at the same time he knew it would just result in frustrating the hell out of him.

But now that he had her alone, he wanted to ask her something. When she turned, he said, "What are you doing next weekend?"

She shrugged. "Just hanging out, I guess." She held the jar out to him. "Why?"

Elec took it and said, "How about you come down to Daytona with me for the Fourth of July weekend and race?"

Tamara stared at him. "With the kids or alone?" she finally asked.

"I was thinking that you could come down a few days ahead of the race by yourself, then the kids could join us. You can stay with me until they get there, then I'll get the three of you a hotel so we're not sharing a bed in front of them."

Her hair had slipped again and she tucked it back impatiently. "Who is going to stay with my kids while I'm gone and bring them down?"

"Your in-laws," he said, willing himself not to fidget. If she said no, she had legitimate reasons and he couldn't take it personally. "Don't they always come to Daytona for the race?"

She nodded.

She didn't give him an answer for a second, and Elec knew she knew what he was asking her. To tell her in-laws the truth. They weren't going to be able to hide it much longer anyway since he was spending time with her kids. But he knew it was a lot to ask of her and he wasn't going to be surprised if she said it wasn't possible.

But Tamara glanced toward the back door, then toward him, and she nodded. "Yes. I would love to go to Daytona with you."

Well, hot damn. They were going to be sharing a bed for two or three nights. All night.

His body reacted to the thought and he got an immediate erection. "That's awesome. Good. We'll have a great time."

Tamara glanced down at his erection, her eyebrows raised. Then she burst out laughing. "I'm guessing we will."

"What can I say? I'm a guy. We don't hide our emotions."

"Yeah, right. *Emotions* is what you're calling that these days?" She rolled her eyes.

Elec leaned in and kissed her gently. "God, I . . ."

"What?" She pulled back and looked up at him, her eyes wide.

He chickened out. "I can't wait to be alone with you."

He could only hope that wasn't disappointment in her eyes. But she just nodded. "Me, too."

Elec held up the jar. "Now let's go catch us some fireflies."

CHAPTER
FIFTEEN

TAMARA had decided her best bet was to go to Beth, who would be more rational than Johnny about her request, but she was still shaking like a leaf and having a hard time forcing the words out of her mouth.

"What's the matter, Tammy?" Beth asked her as she cut some blue hydrangeas off the bush to take into the house.

Tammy was sitting on Beth's back patio watching her kids run through the sprinkler and trying to work up the nerve to confess the truth to her mother-in-law. "I have a favor to ask you, Beth," she said, settling on the roundabout approach.

"Sure, sweetie. You know if I can help in any way, I will."

She did, which was why she felt like garbage asking Beth to watch her children so she could play porn star in Elec Monroe's coach. "I was thinking of going to Daytona this weekend, on Thursday, actually. By myself. I was hoping you could watch the kids and then bring them down on Saturday with you when you and Johnny come down."

Beth looked at her in surprise. "Why are you looking to go early? Are you planning a girls' weekend with Suzanne?"

"No . . . I've been seeing someone. A man."

"Is it Geoffrey again?" Beth said, and her opinion on him was clear on her face. She placed another bloom in her basket, her floral gloves, tight ruffled blouse, and Capri pants tidy.

It amazed Tamara that Beth could manage to look like she was going for cocktails when she was working in her own garden.

"No, it's not Geoffrey."

"Thank goodness. So who is it? How long have you been seeing him?"

"About five weeks. Which I know isn't really all that long, but he's such a great guy, Beth. And he's been so good to me, I just can't tell you how much fun I'm having with him."

"That's wonderful, Tammy." Beth smiled. "I can tell by the look on your face that this one is going much better than the last one."

"It is. So, so much better." That she could say in all honesty.

"So who is it?" Beth asked, turning back to the bush and taking hold of a stem.

"It's . . ." Tamara bit her fingernail and willed herself not to vomit. "Elec Monroe."

Beth dropped her shears in the bush. Her head whipped around. "Elec Monroe, are you serious?"

"Yes," she practically wailed. "I didn't mean this to happen, we met again by accident, and I tried to tell him no when he asked me out, I did, but then I just couldn't resist him, and he's just *wonderful*." Oh, Lord, she was gushing. Tamara leaned against the porch post and tried to control herself. "Beth, I keep trying to be rational, but all that's happened is that I've gone and fallen in love with him."

She had.

And it was utterly ridiculous that the first time she would admit that to herself or out loud, it was to her mother-in-law, the woman whose son she had previously been married to.

She had lost her mind.

"Oh, my," was Beth's opinion.

"What am I going to do?" Tamara asked, giving a heavy sigh.

"What do you mean, what are you going to do?" Beth turned and took both of Tamara's hands in hers and squeezed them. "You say he's been wonderful to you?"

"He has."

"And the kids? Has he met them?"

"Yes, and he's fabulous with them. He plays with them, and has them wash their hands before they eat, and makes sure Hunter isn't falling into the fire pit. He brought them gifts when they had chicken pox—an art farm for Petey, a die-cast car for Hunter. He listens to what they like, and he never does anything inappropriate with me in front of them."

Not in front of them was another story, but she wasn't going to go there.

"Does he make time for you?"

"I would say all his free time goes to me. And he calls me and texts me from the road."

Beth smiled at her. "Then, sweetie, I'd say where you're going is to Daytona for a romantic weekend with your new man."

Tamara blinked. "But . . . Johnny hates the Monroes. And I know this has to be uncomfortable for you. You know I loved Pete."

"I know that, Tammy. But you're a young and attractive woman with a lot of years in front of you. I don't expect you to be a martyr and spend those alone. All I want is for you to be happy and for Johnny and me to continue to be a part of our grandkids' lives."

"Of course. Absolutely. I can't imagine my life or the kids' lives without you in it." She meant that sincerely. "I love both of you."

Beth teared up and squeezed her hands harder. "We love you, too. You're the daughter I never had."

"That's not going to change."

They hugged, and when Beth pulled back, she tried to blink away her tears as she told Tamara, "Pete would have wanted you to be happy, too."

"I know." She did. Pete had been self-absorbed, but he had loved her, and his children, and he wouldn't want her to be miserable.

Beth studied her. "You really are in love, aren't you?"

Tamara nodded and gave a fresh sob. It's seemed like a good reason to shed some more tears.

"Oh, no." Johnny's voice came from behind them. "What the devil has you two crying now?"

Tamara froze. She did not want her father-in-law's wrath coming down on her right at the moment.

But Beth just smiled and whispered, "Don't worry. I'll handle it. You just make your plans. It will all be fine."

TAMARA had no idea what Beth had said to Johnny, or done to him, she supposed, but whatever it was it had worked because despite the fact that Beth had picked up her kids solo, Tamara had just arrived in Daytona with Elec in Ryder's private plane.

Contrary to Ryder's teasing suggestion, they hadn't used that particular piece of his property to have sex, but to be fair, they probably would have had Ryder, Ty, and Evan not been sitting in the plane with them.

Elec was clearly chomping at the bit to get her alone and have his way with her, and she couldn't say she objected to that in the least. He had reminded her at least twelve times that it had been ten days since they had had sex.

She was well aware of that fact and wished he would stop referencing that unfortunate little reality.

When they got to the hotel, Elec didn't waste time stating the obvious anymore. Nor did he give her a chance to do more than give the room a quick glance before he had dumped their suitcases on the floor and pulled her into his arms.

"Whoa," she said, when he squeezed her so tightly she feared for her ribs. "Slow down."

"No." Elec kissed her mouth, her temples, her nose.

Tamara laughed, then pulled back and looked at him. What she saw on his face cut her giggles short. He was so intense, so serious, so focused on her. There was something in his eyes that was different, that was beyond desire. It was a look that told her what they were sharing was special, that their connection was real, solid, wonderful.

Any reservations she might have still had about dating a race car driver disappeared. She was willing to push aside fear to be with him because that look made everything inside her soften and hush in appreciation, and in reciprocation. God, she had fallen in love with him, and she wanted to show him that.

There was one action that she knew would speak louder than words.

So she stepped back and pulled off her sleeveless red shirt and tossed it to the floor.

Elec's eyes darkened. "I'm liking that," he said.

"Then you should like this even more," she said, and undid her jeans and stepped out of them.

"I do," he said.

When he tried to reach for her and pull her against him, Tamara backed up to evade him and smiled. "Just a minute. I'm not naked yet."

Elec groaned. "You're killing me."

What she was doing was setting aside her insecurities and letting him know that she trusted him, that she loved him, that she felt absolutely sexy and beautiful in front of him. To that end, she licked her lips and slid her bra straps down her arms. Watching him watching her, enjoying the way his breath hitched and his gaze darted over her body, she undid her bra and let it drop.

A little push and her panties were gone, too. Tamara didn't know a damn thing about modeling or posing, but she figured good posture always helped, and when she dug her hands into her hair to pull it back off her face, she was rewarded with a curse from Elec. It really wasn't all that difficult to be totally naked in broad daylight with Elec.

As a matter of fact, she was kind of enjoying it.

It felt sexy, powerful, to turn and walk to the bed, his eyes on her the whole way. Tamara climbed onto the mattress, taking satisfaction in the growl he gave as her tail end went up. She rolled onto her side and propped her head up with the palm of her hand.

"You can touch me now."

Before she could even blink, he had his T-shirt off over his head, shoes and socks kicked off, jeans and boxer briefs down and out of the way, condom on. His efficiency amazed her, at the same time she wished he would give her just a little more time to check out his abs, his biceps, his rock-solid thighs.

But he clearly had a goal in mind and with no detour, Elec got on the bed and spread her legs.

"Do you mind if I take you hard right now?" he asked, poised over her, his erection resting against her wetness. "I want to feel you. I *need* to feel you."

Like she was going to say no to that? "Take me," she whispered.

"Thank you," he said, and thrust inside her.

Tamara moaned as he filled her. The stretch and give as he buried himself deep inside her was pure eye-rolling ecstasy. She lay slack on the bed, overwhelmed by sensation as he moved slowly, in and out, his arms surrounding her.

Looking up at Elec while he moved his body with hers, Tamara wanted all of him, harder, faster, wanted to be the one to move, to show him that she needed to feel him, too.

"Roll over," she told him.

Elec didn't even hesitate. Barely breaking rhythm, he took her in his arms and flipped their positions so that she straddled him. Lifting his head up, he kissed her, nipping her bottom lip, then he just lay back and waited for her to take control.

Shifting her knees a little for better leverage, Tamara moved herself on him, up and down slowly at first, then faster. She had none of her previous fears about being exposed in front of him. One glance down at Elec showed that he cared deeply about her, that he thought she was sexy and attractive. Better yet, she felt sexy. For the first time in her adult life, she understood that sexy was more a matter of confidence than physical appearance. That knowing her worth, being with a man like Elec and saying hell yeah, she was entitled to every inch of him, in return made her sexier to him.

So she put her palms flat on his muscular chest and rode him hard, until they were both moaning and Elec's skin was glistening with sweat. He met her rhythm, thrusting up into her to meet her hips with a hard slap.

"Oh, baby, that feels so damn good," Elec said.

It did. And Tamara couldn't hold back. Staring into those dark eyes that did such amazing things to her insides, overwhelmed by love, she came with a cry. Letting the sensation own her, she just held on as Elec thrust deep up into her and joined her with his own orgasm.

When the shudders had slowed, Tamara loosened her

death grip on Elec and gave a small, satisfied laugh, all her muscles slack, her mind empty except for thoughts of him.

She decided she liked being on top after all.

ELEC thought the little laugh Tamara had given after she'd come had been the sexiest damn thing he'd ever heard. It had said to him that she totally trusted him, that she was comfortable enough, cared enough about him to let it all go.

As she lay on his chest, he pondered that, and what to do about all the feelings zipping around inside of him.

Elec didn't know if the timing was right. Hell, he'd never told any woman he loved her, ever, not even as a teenager, so he had no idea what was good timing. But all he knew was that he was so overflowing with emotion at the moment, that it made it right.

He loved her, deeply and intensely, with everything in him, in a way he had never thought possible, and he had to tell her.

So he rolled up on his side so he could look down at her and he said, "Tamara?"

"Yes?" She smiled up at him, her expression satisfied and sleepy and bemused.

It didn't matter if she didn't answer him in kind. He was okay with that. She had different baggage than him, and she had reasons to keep a tighter lid on her emotions, so he was prepared to get a smile or an "Oh, Elec," and nothing more.

But that wasn't going to stop him from saying what he needed to. "Tamara, I want you to know that I'm in love with you. I love you."

Her eyes went wide, then filled with tears.

Good tears, or bad tears, he wasn't sure, and he started to panic as he took his thumb and wiped them away when they slid down her cheeks. "Don't cry, darlin'. I'm sorry, I shouldn't have said anything." He felt like a complete jack-ass. He knew she had gone to bat with her in-laws, admit-ting their relationship so she could come with him, and that had taken a lot of courage. She was already risking a lot to be with him, and then he had to go and dump the *L* word on her?

It was likely he had just overloaded her.

She shook her head, and just cried harder. "No, no."

What did that mean? Elec started to pull back, to go where he didn't know, but to give her space, to let her put clothes on, something.

"No, don't go." She reached out and grabbed his arm. "I'm sorry, I don't know why I'm crying. It's just, I wasn't expecting you to say that." She sat up and touched his cheek. "Elec."

"Yeah?" He was going to get dumped, he just knew it. He had crossed the line into emotional and now she was going to bail because she couldn't deal with his moony-eyed adoration.

He was a royal fuckup.

"I love you, too."

Come again?

"What?" he asked, because after all the anxiety that had just churned through him, he found it hard to believe he was actually hearing her correctly.

"I love you."

He expelled the breath he'd been holding. Wow. She loved him? She loved him. He had heard it. She had said it. And it was awesome.

Then she made it even better by sighing, a pretty little sigh of wonderment. "Oh, God, I do. So much. I love you."

Elec rested his forehead against hers and kissed her softly. "I love you, too," he said again, just for good measure.

She kissed him, a long, trusting kiss that was the same

but was different. It had the same taste, the same passion, the same intensity as before, but now they *knew*. Now they were saying they shared love, a relationship, a life.

They were going to be together.

And he needed to show her all over again how much she meant to him.

CHAPTER
SIXTEEN

ELEC was aware his cell phone was ringing but he was choosing to ignore it. He and Tamara had stayed up way too late considering he had to be at the track for test-drives that day, but he wasn't going to regret it.

How many times in his life did a guy confess he was in love and spend all night making love to the woman he could now legitimately call his girlfriend?

It was a first for Elec, and if the phone would stop ringing, he could grab ten more minutes of sleep.

"Shouldn't you get that?" Tamara asked, rolling over onto his chest and yawning. "That's the second time someone has called."

"It is?"

"Yes." She kissed his chin. "Just see who it is."

Elec felt around for his phone, held it in front of him, and squinted. "It's my sister."

"Maybe it's important. She is your PR rep."

"You want me to answer it, don't you?" He could personally care less what Eve had to say.

"Yes, you should answer it."

"Yes, ma'am."

Tamara smacked his arm. "Do not call me 'ma'am.' Ever."

Elec laughed and answered his phone, "Hello?"

"Where the hell are you?"

"In bed in my hotel room."

"Turn on the TV, the computer, something. They're doing coverage for the race this weekend and your name has come up."

Eve sounded angry. "Come up, how?"

"Oh, you don't even want to know."

"Then why should I turn the TV on?"

"Don't make light of this!" Eve snapped. "Just tell me the truth . . . can you get a woman pregnant?"

"*What?*" Elec lost all remnants of sleep and sat straight up in bed, knocking Tamara in the shoulder. "Sorry," he whispered to her.

Eve heard. "Who is with you?"

"Tamara Briggs."

"Oh, my God." His sister was groaning on the other end of the phone. "Elec, I'm serious, can you or can you not get a woman pregnant?"

He didn't know why she was asking when she knew the truth and it was making him both angry and unnerved. "No. I absolutely cannot. Why? What the hell is going on?"

"Some blond woman named Crystal has contacted the media to let them know she is pregnant with your child, and that you're refusing to accept responsibility."

"What?" he said again, feeling completely blindsided. "You can't be serious!"

Tamara was looking at him in concern. "What's wrong?" she asked him.

He couldn't even answer. He felt sick to his stomach. He had known Crystal was aggressive, but how could she claim she was having his baby? Even if he could have children, which he couldn't, they hadn't even had sex. It was totally insane.

"Oh, I am so serious. I take it you know who I'm talking about?"

"Yes. We went on three dates. That's it. Three dates. We didn't even, um, you know."

"Are you telling me the truth?" his sister asked him sternly.

"Yes! Why would I lie? And you know the truth about my situation. It couldn't be possible anyway."

"Alright, alright, I need to think about this. We need to come up with a strategy to combat this crap. I'm going to think about it and call you back. Turn on the TV and watch this tramp at work."

Did he have to? "Okay. I'll wait to hear from you."

He hung up the phone and turned to Tamara, who was clutching the sheet to her and looking extremely worried.

"What's the matter?" she said.

"My sister says that Crystal contacted the media and told them she's pregnant with my baby and that I'm refusing to accept responsibility." Just saying the words out loud made him want to throw up. If he could get a woman pregnant, even someone like Crystal, he would never, ever turn his back on that child. In fact, he would probably want full custody if the mother was Crystal.

Tamara's mouth dropped open. "Oh, no. Are you serious?"

"Unfortunately." Elec fished around for the remote and turned on the TV, trying to find ESPN.

"Could it be true? Could she be pregnant with your baby?" Tamara asked, biting her fingernail.

He wanted to snap at her, frustrated with the whole crazy situation, but he realized it was a legitimate question. He stopped on the sports channel and turned back to Tamara. "No, it's not true. I told you I did not have sex with her."

"Yeah, but sometimes women can get pregnant just

from being in the area . . . from pre-ejaculate next to the vagina."

Elec rubbed his temples. This so wasn't the conversation he wanted to be having with her the morning after they had admitted they were in love and were going to be a couple. "Tamara, I know you're just trying to be thorough here, but trust me. At no point in her presence did I ejaculate, have pre-ejaculate, or take any of my clothing off. What she's claiming is physically impossible."

And the word *ejaculate* in relation to Crystal was kind of grossing him out.

"There it is." Tamara pointed to the TV.

There was a caption that said "Baby Daddy News from Daytona."

Baby Daddy? Yeah, he was going to throw up.

The reporter was talking and Elec tried to focus on what she was saying.

"A lingerie model has stepped forward today to say she is suing rookie race car driver, Elec Monroe, for paternity and child support of her unborn baby. She claims the driver is refusing to pay for her medical care and is denying the child is his. Crystal Collins has been diagnosed with an incompetent cervix and needs thousands of dollars in medical care in order for her baby to come as close to term as possible. In a sport that strives for a family image, this calls into question the possibility of retaining major sponsorships for the driver."

"Oh, Lord," Tamara whispered.

Elec prided himself on being calm and rational, but he exploded. "There was not one goddamn word of that that was true! Incompetent cervix, my ass. She's not even a lingerie model! She's a bartender. Why would she do this? All of this can be proved a lie, including that she's not suing me, nor is that alleged baby mine. She's probably not even pregnant!"

"I'm sure she's doing it for attention. And to punish you for rejecting her."

"Just because I wasn't interested in her, she's going to drag my name through the mud?"

"It gives her the fifteen minutes of fame she's looking for. People make careers out of scandal." Tamara tucked her hair back. "And I might have contributed to the problem. I actually ran into her last week and I, uh, made it known that you were with me now."

"You did?" That surprised him for some reason.

"Yes. She was just so nasty and not only did she claim you're her boyfriend, she said she slept with Ryder, and implied it was while he was still married to Suz. I saw red, Elec, and I stooped to showing her text messages from you. I'm sorry."

"You got jealous, didn't you?" He grinned, despite the gravity of the situation.

"Yes. She pissed me off, acting like you were with her, when I happen to know that you spend all your spare time with me."

He kissed the top of her head. "Yes, I do."

"Can they do paternity tests before babies are born?"

"I don't know. But I guess our lawyer needs to look into it. And shouldn't she have to prove she is even pregnant?"

"Yes, I'm sure, but it will take a few days to sort through and report all that information. In the meantime, she gets to say whatever she wants."

Elec didn't like the timing, but he wanted Tamara to know, even before proof of a paternity test, that he was absolutely convinced this couldn't be his child. That Crystal couldn't have even somehow stolen his sperm, because he didn't have any.

"I need to tell you something," he said.

"You did sleep with her?" Tamara asked.

"No! I really didn't. But even if for some reason I had lost my mind and slept with her, that baby still couldn't be mine." Elec swallowed and dropped his eyes to her lap, where the sheet was bunched up in her fingers. He forced himself to look back up and meet her gaze. "Tamara, I can't have children. I'm sterile."

"What? How do you know that?"

"I got tested at nineteen. I'm shooting blanks, babe."

"Oh." She blinked a few times, then she reached out for his hand. "Oh, Elec, I'm sorry. That really bothers you, doesn't it?"

He nodded, a lump in his throat. "Yeah. I thought I could be okay with it, but it's hard. I like kids," he said simply.

"I know you do," she said softly, tears in her eyes. "You are amazing with mine."

"That's why I dated the women I did, you know? Because they were not the settling-down kind. I figured why fall in love with a woman who wants to have kids, then have her dump me when I can't give them to her?"

Tamara saw the pain on Elec's face that he was trying valiantly to shrug off and she wanted to weep for him. She could see the logic, the horrible, empty logic to what he was saying. But to deny himself love? And what kind of woman would give up a man like Elec simply because he couldn't give her biological children? Hadn't anyone ever heard of adoption? But then, that was easy for her to say. She had her own birth children already.

Which was why she and Elec were even more perfect for each other than she had realized the day before. She touched his cheek, loving the rough morning stubble there. "If you loved a woman, she would be a total idiot if she let you go."

"Yeah?" he said, and he looked so hopeful, so earnest, that Tamara kissed him.

"Yeah. And you love me, and I'm not an idiot. I'm not letting you go. Ever."

"No?"

"No."

Elec dug his hand into her hair and pressed his lips to

her forehead, hard. "Tamara, would it be crazy if I asked you to marry me right this minute?"

Her heart just about stopped. "Why don't you ask me and see what happens?"

He pulled back and stared at her with those rich brown eyes she could get lost in. Hell, she had gotten lost in them, the very first night she'd met him.

"Will you marry me?"

"Yes," she said simply, without thinking it through, without questioning it, without worrying. It was what she wanted, and that was all that mattered.

"Corny as it sounds, you've just made me the happiest man alive," he said, and he kissed her.

Tamara loved his kisses, loved the way his mouth covered hers so confidently, so tenderly. Neither of them had bothered to dress after sex, and his bare arms wrapped around her, strong and masculine. Tamara stroked his chest and sighed.

Damn, she did love him. And now she was going to be his wife.

Just the thought had her toes curling.

But they had a problem to deal with, the sooner the better.

"Okay," she said, pulling away and touching his lips. "Reality rears its ugly head. We have to deal with Crystal's little announcement."

"How do we do that?"

"This is what I think we should do," Tamara said. She just absolutely refused to let Crystal have even one more day to malign Elec, nor one more day to interfere with their happiness. "We're going to come out as a couple and deny Crystal's accusations."

"You would do that?"

"Of course. We present a united front. And while we're doing that, you have your lawyers looking into Crystal's background, see if she's been treated by an OB/GYN, see if she has filed any papers, see if we can get a paternity test done before birth, all of that. But I think if I'm standing next to you, your brother, your sister, your father, and we're all saying it isn't true, it will set off alarms. The media will start scrutinizing her story closer."

"Shouldn't I just have my lawyer say it's not true? I don't actually have to do interviews, do I?"

"I don't know. Let's call your sister. She's the expert." Tamara squeezed his hand. "But no matter, I'm here with you. And if you have to do interviews, you'll do them with me standing next to you."

ELEC needed a beer. Hell, he needed a whiskey. He had retreated to his coach with Tamara, Eve, and Evan, and they looked almost as lousy as he felt.

"Dude, that was awful," Evan said in sympathy. "Can I get you a beer?"

"Jack Daniel's," Elec said. He had just suffered through reading a statement to the media, then a round of grueling questions before Eve had pulled the plug on the reporters. He was feeling battered and bruised and disgusted with Crystal, the gossip-hungry media, and himself for even going out with the woman in the first place.

Evan glanced at him in surprise. "Are you serious?"

"Oh, yeah." Elec collapsed on the couch, and pulled Tamara down next to him. He needed to feel her hand in his. "How do you think it went?" he asked Eve.

"I actually think it went fine. The statement I wrote was neither defensive nor unsympathetic. Saying you feel for Crystal's situation and wish the best for her and her child, but that you are one hundred percent certain you are not the father, was the only tactic you could really take. You can't say much more than that and you don't want to sling mud back."

"I blew it when they started asking me questions." He

had never been able to get his precise meaning across with words, and in his determination to make sure they understood the truth, he was pretty sure he had rambled. But it had helped tremendously to know that Tamara was standing behind his right shoulder through the entire thing, silently supporting him.

"No, you didn't," Tamara said, squeezing his hand. "You did just fine."

"Thank you," he told her with a smile. "But you're biased. Eve will tell me the truth." He looked at his sister, who was pacing, as usual. "What do you think?"

"The first few questions were fine, and it was awesome that Tamara was there with you and you got to introduce her. I think that leant credence to your clean image. But then you got a little overwhelmed, so I just pulled the plug. All in all, not bad considering how much you hate these and the shitty nature of the interview."

High praise from his sister. "Thanks."

Evan handed him a shot of Jack and raised a second glass. "Cheers, man. We'll get you through this."

"Thanks, Bro." Elec tossed it back, and let the whiskey race down and settle into his gut, spreading out in fiery tendrils. That was better.

"How come no one offered me a shot?" Eve asked.

Trust his sister to get ticked off. Eve never liked to feel like she was being left behind or slighted.

"Do you want one?" Evan asked, not really answering the question of why he hadn't offered her one in the first place.

Most women would say no at that point, that it was the principle of the thing, but Elec could have bet money that Eve would say yes, and she did.

"Yes." Her chin came out and she stuck her hand on her hip. She was wearing a summer floral dress that hit right above the knee and showed off her thin frame and her toned shoulders.

It struck Elec as funny that she was going to insist on shooting whiskey at two in the afternoon dressed like an ad for *Working Woman*.

"Alright, but don't blame me when you have a headache." Evan walked back into the kitchen. "Tamara, how about you? Want a shot?"

Tamara gave Elec an amused smile. "No thanks, Evan, you'd be peeling me off the floor if I did a shot."

"Chances are we'll be peeling Eve off the floor," Elec told her. "But that doesn't stop her."

"Shut up," Eve said, with all the love of a sister.

There was a knock on the door, then it opened and Elec's father strolled in wearing jeans, a T-shirt, and a ball cap. Monroe men's uniform.

"Well, that does a man proud," he said by way of greeting. "Walking in and seeing my only daughter throwing back a shot in the middle of the day. Good Lord, Eve, what are you doing?"

She was choking, is what she was doing. Eve had tossed the shot and now her face was in horrible contortions, wincing and grimacing and shuddering, her eyes watering and her hand waving wildly. Elec and Evan started laughing. That was funny, Elec had to admit.

Eve finally caught her breath and said, "Damn, that's horrible. How do you drink that crap?"

"We have balls," Evan said. Then he glanced over at Tamara. "Sorry, Tamara, don't mean to be crass."

"Yes, you do," Eve said, wiping her eyes and sniffling.

"That's okay," Tamara said. "I've spent plenty of time in the company of drivers." She stood up and went over to his father. "I'm not sure if you remember me, but I'm Tamara Briggs."

"Of course I remember you," his father said, taking her hand in both of his. "It's good to see you again, sweetie. So how exactly did my youngest son manage to snag a beautiful woman like you?"

Elec unfurled himself from the couch and stretched. Every muscle in his body was sore from all the tension of the day. God, this wasn't how he wanted to spend the day after getting engaged. He had wanted to introduce Tamara to his parents under much better circumstances, not have them see her hovering behind him on camera. But then again, if Crystal hadn't gone to the media, Elec might not have actually proposed to Tamara, and he was so glad that he had.

That alone was what was getting him through the day. He was going to have Tamara as his wife. They were going to be married and share a bed and he could make love to her whenever he wasn't on the road.

"He gives a mean massage," Tamara told his father, which made Elec laugh.

Elec extracted his girlfriend's hand from his father's and said, "We're getting married, Dad." He knew he was grinning like a fool, but he couldn't help himself.

Evan threw his hands up in the air and shouted. "Yes! I am so good." He pointed to himself. "I rule."

"Does that mean you're happy for me?" Elec asked wryly.

"Of course." And Evan, his stupid, crazy-ass brother, actually came over and gave Tamara a kiss on the cheek. "Welcome to the family," he told her. "You make Elec happy and that makes me happy."

Wow, who knew Evan was capable of that?

His father said, "Getting married?" He took Tamara's left hand and studied it. "I don't see any ring on this girl's finger. Lord, Elec, didn't I teach you better than that?"

"There hasn't been time," he said defensively.

"Good cause to angle for a bigger ring," his father told Tamara. Then he gave her a big hug, actually lifting her off the ground. "We're glad you're going to be a part of the family, sweetie. Guess I need to call the wife and have her come over. She'll be pleased as punch."

"Congrats," Eve said, leaning forward to give Elec a kiss and misjudging the clearance around the end table and knocking into it. "Ow, damn it."

Elec and Evan laughed again. "You're drunk, aren't you?"

"I don't think so," Eve said with great dignity. But she ruined the regal pose by covering her mouth and burping. "Excuse me."

Their father rolled his eyes.

Evan laughed.

And Elec took advantage of the distraction to pull Tamara close to him and kiss her. Crystal's accusations didn't matter anymore. He was deeply, truly happy.

CHAPTER
SEVENTEEN

TAMARA didn't think she could recall another weekend of so many ups and downs. Having the special moments with Elec, hearing him say he was in love with her, his proposal, those were amazing and wonderful and everything she could have ever asked for.

The "Baby Daddy News in Daytona" story? She could have done without that, but she figured since it was all bald-faced lies, they'd survive it.

The phone call from her father-in-law? Not a good time.

Elec had just dropped her back at the hotel after meeting his family so he could go to the track for practice, and she was looking forward to a long, hot shower. Eve had invited her to go shopping and she had two hours before they were supposed to meet.

Her cell phone rang and she winced when she saw it was Johnny, not Beth, calling her. That didn't bode well. Beth was fine with her relationship with Elec, but while Johnny had agreed to watch the kids and bring them to Daytona,

Beth had warned Tamara he wasn't thrilled with her being with Elec.

"Hello?"

"Tammy, it's Johnny."

"Hi, how are you? How are the kids?" Tamara pulled clean clothes out of her suitcase and tried to sound chipper and nonchalant.

"The kids are fine. I've been better."

"Why? What's wrong?"

"Tammy, you know that I care about you a great deal. You've been a part of my family for a long time and you were a good wife to my son."

Uh-oh. She could hear the big "but" on the end of this and she swallowed hard.

"I can appreciate that you have the right to date. It's been more than two years and you're a young woman. I get all of that, I do."

Tamara just waited for him to continue and he did.

"But why in the hell does it have to be Elec Monroe? Bad enough that you've been seeing him on the sly for months, knowing it would upset Beth and I, but for God's sake, standing behind the man when he does a press conference? What the hell are you thinking? No one even knows you're dating and now he's all caught up in a major scandal—with a lingerie model, for Chrissake! I don't think you realize what this does to your reputation, to the Briggs name, to your children."

Tamara tried to interject, knowing he wasn't going to understand, but having to try. "Johnny, Elec is a good man. He didn't father that child, and he shouldn't have to even defend himself. But since this is a gossip-crazy world we live in, he does, and I need to show my support. I know you have a feud with Elliot Monroe, but the thing is, we can't control who we fall in love with. And I'm in love with Elec."

"That's all fine and good, except when it affects your

children. For the first time since Petey's birth, I can honestly say I'm calling into question your mothering. I'm completely disappointed in you."

The insult of that hit Tamara hard, and she was equal parts furious and devastated. Her whole adult life had focused on what was best for her babies, and the one thing that had held her back from Elec had been her children. But she had realized that Elec only added to their lives, and they were all better off for knowing him, and to have Johnny accuse her of not taking their feelings into account, well, it shredded her. "I'm sorry you feel that way," she said.

Then she added, "I'll talk to you later," and hung up so she could sit down on the bed and cry in private.

RYDER took his place in the lineup at drivers' introductions on Sunday and watched all the cameras focusing in on Elec Monroe, who was four down the line from him, Tammy standing with him. The rookie had qualified in the eighth position, despite having all the media distractions of the past few days. Elec's brother Evan was standing next to Ryder in the fifth position.

"So, your brother's marrying Tammy, huh?" Ryder said to him, not really surprised by the news buzzing all over the track. Elec and Tammy were both the marrying kind.

"Yep. I predicted that one."

"They look damn happy, despite all this lawsuit bullshit everyone's talking about. I'm almost jealous of them." Ryder shifted in his uniform, hot already. That was one thing he would never get used to—the heat inside his flame-retardant suit.

"Jealous of marriage?" Evan snorted. "Not me. But I think they'll be good at it."

That made Ryder frown. Apparently he hadn't been good at it, though he wasn't sure why not. Whenever he tried to talk to Suzanne about it, they just seemed to go around in circles until he got a pie in his face. It wasn't good.

But Elec and Tammy were beaming at each other, and he wished them happy.

Having her stand with him at drivers' intro was a good strategy. It was a gauge of how serious a driver was about his girlfriend. She only walked across that stage with him if she was around for the long haul, and for Tammy to choose today, of all days, to walk and wave with Elec, was good timing. It would show they were standing tall in the face of what would ultimately turn out to be just false accusations.

When the dust settled and the blonde was proven to be a liar, Elec would be in a better position with his image than he had been before. He'd be seen as decent, hardworking, a family man taking on a couple of kids that weren't his, all at the somewhat tender age of twenty-five.

And what would Ryder be doing?

He'd be winning races.

TAMARA tried not to squirm as Hunter bounced in her seat and told her grandfather, "Elec made a fire and we roasted marshmallows. He helped us catch fireflies. And look, did you see that? He just moved into tenth place. Bet he wins. He's an amazing driver."

It seemed that since Hunter had been given the green light to talk about Elec, she was trying to make up for lost time. She had peppered Johnny with Elec stories all day, and Tamara was just waiting for her father-in-law to blow. Even Petey, who usually paid more attention to what was going in his mouth than the race, kept making comments about Elec's driving.

"Mom, can we fly back home with Elec?" Petey asked.

That was the last straw for Johnny. Tamara saw his jaw

lock and she hastily stood up. "Let's go for a walk, guys. I could use a little snack. Are you hungry?"

"Yeah," Petey said immediately, which she knew he would. He was always hungry.

"Okay," Hunter said.

"We'll be back," Tamara said with a smile at Johnny, who ignored her. Beth shrugged her shoulders and gave her a sympathetic look.

She had her hands filled with popcorn and hot dogs and soft drinks when her cell phone rang. Passing most of the food off to the kids, she pulled out her phone and answered it. "Hello?"

"Hey, Tamara, it's Elliot, Elec's father. My wife and I heard you have your kids here at the track and we were hoping you could drop by the suite with them so we could meet them since they are going to be our step-grandchildren."

Touched by the gesture, Tamara said, "Sure. We're at the snack bar right now. When they're done eating, I can bring them by."

"Oh, bring the munchies with you. That way they can sit down and eat."

"Okay, great, I'll see you in a few minutes."

Tamara hung up and looked at her kids. "We're going over to meet Elec's parents. Best manners, okay?" She hadn't told them yet that she and Elec were getting married. She had wanted a private moment with them to discuss it and she hadn't had one yet. She would have to pull Elec's parents aside and give them the heads-up not to say anything just yet.

When they got to the suite, Hunter was true to form, marching in and settling herself outside the box with the best view of the track, inviting Elliot to join her. Petey hung back munching on his hot dog and running his fingers along the impressive selection of soft drinks sitting on the bar.

Kathy, Elec's mom, gave Tamara a big hug. "I knew you were something special weeks ago when he was mooning over you," she said with a smile.

"He was mooning over me?" That was awfully nice to know.

"Oh, yeah. He went around and around on whether or not he should stop by when your kids had the chicken pox. Took him the better part of an hour and lots of coaxing from me to decide to go for it."

Now that was just damn cute to know Elec had put that much thought into it. "Well, thank you. And while I have a quick second, I just wanted you to know that Elec just proposed to me, but my kids don't know yet, so if you could not mention it in front of them for a few days, I'd appreciate it. I need to tell them alone."

"Of course, sweetie. I understand. And then I can't wait to dive into wedding plans with you. Where is your mother?"

"She's in Seattle." And needless to say, when Tamara had called her the night before, she had been stunned to hear her daughter was marrying yet another race car driver. "She only gets out here about once a year."

Kathy opened her mouth to say something but stopped short when they heard a shriek from the seats by the track. Tamara didn't wait to turn all the way around before she was running. That was Hunter and that had been a blood-curdling scream of terror.

"What? What is it?" she said, frantically moving toward her daughter and expecting blood, a broken arm, something.

Elliot was already carrying a white-faced Hunter into the suite on his hip. "Turn up the TV," he demanded. "Elec got caught in a pileup."

Tamara felt the fear for her daughter shift to Elec. Oh, Lord.

Elec's uncle had the remote and he turned the volume up while she prayed it was just a dustup, nothing serious. But she knew it had to be, given Hunter's scream of terror. Hunter was a race fan. She knew all about bumps and spin-outs and they wouldn't upset her.

"Wow, what happened there, Rick?" the announcer said. "Let's get a rollback on that clip."

It happened so fast, that Tamara had a hard time follow-ing which car was which. She spotted Elec's 56 car and tracked it as one car bumped another and they spun out, hitting a third car. The hood of the first car collided with Elec, who was trying to avoid the wreck on the apron, and in a split second his car went from in control to a full-out roll into the grass. He turned twice before coming to a stop right side up, engine dead. The caution flag went up, and the announcers started the clip all over again as they dis-sected what had happened.

She didn't care what had happened. She did not give a damn who did what and why. All she cared about was that the man she loved was in that smashed car and she wasn't sure she could survive losing him when she had just found him.

"It looked to me like the lead car started out slow when they lifted the caution flag, and when you have all these cars sitting in tenth, eleventh, twelfth place, they jam up on top of each other when they can't get enough speed. Wow, what an accident for the fifty-six car. Let's hope rookie Elec Monroe is okay. They've had no radio contact with him but they're pulling him out of the car now."

There was bile in Tamara's throat and she struggled against the need to throw up.

Elec's mother tucked her arm through Tamara's and whispered, "It's okay, sweetie. Wrecks happen. He's fine. Put on a brave face for your kids."

Tamara blinked and nodded. Kathy was right. She could see that Hunter and Petey were scared. "It's alright," she told them, even if her voice was shaky. "Just a little wreck, happens all the time." She reached out and took Hunter from Elliot. Her daughter was too heavy for her to carry, but she gave her a hug before setting her back on her feet. She reached for Petey and squeezed his shoulder.

Glancing back at the TV, she saw paramedics were pulling Elec out of his car. The camera panned in as they were removing his helmet. His lips were moving, though he was clutching his ribs with his right arm.

Relief flooded her.

"He looks just fine," Elliot said and the relief was evident in his voice as well. "Talking and everything. They'll have to take him down to the medical center, per the rules. What do you say we all go down and check on him and let him know that next time he shouldn't be daydreaming behind the wheel?"

"I don't think it was his fault at all," Hunter said, some of the color restored to her face.

Petey hadn't said a word at all and that worried Tamara. "It's okay," she told him. "Elec is fine."

He just nodded and crammed a handful of popcorn into his mouth.

The wide eyes and white faces of her children hit Tamara hard. They cared about Elec. He had filled a void in their life and they would be devastated if something happened to him.

That scared her.

All of a sudden a lot of things scared her.

ELEC rested his hand on the tape binding his ribs as he sat on the gurney, and tried not to be annoyed. He hated, absolutely hated, not being able to finish a race. It was one, a matter of pride, and two, a matter of losing points in the cup race. He had considered going back out there and running his last eighty laps since finishing last still gave you points, whereas not finishing gave you none. Then he had tried to stand up and walk across the room and nixed that idea. It felt like he had a bear on his chest, and he didn't think he could climb into his seat.

Next week, though. The doctor said it would take six weeks for his four cracked ribs to heal completely but he figured he would be pretty pain-free by the following week and all he was doing was sitting. He could handle a few hours in the car, no problem.

There was a knock on his door, which he assumed was the nurse with his discharge instructions.

It was actually his family, who were all smiles to see him sitting up. He knew a wreck was scary for loved ones sitting and watching, and he had had his crew chief call his parents and Tamara as soon as he was out of the car and pretty sure there wasn't all that much wrong with him.

"Hey," he said. "How was that for a roll?"

His father said, "Had a little trouble in turn two, did you?"

It was an old racing joke. Everything was blamed on turn two.

His mother shook her head, bemused.

Eve said, "I think you're a publicity hog. All anyone's been talking about all weekend is you."

"Yeah, I wrecked just to get the spotlight. And I paid off the other two cars to take me out so I could land on camera." Elec grinned at her. "Brat."

Hunter and Petey came into the room then with Tamara, and Elec waved them over to him. "Hey, guys, what's up? How's the race? You see who won?"

"Can I hug you?" Hunter asked, looking nervously at his bandaged chest. He hadn't put his shirt back on yet because he wasn't sure he could manage the sleeves.

"Of course you can hug me," he said, and opened his arm so she could slide in between his legs and hug his waist. He fought the urge to wince as pain shot through his chest, but he hugged her back, tweaking her ponytail. "Thanks for coming to visit me."

He turned to Tamara's son. "What's up, Pete?"

Pete didn't say anything, just looked warily around the hospital room. Elec wondered if he was remembering his father's wreck. Tamara had never told him if Pete had been there. Somehow he had assumed he wasn't, but he didn't know that for a fact.

Elec looked past him, and met Tamara's gaze. She looked pale and pinched, her arms across her chest. "Hey, beautiful," he told her. "Forgot to look where I was going today." He smiled at her, but she didn't smile back.

His mother noticed the look on Tamara's face and she said, "Elliot, Eve, let's take these kids for a snack and give Elec and Tamara a minute alone."

"Right. Good plan," Elliot said.

Hunter gave him another squeeze but she went with his parents willingly enough, which made him happy. Petey followed, although he was still way too quiet for Elec's tastes.

"Hey," he said, trying to slide off the table to get to Tamara since she was still hovering in the doorway. "I've had a hard day, baby. I could use a kiss."

She did come to him then, and she touched his cheeks, brushed his hair back off his forehead, glancing down at his bandaged ribs and wincing. Then she kissed him softly, her arms twining carefully around him.

"The good thing is I'll have some extra free time this week. We can go ring shopping," he told her, trying to inject some levity into the situation. He wasn't that banged up, all things considered, and he didn't want it to be a big deal.

To his shock and horror, she started sobbing in his arms, her shoulders rocking, her tears wetting his cheeks.

"Hey, hey, it's okay. I'm alright. It's not a big deal."

She just shook harder and Elec lifted his arms carefully

and rubbed her back to try and soothe her. It made him feel wonderful that she cared that much at the same time it terrified him. He didn't know how to deal with this, nor did he like that he had scared her that much. "Shh. It's alright."

But then she pulled back from him and her face was contorted in anger. "It's not alright!" she said, swiping at her face. "It's not even remotely alright. You could have died out there!"

Uh-oh. How the hell did he answer that one? "I'm fine. It's just a few cracked ribs."

"But you could have died. It's a huge risk you take every week going out there."

Shit, this was about racing. He needed to nip that in the bud. Racing had its dangers, but so did life in general. "I could die choking on a piece of chicken."

"Oh, don't give me that stupid argument!" she said, throwing her hands in the air and turning her back on him. "The probability of a serious wreck in stock car racing is much higher than choking on your damn food and you know it."

"Tamara, what do you want me to say?"

"Nothing. Nothing." She wiped at her cheeks and said, "I can't do this."

"Do what?" There was a sudden pain in his chest and it had nothing to do with cracked ribs.

"This. I can't be a driver's wife again. I can't live with this fear, this uncertainty. I can't stand to see my kids terrified like that. I told you that way back when, I warned you, but we did this anyway, and now I know I should have never let it get this far."

Elec was starting to panic. "Baby, you don't mean that. I *love* you. We're amazing together. We belong together."

"I love you, too," she said, crying in earnest again.

It broke his heart to see her like that, and he went for her, but she dodged his touch. "Tamara, I know this was a scare, but I am okay. We're okay." Maybe if he said it enough, it would be true.

But she just shook her head and sobbed. "I can't, Elec. I just can't. I can't marry you."

Then she turned and ran out of the room and his heart cracked just as surely as his four ribs.

CHAPTER
EIGHTEEN

TAMARA ran down the hallway, hoping to avoid her kids for the moment. She was a mess, and she needed a minute to get ahold of herself. Unfortunately, there was really nowhere to go. One way led to her kids and Elec's parents, the other way to the track and a crowd of almost two hundred thousand people. Not to mention the cameras and reporters, who would be dying to get her reaction to Elec's wreck.

Her reaction sucked. She knew she was being unreasonable to him, knew it was shitty to break off their engagement in a hospital cubicle, but she had panicked. Seeing the accident, his car roll like that, seeing the expressions on her babies' faces, then seeing him sitting there shirtless and wrapped in tape, a deep bruise under his eye from his helmet, had all welled up inside her.

She couldn't do it. She had said yes to marry the Elec who sat on her wicker patio furniture with her and roasted marshmallows. She'd said yes to the Elec who made her feel sexy as hell in bed, who thought she was beautiful, and who was capable of loving her children as his own.

But first and foremost, Elec was a driver, and even after standing side by side with him through the media circus of the weekend, the truth of that hadn't really hit her. She couldn't love him only to lose him. She just couldn't.

She just wasn't strong enough to stay standing if it happened a second time.

Ducking down another hallway to find the restroom and splash water on her face to try and get a grip, Tamara nearly groaned out loud when she saw Pete's father coming toward her in the opposite direction. Johnny was the last person she wanted to see at the moment. But he had already spotted her.

"Tammy, how's Elec?"

"He's fine," she said, clearing her throat. "Just a few cracked ribs and some minor bruises."

"That's good," Johnny said. "Doesn't sound like a big deal."

Of course it wasn't a big deal. No one seemed to think it was a big deal that he could have died. "Yeah," she managed to say, even though her throat was tight and she was fighting fresh tears.

Johnny eyed her and said, "Come on and sit down and have a chat with me, Tammy. I owe you an apology."

She could surely use something. Johnny led her out the back of the med center and they found a bench in what was clearly intended to be the employee smoking area. They couldn't see the track, just the fence, and they were sheltered from the grandstands by the building.

"Have a seat."

Johnny indicated the bench so Tamara sat down and closed her eyes for a second, the heat and sunshine spilling over her. She felt him sit beside her.

"I'm sorry for what I said about your mothering," he said. "That was petty and uncalled for. I've never been anything but proud of the way you've raised my grand-babies."

That caused the tears she'd been struggling against to burst forth. "Thank you," she managed. "I have tried my best."

He patted her knee. "You have, and you've been an excellent mother. A better mother than Pete was a father. It's hard for me to admit that, but it's true. He loved those kids, but he wasn't hands-on and I realize that."

"He did love his kids. And he was a good husband." When he was around. Tamara kept that caveat to herself, though.

"I got upset with you the other day because it's hard for me to acknowledge that my son might be replaced in Petey's and Hunter's lives. Hearing them talk about all the things Elec does with them, well, it's hard."

"I know that. I'm sorry for that. But you know I want you in the kids' lives just as much as you've always been."

"And Beth and I appreciate it. Hearing everything Elec does with the kids and how taken they are with him, it made me realize that while it's hard for me, it's good for them. They need a man in their life. Not that you're not doing an excellent job solo but because life is just easier, more well rounded, when kids have two parents in there pitching in. Elec Monroe seems like a good kid, and you have my blessing."

Tamara wiped her face and shook her head. "I appreciate that, Johnny, but the thing is, I just broke up with him."

Johnny looked at her in amazement. "What? Why the hell would you do that? Did he really knock up the lingerie model? Because, honey, accidents happen."

"No. He never slept with her." Tamara bit her lip. "I broke up with him because I can't deal with moments like today. That fear almost knocked me to the floor. I can't lose another husband, I just can't."

"Well, now I understand fear. But, Tammy, you can't just stop loving people because you might lose them."

"Yes, I can." She didn't know how but she would force herself to stop loving Elec.

Johnny actually laughed. "That's ridiculous. Then if that logic is true, I guess you'd better stop loving Petey and Hunter."

"It's not the same thing."

"The hell it isn't. You could lose them, but would you have wanted to give back one single minute with them?"

Her throat constricted. "No, of course not."

"Then if you love this man, go for it, girl. Grab hold of every minute of happiness and enjoy it. Tell yourself you may only have today or you may have fifty years together, but love him for that time. Love him the way we race—for the joy, for the thrill, for the adrenaline, and for the triumph." Johnny looked at her sideways. "Does he take your breath away?"

Tamara sighed. "Yes. He does."

"And exactly how many times do you think that's going to happen in your lifetime?" Johnny stood up and reached for her hand. "Come on. Go on in there and make up with your man."

Johnny was right. She knew it. She had let fear take over. If she had ten days, a year, a lifetime with Elec, it was better than denying herself him. She loved him.

"Thank you," she told her father-in-law. "For everything. Now and the last eleven years."

He nodded. "You'll always be a Briggs."

ELEC was gone when Johnny walked her back in, and Tamara's heart sank. Pacing back outside by the bench, she called Elec's parents to check on her kids. It turned out they had hooked up with Beth and the kids were back with their grandmother and intending to head to their hotel for the night. Tamara talked to them on the phone for a minute and they seemed tired, but fine. Elec's parents told her they had dropped him off at the hotel. It didn't sound like he had said anything about her outburst, because Elliot didn't mention it, though he did say Elec looked like he was in a fair amount of pain.

"You heading back to the hotel?" Elliot asked. "I'm sure he could use some TLC from you."

"Yeah. I have to run an errand real quick, then I'll be there."

Tamara hung up and called Suzanne, who had been desperately calling her and texting her all weekend.

"Oh, my God, talk to me," Suz said as a greeting. "What is going on down there? There's all this talk about the pit lizard and then you showed up at drivers' intro and then Elec wrecked today . . . it's crazy. First, how is Elec?"

"Fine. Four cracked ribs."

"Good. Now what the heck is up with that Crystal chick? Is she really pregnant?"

"I have no idea. But if she is, it isn't Elec's. She is a total liar. But I don't want to talk about her. Elec asked me to marry him."

Suzanne shrieked. "Holy monkey! That's awesome! When did he propose?"

"Friday."

"And you're just telling me *now*? What the hell?"

"Well, everything descended into chaos with Crystal, then I had a fight with my father-in-law, then Elec wrecked, then I broke up with him."

"What? Why would you do that?"

"I freaked out, plain and simple. I saw that car roll and I just lost it. I said I couldn't handle it and broke up with him."

"Oh, Tammy, sweetie." Suzanne's voice was sympathetic. "I know that fear, baby, even though I didn't lose a husband. You can't let that stop you from being happy with Elec."

"I know. I had a chat with Johnny, believe it or not, and

got my head back on straight. Now I need you to do me a favor." The idea had just popped into her head and she was going to roll with it. It was the gesture she needed to show Elec she was ready to commit to him, to a life together.

"What?"

"Find me a reputable tattoo parlor in Daytona."

"Umm . . . okay. Why?"

"I need to get a tattoo."

"Well, I figured that out. A tattoo of what, and why can't it wait until you get home?"

"I'm getting Elec's car number on my inside wrist like he has."

"Wow, that's incredibly romantic." Suz sounded impressed. "You're getting inked for him. Wow. Okay, I'll call David Busbee's wife. They live in Daytona and he's all tatted up. I'll call you right back."

"Okay, thanks." Tamara took a deep breath and hoped Elec would forgive her for her outburst. She was ready to become Tamara Briggs-Monroe.

TAMARA debated knocking on the hotel door or just using her key, then decided she didn't want to wind up standing awkwardly in the doorway having this conversation if he opened the door and didn't invite her in. So she slid her key in and opened the hotel door.

Elec was sitting propped up on the bed with his shirt off, wearing his boxer shorts and a vacant look as he stared at the TV. His head swung over to her when she stepped inside.

"Hey," she said, tucking her hair back nervously.

"Hey. Did you come to get your stuff?" he asked, his voice stiff. "I packed everything up for you."

Her heart squeezed. "Honey, you shouldn't be bending over like that." Unable to resist, she went over to the bed and pushed his hair back off his forehead. "Did they give you pain medication? You look ashen."

"It's not really my ribs that are bothering me," he said, and the look he gave her was so hurt and so full of meaning that Tamara knew she needed to resolve this before she worried about his health.

"Elec, God, I'm so sorry about earlier. I just absolutely panicked when I saw your car roll. That was one of the worst moments of my life, and Hunter was screaming, and it just scared the daylights out of me." She took a deep breath as she stood in front of him. "But the thing is I realized walking out of that room like that was the last thing in the world I wanted. I don't like the fear, but living with fear is so much better than living without you."

He just stared at her. Finally he said, "Are you saying what I think you're saying? That you do want to be together?"

Tamara nodded, tears in her eyes. Lord, if she cried any more, she was going to dehydrate. "Yes. I absolutely would be honored to be your wife if you'll still have me."

Elec's jaw worked. "Do you really mean that?"

"Yes. I love you. I love the way you love me, the way you love your family, the way you love my children. I love the way you live your life with integrity. I know you're a driver, that's who you are, and I love the sport, too. I'm prepared to deal with all that it brings so that we can be together." She meant every word of that. She wanted nothing more than to share her life with Elec.

Elec listened to Tamara and felt the biggest sense of relief, coupled with joy, that he had ever known. He had been sitting in the goddamn hotel room staring at the TV and wondering how he was supposed to move on from a hit so hard it had knocked the wind out of him. He had felt like he'd come so close to having everything he'd ever wanted in his entire life and had watched it get yanked away.

To have it back, to look into her eyes, and see she meant it, had him reaching for her. He needed to feel her, touch her, and he took her hand. "*Yes*, I absolutely want you to be my wife. God, I thought I couldn't feel any worse than when you called things off this afternoon. I want to be with you, to love you, to build a life and a family with you and the kids."

"Really?" she said, climbing up onto the bed so she could slide in next to him.

"Really." Elec kissed her, ignoring the way his ribs screamed in protest. Tamara was going to be his wife and he wanted to kiss her, injury or not.

He poured all of his love, all of his happiness, into that kiss, and she responded in kind, sighing against him.

"I love you," she said.

"I love you, too."

"And I'm glad you said yes because I was going to have a hard time explaining this to the world if you said no." Tamara held up her wrist and turned it so he could see the inside of it.

It was a tattoo, just like his: 56. Elec lightly touched the brand-new, red, and raw tattoo. "You got my car number?" He was amazed she would do that. Thrilled. It screamed permanency and commitment to him and he loved the sound of that.

"Yes. I have to keep Briggs as a last name because of the kids, so I'll be Tamara Briggs-Monroe. But I wanted a way to show you I love you and back you one hundred percent. That I'm Elec Monroe's wife." She crossed her wrist over his. "And I got the left hand so that when we hold hands, the numbers align."

He could honestly say that having his car number tattooed on Tamara was the sexiest thing he had ever seen in his life. "My number looks damn good on you."

She laughed and snuggled against him carefully, obviously trying not to jar his ribs. "I never saw myself as one to get a tattoo, but it seemed right. And I want you to know that we'll resolve all this business with Crystal. It won't be a big deal."

"Thank you." He kissed her temple. "So about that ring shopping? You busy tomorrow?" Now that she was on board, he was slapping a ring on her finger, pronto.

"Not busy at all. Though you should rest."

"The hell I should." Elec took her hand and put it on his erection. "I was sitting here thinking how we can do it with the least movement possible."

Tamara laughed. "You're ridiculous."

"No. Turned on and in love." He grinned at her.

She smiled back. "Me, too. And I like it."

EPILOGUE

IMOGEN Wilson could honestly say she'd never been to a wedding in Manhattan where the groom arrived in a decaled race car. But she was in Charlotte now, and no one had seemed to blink when Elec Monroe had slid out of the window of his car in his tux at the church.

Nor did anyone seem to think it was strange that the car had been driven to the outdoor reception location and the entire wedding party was having pictures taken in the car, on the car, and around the car. Tamara's daughter Hunter was standing on the hood in her satin and chiffon red flower girl dress, posing first demurely, then using her floral bouquet like it was a guitar. Elec jumped up on the hood with her and picked her up and held her over his head like she was a trophy while she shrieked with laughter.

Imogen thought it was great to attend a wedding where everyone was having fun, no one was stressed out, and the bride and groom were beaming with pleasure. Most weddings in her opinion tended to be uptight and over-planned. Tamara and Elec's wedding was more like a big party.

Not that Imogen was partying. She was standing next to the tent pole watching the picture taking and sipping from a glass of champagne. She didn't know a lot of people at the wedding and she was relegated to either chatting up strangers or just watching, and for the moment she was content to just watch. Tamara's son Petey was standing in his tux holding an empty glass under the stream of the flowing chocolate fountain, and Imogen grinned when he looked up, spotted her, and put his fingers to his lips to indicate he didn't want her to tell anyone. She gave him the thumbs-up to let him know she wouldn't rat him out.

Though she suspected no one would care. It was a go-with-the-flow day, a celebration of Tamara and Elec's love and marriage.

The photographer was taking shots of the newlyweds' matching tattoos when Imogen realized someone was standing directly behind her. She turned and saw it was Ty McCordle. Her heart immediately started to race, and she was annoyed by the reaction. There was truly no reason for her sizzling sexual attraction to him. Granted, he was good-looking, but beyond that, they couldn't possibly have anything in common. Yet she was decidedly aware of the desire to see him naked.

"Hey, Emma Jean," he said with a grin.

"Hi," she said, not sure if he was calling her that to tease her or if he really couldn't remember her name. "Shouldn't you be in the pictures?"

Ty was pulling his tie off. "I've been released. They're doing solo and family shots now, thank God. Now I can grab a beer and some food. I'm starving."

She wasn't sure what she was supposed to say to that, or if he really required a response, so she just said, "Elec and Tamara seem really happy."

He nodded. "Some people are the marrying kind, others aren't. Those two will have a good long run, no doubt." Then he glanced over at her and grinned. "What about you, Emma Jean? You the marrying kind?"

Like he was actually interested in her response. But she answered truthfully. "I don't know. As of right now, I haven't met anyone I'd be interested in being married to, but that doesn't mean I'm opposed to it."

"I should have known you'd give a careful answer."

Imogen frowned. What was that supposed to mean?

Ty added, "Me, I'm not ever getting married."

"For which your future ex-wife is grateful," she said before she could stop herself.

He laughed loudly. "No doubt."

Imogen spotted a thin, surgically enhanced blonde waving and pouting when she couldn't get Ty's attention. "I think your girlfriend wants you."

Ty flicked a casual wave in the girl's direction. "*Girlfriend* is too strong of a word for Nikki."

Imogen thought the term was actually *booty call*, but she wouldn't swear to it. It seemed like a strictly booty-call relationship wouldn't have you taking the woman to a friend's wedding, but she could be wrong. Having never had anything even remotely close to a booty call or a fling, she couldn't be sure of the parameters.

"Well, whoever she is, she wants your attention."

"Guess I should see what she wants."

"Guess you should."

Imogen watched Ty saunter away and wished she weren't so intrigued by the tightness of his backside. It irritated her when she couldn't control her emotions.

Ryder Jefferson had jumped onto the hood of the car and uncorked a bottle of champagne. "Everyone raise a glass for Tammy and Elec!"

Tamara and Elec were snuggling in front of the car, and Imogen saw that Tamara was just beaming with happiness. It was wonderful to see, yet it reminded her of her own loneliness. Shaking the feeling off, she raised her glass, too.

Ryder said, "Here's to life and love in the fast lane."

Imogen would drink to that.

Turn the page for a preview of
the next contemporary romance
from Erin McCarthy

Hot Finish

Coming August 2010 from Berkley Sensation!

I banged the bride. I feel a little funny about standing up for her husband at their wedding."

Ryder Jefferson almost shot beer out of his nose at his friend Ty's words. Swallowing hard, choking on the liquid and his laughter, he said, "Well, it's not like you slept with her after they started dating, so who cares? In fact, as I recall, she was still dating you when she started sleeping with him. So yeah, I guess you're right. That is awkward, McCordle, since you got tossed over."

Not that he would ever rib his friend about that if his heart had been involved, but Ryder knew Ty had been half-heartedly dating Nikki Borden at best. It had been a relief to all parties involved when Nikki had had a tryst with Jonas Strickland and gotten engaged.

Which made the whole thing damned funny now that she had asked Ty to be a groomsman in her upcoming nuptials.

"Screw you," Ty told him, lifting his bottle to his lips, his head propped up on the worn bar with his hand.

"None of us want to be in this wedding," Elec Monroe, on Ryder's right side, said, tossing peanut after peanut in his mouth. "But at least we can all hang out with one another at the reception."

"This is your fault," Ty told him, pointing a finger at him. "You're the one who was friends with Jonas first. You're the one who invited him to your party, where he met Nikki."

"And that's where you met your fiancé," Ryder reminded him. "So I can't see how you're figuring it's a bad thing, because if Nikki hadn't met Jonas, you'd still be with her instead of Imogen. Do you want to be dating Nikki 'where's my brain' Borden?"

Ty's face contorted in horror and he gave a mock shudder. "Point taken. But it's still weird as hell."

"Nobody's arguing with that." None of them were close to Strickland, yet all of them had been invited to participate in his circus of a wedding.

"I don't mean to be a dick or anything," Evan Monroe, Elec's brother, piped up from down on the end. "But doesn't Strickland have real friends? It's not like any of us are really all that tight with him."

"I'm sure he does," Elec said. "But the truth is, Nikki's pulling the strings here and she wants a splashy media wedding. She has half the top ten drivers in stock car racing in her wedding party. Talk about a photo op."

Ryder had already figured out that was her motivation. He didn't really care all that much, but he did have better things to do than waste a whole weekend wearing a monkey suit. Like watching TV and tossing a load of laundry in. And other stuff, none of which he could think of at the moment. But the truth was, he would do it, and not for Nikki or Jonas.

"Well, I for one feel cheapened and used," he said, amused by the whole situation. He also had a nice beer buzz going, which made him feel much more prosaic about the whole thing.

"You know what? I'm not doing it," Evan declared. "I hate wearing a tux and I always get stuck with the married bridesmaid, so there's no chance of even scoring postreception sex."

"I'm not doing it either," Ty said, slapping his fist down on the bar. "I mean, what the hell? It's like incestuous or something for me to be standing there, in church, with Nikki and Jonas, and my fiancé sitting on the bench behind us . . . I'm not doing it. Screw it. No one can make me."

"Well, if you all aren't going to be there, I'm out, too." Elec rattled the peanuts around in his hand and wrinkled his nose. "I hate having my picture taken."

"That's because you're ugly," Evan told him, with all the love and affection only a brother could have.

"So it's settled, then." Ty sat up and adjusted his ball cap. "We all bail."

Ryder hated to break up this antiwedding sit-in, but he was going to have to own it. "Not me, guys. I can't bail."

"What? Why the hell not?" Ty asked.

"Because of Suzanne. She's the wedding planner for this crazy ass mockery of marriage, and I have to do it. I've gotta support her." He did. He had to support Suzanne whatever way he could since his ex-wife had refused further alimony from him.

He had been busted up about that for weeks, worrying about Suz. She was stubborn to the point she made the mule look like a pansy boy.

If she wouldn't take any money directly from him, he was going to do whatever he could to ensure her fledgling wedding planning business got off to a solid start. Even if that meant he had to suffer through a whole day of watching Nikki and Jonas delude themselves into thinking their marriage would last forever.

"Sorry, boys, I have to be there."

His friends and fellow stock car drivers gave him various expressions of understanding, overlaid with obvious irritation that he wasn't falling in line with their plan.

"Damn it," Ty said. "Truth is, I have to go, too. Imogen says if I back out, it's going to look like I still have feelings for Nikki or something. She's probably right, isn't she?"

Ty's fiancé Imogen was a brainiac and Ryder didn't doubt for a minute that when it came to matters of logic, Imogen reigned supreme over four guys in a bar at four in the afternoon. "She's probably got a point. If you're in the wedding no one's going to think for a minute you're busted up about Nikki. If you bail, it might look like hurt feelings."

"Well, I sure in the hell don't want anyone thinking that. Guess I'm going to have to do it, too."

Elec gave a monumental sigh. "If you two are in, I've got no excuse for not being there. Jonas is a buddy of mine, and I can't hold it against the guy that he's marrying a woman whose voice is like a cheese grater on my nuts. He's got to be in love, he must be happy, and I should be there to help him celebrate that."

"He's not happy!" Evan said, gesturing to the bartender for another beer. "Have you lost your mind? The man is drowning in a haze of endorphins, that's all. He's going to wake up from his sex cloud in six months and wonder what the hell he was thinking."

"You're such a romantic," Elec told him. "I can see why your love life is such a success."

"Screw you." Evan threw a balled up napkin at his brother.

"There's nothing wrong with marriage," Ryder said, the words slipping out before he could stop them.

Suddenly all eyes were on him.

"Yeah?" Ty asked, looking at him funny.

"Yeah." Ryder put his bottle to his lip so he didn't expand on his statement. He didn't want to get into it, didn't want anyone to know he was thinking a lot about his ex these days and wondering what exactly had gone wrong.

Evan said, "I still don't want to be in this wedding."

"Guess you don't have to," Elec told him. "But it looks like the rest of us are in."

"What time is it?" Ryder asked, feeling his pocket for his cell phone. "We have to be at that wedding party planning meeting thing at five."

Ty glanced at his watch. "It's a quarter after."

"We need to head out then. Should we all ride together? Elec, you can drive since you only had one beer and you've been nursing it for two hours."

"That's cool," Elec said. "We're all going to need a beer after this anyway, so we might as well leave your cars here. Evan, you going or not?"

Ryder settled his bar tab and stood up, hoping they weren't going to be late. Bitching and whining while belly up to the bar had eaten up more time than he had expected, and he didn't want to disappoint Suzanne. Or more accurately, he didn't want to listen to her reaming him.

"I'll go," Evan said begrudgingly. "I'll look like a total ass if I don't."

"True." Ryder clapped him on the shoulder. "Would it make you feel better if we let you plan the bachelor party?"

Evan perked up. "Hey, I wouldn't mind that. I could do that."

As they headed to the front door, Ryder wished that it was that easy to please himself these days. Something was missing in his life, and he was afraid he knew exactly what it was.

OR who, to be more accurate. "You want fifteen groomsmen and fifteen bridesmaids?" Was she flippin' serious? Suzanne Jefferson looked at her client, Nikki Borden, who arguably had cotton candy floating where she should have brains, and knew the girl was one hundred percent serious.

"Uh huh." Nikki nodded with a big smile. "My big day should be, well, big."

Right.

Nikki's thin, toned, and tanned arms went flailing out, a beatific smile on her youthful face. "Big like the Eiffel Tower. Big like elephants. Big like . . ." She paused, clearly at a loss for more large and lame metaphors.

"Big like the national debt?" Suzanne asked, shifting in her chair at her dining room table, unable to resist.

Nikki blinked. "Huh? What's that?"

Suzanne bit her cheek and squeezed her lips together in the hopes she wouldn't laugh out loud and have Nikki guessing she thought the blonde had bacon for brains. Why the hell Suzanne thought she could go back to being a wedding planner when she'd never been able to hide her emotions worth a damn was beyond her. Oh, wait. She was dead broke, that's why she was pasting on a big old fake smile and listening to the likes of Nikki natter on and on about her perfect man and her perfect proposal and her perfect wedding.

At one time, before her own marriage and divorce, Suzanne had enjoyed the challenge of wedding planning, making sure every last teeny, tiny detail was taken care of, and taking pride in the joy on a bride's face on her big day. There had been annoying aspects, sure, but they had rolled off her less-cynical back a little easier in those days.

But since she'd spent the past four years working as a volunteer on the board of a charity that funded children's cancer research, she was having a hard time seeing the value in picking the perfect shade of pink for bridesmaids' dresses, or suggesting the happy couple spend thousands of dollars on a cake that would disappear in under four hours.

Not that there was any point in whining about it. This

was life, and she had to deal. She was going to squeeze the shit out of these lemons and force them into lemonade. Suzanne made a notation on her notepad. *Fifteen big-ass bridesmaids.*

Then she added a dollar sign on the end.

That made her feel a little better. She could cash in on Nikki's enthusiasm for excess. "Well, that's perfectly understandable, Nikki. You want to share your wedding with those most important to you, and it's very difficult to cut anyone out." Though from the sound of it, Nikki was planning to ask every cousin, friend, and sorority sister she'd ever had, plus the saleswoman who'd sold her her shoes at a discount, and the yahoo who changed her oil to be in her bridal party.

Nikki nodded. "Exactly."

"But normally wedding parties run about four to six bridesmaids and groomsmen. A wedding party of thirty, plus your flower girl and ring bearer, requires a lot of additional planning and coordinating. I'm going to have to increase my fee if that's what you choose to do."

"I understand." Nikki just stared at her serenely.

"By double."

"Sure." Now a smug smile crossed the blonde's face. "Jonas is paying."

"The deposit—do you have it?"

A check signed by Jonas Strickland passed from Nikki's hand to hers and a glance down at it showed it was written for the entire original amount Suzanne had quoted Nikki.

"This is more than the deposit."

"Jonas doesn't like to be in debt. He said to just pay up front. I can get the rest to you in a day or two, I'm sure."

Nikki might claim to love Jonas, but at the moment, Suzanne really did. He had just padded her checking account substantially. Her smile at Nikki was very genuine. "That's excellent, thank you. Now, you said Jonas was going to be here, right? What time are you expecting him? We can go ahead and discuss venues and colors, or we can wait for him."

"He should be here any minute. And I think everyone from the wedding party said they could make it, too."

Suzanne tugged at her red sweater, adjusting her cleavage. Surely she had heard Nikki wrong. "Excuse me? The wedding party is coming, too?"

"Yeah, I thought that would be fun! They can help us make choices." Nikki beamed at Suzanne, clearly proud of herself.

Turning her dining room into sample central was working fairly well. She had access to all her books and menus and fabric samples, but there was no way in hell she could squeeze thirty people into her whole condo, let alone her dining room. There was really only room for her, Nikki, and a fat Chihuahua around this table.

Then again, she glanced down at the check on the table in front of her. For that kind of money, she'd let the best man sit on her lap. She'd squeeze people in anywhere possible for thirty minutes, throw some bridal magazines at them, then she'd get rid of them.

"I'm not good with decisions," Nikki said.

Yet she'd decided to marry a man she'd been dating for six weeks. Huh. That was promising. "No problem. That's what I'm here for, to guide you through the choices. Now let's talk overall tone of the wedding. Do you want it formal, casual, is there a certain location that appeals to you?"

"I want a *Gone with the Wind* theme."

Suzanne's pen paused over her paper, horrific images of hoopskirts, parasols, and skinny faux mustaches popping into her head. "How literal do you want to take that concept?"

Nikki's brow furrowed. "What do you mean?"

"Were you thinking of maybe doing the wedding outside on the lawn at an antebellum home? With simple elegance for the décor?"

"Oh, yeah. That's what I mean. Just like it really was during the Civil War. That was the Civil War, wasn't it? Anyway, whatever. Plus, I want the big dresses they wore in the movie, and the guys in those long coats, and horses, and curled hair, and, well . . . all of it." Nikki beamed.

Maybe she'd like cannons, poverty, and runaway inflation in her wedding as well.

The doorbell rang, praise the Lord. Suzanne had nothing to say at the moment, which was damn near a first for her.

But how in the hell could she slap her name and wedding planning reputation behind a Civil War–themed wedding? She'd be stuck doing theme weddings for the next decade, and everyone who knew her was aware that her well of patience wasn't very deep.

"I'll get that. Excuse me just a sec, Nikki."

Suzanne hustled to the door and opened it. She blinked to see Elec and Evan Monroe, Ty McCordle, and right in front, her gorgeous and annoying ex-husband, Ryder Jefferson.

"Hey guys, what's up? I'm kind of busy at the moment."

"We're here for the wedding planning thing," Ty told her.

Oh, no. That meant that Nikki's fiancé, Jonas, had asked them . . .

"We're the groomsmen."

Damn. Just what she needed. None of them would listen or take her seriously. She'd lose control of the whole situation.

Ryder brushed past her, dropping a soft kiss on her cheek, his familiar cologne wafting up her nostrils and acting like a sexual trigger. She smelled Ryder, her nipples got hard. They were just trained that way.

"Good to see you, babe. And lucky me, I'm the best man in this wedding."

Suzanne fought the urge to grimace. Good God, this fiasco just got even more ludicrous. Now she was going to have to spend a fair amount of time around Ryder for the next month, and she just couldn't deal with that on top of all her worrying about her future. He made her crazy, plain and simple.

And there was no way this best man was sitting on her lap.

Ryder handed her a manila envelope. "Oh, and this came addressed to both of us. It's from our divorce lawyer."

Suzanne looked at it blankly. It did have their divorce attorney's name on the envelope, and it was addressed to Mr. Ryder and Suzanne Jefferson. Ouch. It had been a long time since she'd seen her name linked with his, and damn it, it still hurt, which pissed her off. It didn't matter anymore, shouldn't matter.

"What is it?"

"I don't know. I didn't open it. Figured you'd want it." He moved past her and the other guys did likewise.

Jonas Strickland was coming up her walk and there was a gaggle of Nikki clones behind him, women in their early twenties, tanned and thin and indistinguishable from one another except for the color of their various sweaters. There was red and yellow and aqua and two in white.

"Hi, come on in. I'm Suzanne," she said absently. "Nikki's in the dining room."

Curiosity killing her, Suzanne ripped open the envelope as she walked behind them, their giggles and chatter a buzzing backdrop. There was a stack of papers that looked like their divorce decree. Okay. She read the cover letter from the lawyer.

And stopped halfway down her hallway, the words blurring in front of her.

Oh. My. God.

She was going to kill Ryder. She was going to rip his arm off and beat him with the bloody stump.

This paper was telling her she and Ryder were not divorced.

They were still married.

"Ryder!" she screamed, aware that her voice sounded like a fair approximation of a banshee.

Everyone in the room looked up at her.

"You know," Nikki said. "I had a thought. I'm blonde."

Elec laughed and Ty elbowed him.

"What?" Suzanne looked at the twit in front of her and didn't bother to hide her irritation.

"I can't do a *Gone with the Wind* theme. Scarlett O'Hara was a brunette." Nikki pointed to her head. "And I'm blonde."

Jesus. "Good point," Suzanne managed. "Now would you all excuse Ryder and I for just one teensy minute?"

Ryder gave her an uneasy look, and the guys looked curious, but she didn't care. She had to discuss this with him immediately before her head exploded off her shoulders.

"What's up, babe?" he asked her, moving in really close to her, his hand landing on the small of her back as he guided her into the next room. "If we're going to fight, maybe we should be out of earshot."

Suzanne got two feet into her kitchen then couldn't hold back. She whirled and smacked the envelope and stack of papers against his chest. "This says we're still married!"

Ryder's eyebrows shot up. "No shit? Does that mean we can have guilt-free sex then?"

Oh, yeah. She was going to kill him.